IRON DRAGONS

BOOK ONE OF THE SARAMOND QUEST

DEREK P. GILBERT

Iron Dragons
By Derek P. Gilbert

AVENUE FICTION
514 ROSE AVENUE, CRANE, MO 65633

Published by Rose Avenue Fiction
www.roseavenuefiction.com

ISBN 978-0-9980967-8-0
All rights reserved.

Cover artwork by Jeffrey Mardis
Interior formatting by Kevin G. Summers

Printed in the United States of America
Copyright 2020 by Derek P. Gilbert
First Edition January 2006

To Sharon: Without your love and encouragement I would never have tried to write this story;

To Nicole: You inspire me to be a better man than I am;

To Mom: Thank you for teaching me to love reading and learning;

And to Dad, who told me Mel Gibson should play Davian in the movie: I miss you. You will always be my hero.

CHAPTER ONE

Dragon pee really stinks.

I share this with you as a friendly word of advice should you ever consider a career in dragon extermination. Remember, you have been warned.

I know of nothing that matches the stench of a dragon's urine, except perhaps armor that has been doused with it and then worn into battle on a hot summer afternoon. The stink never washes out completely, no matter how one tries. Good, well-fitted armor is worth its weight in gold in these times, however, so it is better to get used to it, if you can. Suffice it to say that doing battle with dragons is not for the faint of heart or the weak of stomach.

What causes the odor, I do not know, nor do I care. Some function of the beasts' internal workings, I suppose, fueled by a diet so foul that I will not offend the reader with a description of it here. I do know, from personal experience, that the vile creatures seem to enjoy spraying their fluids over opponents in combat, usually at the most inconvenient times. Not only does it stink, but dragon urine also burns the eyes and brings bile to the throat.

The job of exterminating dragons also requires a clear head—something I did not possess on the day my tale begins.

Those who require the services of a dragon exterminator are usually distraught. The arrival of one of my kind is usually an occasion of great relief, and we are greeted by folk willing, almost desperate, to do anything we might ask.

This often leads to situations that require a great deal of self-control.

I was summoned to the village of Marthwee by the local priest, the only citizen with enough courage to risk the four days' journey to my home in Darnaatha. A dragon had recently taken up residence in the hills near the town and immediately began to abscond with pigs, sheep, cattle, and a few of the less agile residents.

Brother Galthorn was a thin, anxious young man with sharp features and a shock of unruly dark hair. Perched atop his spindly frame, his unkempt mop made it appear as though a treeurchin had fallen from its perch and bespattered itself atop his head.

His nervous hands constantly knotted and wrung the sleeves of the dirt-brown robe that hung loosely from his emaciated limbs as he waited impatiently for me to finish assembling my gear. They continued to do so throughout the four days that we traveled the dusty roads back to Marthwee. The only times he ceased his nervous fidgeting were those brief moments when we stopped for simple meals of dried meat, bread, cheese, and wine. And even then, he twisted the crusts of his bread beyond recognition before eating them.

We spoke little during the journey. I am not a conversationalist by nature and the young man seemed intimidated by my presence. That often happens when I meet younger members of the clergy.

My gift, if I can call it that, is viewed with something approaching awe by some of those who serve the Creator. Others, usually elder members of the priesthood, tend to take a darker view of my abilities. So be it.

I know not the source of my power, whether good or ill. It is what it is, and I must live with it.

In any event, we arrived at Marthwee, parched and fatigued, late in the afternoon of the fourth day. The heat was sweltering, without a cloud in the sky or tree along the road to shield us from an angry sun. Although it is a simple enough task to cool myself on days such as this, I felt it best not to expend energy unnecessarily. Dragons have an uncomfortable habit of presenting themselves when one is least prepared.

The village is situated on a slight rise overlooking miles of flat prairie, farmland, and a wide, slow-moving river. The homes were built with smooth stones pulled from the water and roofed with thatch. They appeared sturdy and well maintained. A small square in the center of the village was marked off with timbers hewn from the forest on the far side of the river. Beds of flowers surrounded an immense oak tree with a trunk so broad that two men might stand on opposite sides without being able to grasp hands. The flowers drooped for lack of water, and it was clear the beds had not been tended in some days.

Marthwee should have been a bustling, prosperous community, and perhaps it was, under normal circumstances. This day, however, there were no obvious signs of human habitation out of doors. I was not surprised. People living near a dragon's lair stay out of sight as much as possible. Entire communities have been forced underground to avoid a dragon's insatiable hunger.

But that only works for a time. Sharing an enclosed space with one's livestock is difficult. The animals need food and water, and their needs—as well as their smells—soon force their masters back into the open. It is good that dragons are rare; else there would be no safe place for men anywhere in this world.

That is why I do what I do—to ensure that the dragons do not overwhelm us.

Brother Galthorn quietly led me through the deserted village, glancing nervously at the sky every few paces, until we arrived at the local inn. His sandaled step was jarring in the eerie silence, for even the birds did not sing that day in Marthwee. Whether it was due to the oppressive heat or the sense of dread that lay like a coverlet over the town, I cannot say.

The innkeeper greeted me warmly but quietly once inside. Brother Galthorn departed to attend to his duties at the small church at the edge of the village. He trembled as he took his leave, but he resolutely made his way homeward, trusting in the Creator to protect him from the evil that lurked somewhere among the hills beyond the river.

The innkeeper, Panderthan, a bear of a man with curly black hair and beard, bade me sit and offered what he could in the way of food and drink. As I mentioned, I have found my hosts through the years to be deferential, sometimes to the extreme. The people of Marthwee began to appear at the inn as news of my arrival spread. Their hope filled the air of the small stone building like the scent of the incense burning at Brother Galthorn's tiny church. It seemed that every man in the village felt obliged to provide another draught to quench my thirst from the long, hot journey.

Therein lay my difficulty.

While I am not opposed to a drink or two, especially on a hot day, I do not tolerate spirits particularly well. In fact, I am usually content to nurse one or two mugs of ale for an entire evening. More than that and I soon find myself asleep; much more than that and I regret it for the better part of the next day. Such was the case in Marthwee that day.

The people were so desperate! I sensed it from the moment I arrived, and I felt that I was doing good by reassuring them as best I could. It seemed wrong to refuse, especially when men I took to be leaders in the community placed new tankards before me.

There is too much superstition about my kind already. I have long since learned the value of a bit of empathy and good fellowship when I am among those who request my help. And the ale tasted especially good after the heat of the day—although, as is well known, heat and cold do not always affect those like myself as they do most folk.

Perhaps it was just that I sensed the power of the one I would soon confront, and I was apprehensive about the task.

Whatever the reason, I awoke at dawn the next day, as is my custom, with a pain behind my left eye that I felt certain would split my skull. I opened my right eye in the lifting gloom and quickly closed it again, hoping against hope that hours still remained until daybreak. I lowered my head gently onto the straw that comprised my bed in the small room at the back of the inn.

The slam of a door hitting the stone wall simultaneously drove a spike through my temples and stilled the beating of my heart.

"Master Davian! Come quickly! Oh, please, come quickly!" I opened my right eye again. It was Brother Galthorn, shaking and knotting the sleeves of his robe.

I arched an eyebrow in question. Brother Galthorn was positively frantic. "The dragon! It's coming!"

I closed my eye and sighed. So, it was to be one of those days.

CHAPTER TWO

I was irritated and I wanted an answer, quickly.

"Who is the idiot responsible for staking the goat in the field?" I scowled at the dozen or so villagers gathered in the close quarters of the inn. It was a look that needed little embellishing because the throbbing in my head made it impossible to open my eyes farther than a squint.

It took only a moment to learn the answer; all eyes slowly turned to focus on Brother Galthorn.

Panderthan interjected, "Don't be too hard on him, sir. He was just trying to help."

I grunted, partly in answer and partly due to exertion as I struggled into the stiff dragonskin jerkin I have worn into battle for more than ten years. "It is considered prudent, Brother Galthorn, to learn the lay of the land and set one's defense before engaging the enemy."

The priest's shaking was more pronounced than I had heretofore seen. "I thought… I thought you would want to draw the beast into the open," he stammered.

"Yes," I spat. "When I was ready. More tea!"

The innkeeper's wife, an ample woman of indiscriminate age, scurried into the kitchen to fetch another cup of the bitter tea brewed from the leaves of an herb I had collected and dried myself. It helped to clear my head. I generally start each day with a cup; today I had finished three already and I needed more.

Panderthan's expansive face wrinkled with distaste. "Might I ask, sir," he said, "What is that smell? Is it some potion to guard you against the dragon's flame, or is that the natural odor of dragonskin?"

"Neither." I continued lacing the jerkin without looking up. "It's dragon's urine." Although, in truth, I did not say "urine." Brother Galthorn coughed nervously at my choice of words.

Normally, I am more tactful in the presence of a priest. Some of them can be enough of a bother without annoying them.

Then a quiet voice, unheard by the others, intruded into my mind.

I know you are here.

It was cold, dry, and full of sibilance—a serpent's hiss slicing into my thoughts like the blade of a frozen knife.

The eyes of those around me were suddenly wide and staring. They had seen my reaction to the dragon's call.

"What is it?" Brother Galthorn was at my side, gripping my arm, his shaking stilled and concern etched into the sharp angles of his face.

"It speaks to me." Brother Galthorn gripped me more tightly.

Come to me. I would have thee to break my fast.

"You will find me not so easy to digest." I spoke aloud in spite of myself. The effect was immediate: The villagers edged away, pressing against the walls, caught between their fear of me and of the beast lurking somewhere outside. Several made gestures with their hands, superstitious charms supposed to protect them from evil.

No matter. 'Tis the eating I relish. Mayhap I shall vomit thee out to display your entrails about my neck as an ornament.

Despite my aching head, I laughed. The sense I had of this beast was powerful, an old worm of size and strength. Dragons are arrogant by nature, and the largest ones are the most taken with themselves. Pride is often their greatest weakness.

"Others have tried, old one." Again I spoke aloud, this time not caring whether I frightened my audience. "I am still here."

Others of your kind have filled my belly, it replied. You are just one more.

I blocked the beast from my mind and finished lacing my jerkin. The stiff dragonskin creaked as I turned to accept a steaming mug of fresh tea from the innkeeper's wife. The pain in my head was beginning to dissipate, but my head still throbbed behind my left eye. I sipped at the bitter brew and let its warmth trickle down to my gut.

A low murmuring in my right ear caught my attention. Brother Galthorn, head bowed, was praying. I looked around the room and noticed several others in silent prayer. They seemed to be calm. The rest looked terrified.

There is normally a rush of emotion and energy as I prepare to face one of these creatures, as I anticipate the monumental task of matching will and skill against the most dangerous of all things living on Saramond. Instead, I felt only the throbbing of my temples, and I wanted nothing but to return to bed until my head was ready for the fight.

Addressing the gathering, I said, "Let me be clear: No one is to venture outside until I return. Dragons have no honor. They think nothing of making off with curious onlookers or using them to gain an advantage. More than once I have destroyed one of the beasts, but at the loss of several spectators who did not heed my warning. While you may never have another chance to witness a Master of The Order do battle with a dragon, I advise you in the strongest possible terms to stay away and well hidden. And you should pray that this is the only time such a battle occurs so close to your homes."

I gulped another swallow of the tea. Brother Galthorn looked up from his prayer at that moment and frowned. It was easy enough to perceive his thoughts. "Yes, brother," I said quietly, "The tea steams as though it is nearly hot enough to boil. So it is. No, it does not burn me, though it would you. One of the small advantages of the Gift." The young man's eyes grew wide with wonder. It is an expression I see often enough.

Turning again to the men, I said, "Your places are with your families, somewhere safe, preferably below ground." I bent and picked up the fire-hardened ash spear I had carried from Darnaatha. At nearly one and a half man-heights, it was roughly a quarter of the width of the inn.

"One other thing," I added. "Stay away from objects made of metal until I return. Oft times, during a battle, objects of metal will behave—strangely. Best that no one save the dragon be hurt." With a final pull on the tea, I hefted the dragonspear and nodded to the man closest to the exit to open the door.

The morning was damp. Silvered beads of dew clung thickly to the blades of grass as though determined to defy the sun and remain in place until nightfall. A faint mist rose from the languorous water of the River Cimlar, marking the village's border to the west with a thin veil of gray. I breathed deeply of the cool, moist air as I walked, trying to clear my head.

Though I had not been to the field where Brother Galthorn had tied the goat during the night, I did not need to ask the way. My very being sensed the malevolent presence that awaited me there. The confidence it radiated had not unnerved me; to tell it honestly, I was annoyed that the beast, if it proved a worthy foe, would only delay the nap for which I longed.

Mind, I do not underestimate the danger these beasts pose. I knew very well the creature might prove to be my end. It is simply a measure of my illness that day that I did not care. Death would at least bring relief from the agony in my head.

Again I opened my mind. The energy required to screen myself from the beast was not great, but everything that morning was a strain. It was not long before the thing resumed boasting.

Ahh, excellent. I grow peckish. And I tire of toying with this bleating thing the humans sacrificed to summon me.

"What is your name, beast?" The effort of thinking at it was painful, and I squinted through my left eye as I neared the edge of the village.

Speak more respectfully to the one who will help thee cross the barrier to the next world.

"It is you who will fall today. What is your name?"

You are food, nothing more. Come to me. I hunger. Mayhap I shall mix thee with goat. It may improve thy flavour.

The ground fell away slightly at the edge of the village and the road curved away to the left. The field was obscured from view by a small stand of oaks and poplars. Hidden by the trees, the dragon lay resting in the dew-soaked grass.

The bleating of the goat carried far in the still morning air. The poor thing was frantic, its senses overwhelmed by the presence of an evil far beyond its ability to comprehend. I tightened my grip on the spear and began to focus my thoughts. My breathing grew deeper and more regular as I performed a mental exercise to quiet my nerves and focus my thoughts.

My pace was even and measured. I did not hurry, nor did I tarry. The process of fighting a dragon is primarily mental, spear notwithstanding. I sensed the beast with every fiber of my being, a tingling, a prickling similar to the feeling when the hair on one's arms rises on a dry winter day.

As I focused on the beast, the pain behind my eyes faded. It would return later, I knew, and with more intensity. I pushed the thought away. There would be time to rest later.

Yessss. A little closer.

The beast was the largest I had seen, at least five man-heights in length, excluding the tail. Its greenish-gray scales glinted dully in the early morning sun. In its arrogance, it lay indolently in the center of a large pasture, which was bounded on two sides by a low stone wall, on a third by the road, and on the side nearest to me by trees. A plot of cultivated land lay opposite the meadow, showing signs of recent neglect. The terrified goat strained frantically at its rope in a vain attempt to escape the horror crouching nearby.

At my approach, the beast slowly reached out, and with a flick of a razor-sharp front claw, cleanly removed the head of the goat, ending its misery. Before the poor creature toppled, the dragon rose, spun, lashed out with its spiked tail and batted the carcass at me. Its aim was excellent, but the distance between us allowed me the time to quicken my pace and avoid the broken, bloody mass. It sailed less than a man-height over my head.

So shall you be.

When confronting a dragon, I normally allow the beast to take the initiative. Often, its overconfidence at facing a creature so much smaller than itself will draw it into a fatal mistake. I encourage this feeling of superiority by feigning weakness until a time of my choosing. This day, however, I was in no mood to draw out the affair. Focusing my mind, I quickly directed a small charge of superheated energy between the dragon's eyes. It recoiled, bellowing in shock and surprise. Thin wisps of smoke curled into the air from a darkened spot in the middle of its knot-encrusted forehead.

With a roar and a rush of air, the beast launched itself into the sky. Its great, leathery wings unfurled and carried it upward, above the level of the treetops. It circled away from me and then doubled back, gliding elegantly through the air like an eel in the river. The creatures, dangerous as they are, are truly beautiful in their grace and economy of movement. What a different world if we could live together peacefully!

But no. The dragon bore down on me from above like the very wrath of the Creator. A crimson blast from its nostrils bloomed and grew to envelop me. I pushed it aside with my mind, barely feeling the warmth of the flames that surrounded me. Drawing on the heat of the dragon's breath, I redirected the energy and sent it back in the direction from which it had come.

Ah, but this was a crafty one. While my vision was obscured, the dragon changed its path. It was only a few degrees from where I had expected it to be, but the difference was enough that my bolt missed—and the beast was nearly on me. Curse my aching head! If I had been thinking clearly I would have sensed the creature's deception and I would not have missed.

I ran toward it. I doubt this dragon had seen a man run toward it in many years, if ever, and the beast had calculated its angle of attack accordingly. My reaction changed the equation, and by dropping the spear and executing a tumbler's roll, I evaded the dragon's claws by mere inches.

And then I was soaked.

The males of certain species of mammal will "spray" during combat or to mark their territory as a warning against intruders. Personally, I believe dragons do it simply to be nasty.

The exertion of the sudden movement roused the pain in my head, and the throbbing returned behind my left eye. Gritting my teeth against the ache and the stench, I wiped my face with my hands and tried to focus. I should have anticipated this dragon's experience and reacted to its initial attack with more force. A dragon this large had seen many more summers than I, and it had done so by besting others of its kind—and perhaps several of my brothers in The Order.

Why, of all days, had I chosen last night to drink myself to sleep?

Come, now. You merely delay the inevitable. Let me end thy suffering quickly.

I retrieved my dragonspear and forced myself to calm my breathing again. The dragon, over the trees now, brazenly rolled completely over before slowly turning to its left in a lazy half-circle. So cocksure was the beast that it performed tricks in mid-air!

So be it. I let my shoulders sag and leaned against the big wooden shaft of the spear. A mental groan of pain and despair escaped my mind, one I made sure it would hear.

Do not fret. I am coming. This will be over soon.

The dragon completed its turn and prepared for another charge. I felt the energy of the beast as it pumped its mighty wings, gaining speed as it began its descent. Clearly, it intended to kill or cripple me with this pass.

Unmoving, looking as forlorn as I was able, I gauged the amount of energy I would need to blast the foul creature out of the air.

The brute reared back its head as it approached, chest expanding as it prepared to discharge another volley of flame. I focused on the approaching monster, seeing nothing but the reptilian nightmare hurtling toward me, and I marshaled my strength for the blow I would strike with my mind.

Precisely at that moment, a desperate cry pierced my concentration: "Nooooo!"

The dragon heard it, too. We turned and beheld a sight I shall never forget as long as I draw breath: It was the preposterous, stick-thin figure of Brother Galthorn, flapping down the road in oversized sandals, robe whipping madly about his underfed frame like a pennant in a gale. I do not know who was more surprised, the dragon or me. I do know that I recovered first.

The dragon, however, interrupted at a critical moment in its descent, discovered with a shock that it was impossible to redirect its bulk away from the rapidly approaching turf.

Unfortunately, I stood at the projected point of impact.

Quickly letting fly my spear, I leaped to my right, rolling as I hit the turf. The ground shook as though beneath the feet of the Creator himself. My head was slammed to the ground, and an unbearable weight fell atop me, crushing the breath from my motionless body.

All was still. Unable to move, I saw nothing, heard nothing, felt nothing. And as I slipped beneath the surface of a liquid blackness, I heard in my mind the dragon's voice, eerily quiet: *My name... is... Sennthurnisss...*

CHAPTER THREE

The world returned to me slowly, painfully, and by degrees. First sound, and then light, and gradually, shapes in the fog that resolved themselves into forms resembling human. Carefully opening my eyes, I saw the innkeeper, Panderthan, Brother Galthorn, and the village headman, Tarn, in a semicircle above me.

"Ah, he has returned to us," Tarn said. "And how do you feel, Master Davian?"

After briefly surveying my condition, I gave him my assessment. "I feel as though a building has fallen on me."

Tarn laughed, with that hearty but insincere chortle that is universal to politicians. "Well said, Davian! From Brother Galthorn's telling of the event, the dragon was very nearly impaled on you as well as your spear!"

I looked at the priest. "Then the beast is dead?"

He nodded emphatically. "Oh, yes, Master Davian, praise the Creator! I have never seen the like. You were magnificent! What bravery! To allow the beast to come so close to assure a killing strike with your spear—'twas the stuff of legend!"

From the beaming faces of Panderthan and Tarn, it was plain that Brother Galthorn had relished the telling of his tale. In truth, I had never had a battle with a dragon end so quickly, and rarely had one ended with my survival such a near thing. I am not reckless. One does not grow old in my profession by taking unnecessary risks.

I closed my eyes. The whole of my body felt bruised, and my right shoulder ached terribly, as though it had been wrenched when I fell. My dragonskin vest might have saved me from broken ribs or worse.

"How did I…" I began to ask.

"Brother Galthorn here," Panderthan interrupted. "He come high-tailing it back to the village with the news, and brought eight of us a-running back with him. You were pinned beneath the creature's tail for near half an hour before we could pry you out. We had to saw the blasted thing's tail off to get you loose," he finished with a chuckle.

The fact that they were able to cut through the dragon's tough hide was proof enough that it was truly dead. Metal implements have little effect on the beasts while they are alive.

Another question presented itself to me. "How long have I…"

"The rest of the day and all of the night," the headman interrupted. "You gave us a bit of a scare."

"I appreciate your concern." I tried to sit up and found the effort exhausting. I am often drained, physically and mentally, after doing battle with one of the creatures, but not to such an extent. Of course, I do not normally allow a dragon to come as close as Sennthurniss had been. Even for one of The Order, such intimacy with the enemy is as good as cutting one's throat, but not as mercifully quick.

Dragons, like cats, enjoy playing with their food.

I surveyed my surroundings. The room seemed too austere to be part of the inn. "Where…" I began.

"The church," interrupted Brother Galthorn. "A small guest room in the rectory. We use it for guests, travelers, and sometimes for those who are ill."

The room was small, with whitewashed stone walls and simple furnishings. The only furniture in evidence was the bed and a small rough wooden table next to it. A half-melted candle and a curved serrated tooth as long as the width of my hand sat on top of the table.

Brother Galthorn noticed the direction of my gaze. "I thought you would want a memento from your gallant victory."

"Thank you, Brother Galthorn. I would prefer that you keep it."

The young clergyman stammered, "Oh, n-no, sir. I c-couldn't."

"You deserve it more than I."

Galthorn flushed, his face crimson against the nut brown of his robe. "R-really, Master Davian, I could n-not accept it."

Conscious of the assorted aches in my body clamoring for attention, I asked Panderthan, "Might I have a pot of boiling water? I would have some of my tea—and perhaps some bread, if you have some."

"I'll do better than that. You just stay right there, Master and I'll be back in no time at all." The big man departed, rubbing his hands, a man who clearly enjoyed playing the host.

"So what will you do now?" Tarn asked. The head man was shorter than Brother Galthorn, with dark, close-cropped hair, and a neatly trimmed beard and mustache. His clothes, I noticed, were of a fine linen, certainly not the product of a local weaver. His appearance and manner of dress were more cosmopolitan than I would have expected in a small village of no more than two hundred souls.

Tarn's question was anticipated. Those of us with the Gift are usually welcome as long as there is a need. Once the need was met, however, old fears and superstitions quickly return. Among those in power, the fears are commonly not about superstition, but about the security of their positions. A man who removes the threat of a dragon from a district is usually quite popular for a time. The support of the people, combined with the powers we possess, might tempt one to sweep aside an incumbent ruler. It has been known to happen.

"I will rest a short while, and then I will return to my home." Tarn nodded sagely, as though agreeing with the wisdom of my decision. To his credit, he managed to hide his relief almost completely as he bade me good day and made his exit.

For his part, Brother Galthorn seemed less enthused about my imminent departure. "Is something wrong?" I asked.

Brother Galhorn's fingers went to work on the sleeves of his robe once again, twisting and rolling. "It's just… well, I believe I might have put you in danger today."

After debating a moment whether to soften the blow to spare his feelings, I decided against it. It's not that I disliked the young man, but the world is hard and often unforgiving of mistakes. The sooner he learned, the better.

Or so I said to myself. Perhaps I was still irritated that I had nearly being flattened by a flying lizard the size of a barn.

"You put it too mildly, brother," I said. "Your shout broke my concentration at a critical moment. You very nearly witnessed my death."

The young priest paled and stared at the floor, nervously working the sleeves of his robe through his fingers. "I am terribly sorry," he said quietly. "I could not help myself. When I saw that spawn of hell descending upon you, I thought…"

I held up my hand to stop him. "You have never seen one of The Order engaged in battle with a dragon."

"No."

"Then you should not have assumed that you understood what was happening. The beast would not have touched me as long as I was able to focus upon it. That is why I told everyone to stay away, Brother Galthorn. The greatest danger to me is when I am distracted by the threat of danger to someone else. So why, may I ask, were you out there at all?"

"I… I couldn't stand the thought of you fighting that thing all alone."

"You were unarmed. You do not possess the Gift. What in the world were you going to do?"

For the first time in the six days that I had known him, I saw some grit in Brother Galthorn. He looked up and trained his eyes on mine. "Pray," he said, evenly.

"You could not do that from the safety of the village?"

"I, uh…" He cast his eyes downward again and was silent.

I sighed. "You do understand that exterminating dragons is my calling."

He nodded penitently.

"And you understand that I have trained for this my entire life."

He nodded again.

"Then please, Brother Galthorn, if you should be unfortunate enough to see another dragon in your lifetime, and another like me is called to dispatch it, please do not try to help!"

The door to the room opened and Panderthan entered, carrying a tray loaded with fruit, bread, cheeses, a pitcher of ale, and a steaming pot of water for my tea. I suddenly realized that despite my aches and bruises I was terrifically hungry, and I proceeded to eat my fill of Panderthan's hospitality.

* * *

That evening, the townsfolk of Marthwee hosted a feast to celebrate the demise of the dragon, and it was insisted that I be present as the guest of honor. Attend I did, but only reluctantly. I did not feel particularly honorable. That the dragon was dead was beyond doubt, but its death had been achieved through no great effort of mine. By my reckoning, my only contribution had been to induce the dragon to fly, which allowed Brother Galthorn to startle it to death.

The evening's main course was, of course, dragon, a dish for which I have long since lost an appetite. I know too much about their eating habits to find dragon steak appealing. I also find it difficult to eat a creature, evil though it may be, that is capable of intelligent thought.

There were several others that chose not to partake of the dragon. At least two, I was told, were relatives of those consumed by Sennthurniss. Presumably they found that the links in this particular food chain had been forged too close to home.

The ale was cold—I saw to that; it was the least I could do—and the people were exuberant. Panderthan's inn, the Merry Fisherman, served as the hub of the celebration. The festivities soon spilled out into the main street as the villagers sought relief from the crowd indoors, or room to dance as the local bard, Tewdrig, warmed to the task with his harp and a strong, resonant baritone voice.

The night air was pleasant, freshened by a light breeze from across the river. This was fortunate, as a glow behind the line of trees to the south marked the place where the dragon had fallen. After spending the day harvesting the skin and edible meat from the beast, a crew had built a bonfire and was busily rendering the fat and burning the offal. The bones of the great beast would be used to produce tools and provide artisans with raw material. Very little of a fallen dragon goes to waste. Still, it was small compensation for the losses the village had suffered.

Torches had been lit and positioned in the street outside the Merry Fisherman. As near as I could tell, all of Marthwee's two hundred inhabitants had joined in the celebration, and some from the surrounding countryside, as well. Alone outside the inn, I enjoyed the cool night air and watched the happy people. I am not one who enjoys crowds or mindless chatter, and there was too much of both inside the inn. Still, I was relieved that the dragon was no more and pleased that these simple folk could soon return to their normal routines.

A man stepped out of the patch of light marking the entrance to the inn, looked about for a moment, and fixed his attention on me. Weaving through the score of dancers in the street, he approached. It was Tarn.

"Ho, Master Davian," he said with a contrived laugh. "I dare say our town is a bit more lively than when you first arrived."

"True, true," I said. "Thankfully so."

"Eh?"

"I mean, were the dragon still about, there would be no cause to celebrate."

"Right you are, right you are," he laughed, slapping me on the back. I winced.

An attractive young woman separated herself from the crowd and began walking slowly toward us. She was half a head taller than Tarn, which made her about a hand shorter than myself. Long, dark hair framed a lovely oval face with large eyes and a narrow mouth with full lips. I was riveted to the spot, unable to move, breathe, or even contemplate a response should she desire to speak.

Raising an eyebrow as he noticed the direction of my eyes, Tarn beamed and said, "Ah! Allow me to introduce my pride and joy. Master Davian, this is my eldest daughter, Lareina."

As she moved closer, her delicate features were gradually revealed by the dancing torchlight. Rather than being enhanced by darkness, Lareina's beauty was magnified as she was more clearly seen. A flock of sparrows took wing through my insides, and I realized that I faced the most intoxicatingly beautiful woman I had ever seen. With effort, I managed to summon just enough composure to speak: "I am honored to meet you, Lareina."

Rather than responding to my greeting, or even slowing her approach, she reared back and delivered a punishing roundhouse punch to my nose.

"That is for Reneiver! He is dead, thanks to you!" With that, she spun on her heels and walked away. Stunned, I didn't move even as the blood rushed from my broken nose and dripped from my chin to the dusty street.

It was then I realized that dragons are easier to understand than women.

The look of horror on Tarn's face would have been comical had it not been for the flood of crimson down my face, not to speak of the intense pain. From the edge of my vision—for I was unable to look away from the retreating form of the lovely Lareina—I was dimly aware that the direction of my nose had been shifted by several degrees to the right.

"I must apologize for my daughter! I am so terribly sorry! Please, let me help you!" Tarn was nearly frantic in his apology.

As the initial shock wore off, the pain grew more intense with each passing moment. "Please," I said, "Just get me some water." I gingerly pinched my nostrils shut to stop the flow of blood.

"Water?"

"Water. Please. Quickly."

"Yes, yes, of course! Please, come with me."

"No, I would rather not."

"Eh?"

"I would rather not be seen like this." Call it a vanity, if you will. I had no wish to show myself to the merry townsfolk, bloodied, eyes tearing, and nose out of place. "Please just bring me some water, and ask Brother Galthorn to join me, if you would."

Tarn nodded and scurried into the inn. Moving further into the shadows, I did my best to be inconspicuous. The head man returned a few moments later with Brother Galthorn, who was carrying a pitcher.

Brother Galthorn's face was drawn with concern. "Oh, my. What has she done?"

"She has broken my nose, Brother Galthorn," I said, voice muffled through my pinched nostrils. "That would appear to be obvious."

"Yes, but… well, she has a bit of a temper. You must admit that, Tarn."

Tarn nodded vigorously. "Yes, yes. Just like her mother."

"Brother Galthorn," I said, cupping my hands, "Pour some of the water here."

He did as asked. I pulled energy from the water and released the heat overhead where it would do no harm. The popping sound caused Tarn and Brother Galthorn to jump with surprise. Grimacing, I applied the ice to the bridge of my nose.

Eyes wide, Brother Galthorn said, "Truly your power is a gift from the Creator."

"Perhaps. It has its uses." I had no patience for company that night and no desire to discuss theology, especially as it concerned my abilities.

"Are you in pain? Shall I fetch the doctor?"

"Yes, I am; and no, thank you, Brother Galthorn," I said. "Perhaps you can accompany me back to my room at the church. I think I should rest for the night." I turned to the headman. "Tarn, who is—or was—Reneiver?"

"He was her betrothed," he answered. "They were to wed in a fortnight."

"Why does she blame me for his death?"

"I do not know that she does, for certain." Tarn looked as puzzled as I felt. "I know she is distraught, but…"

Brother Galthorn said, "It may be that she resents a night of celebration so soon after Reneiver's death, and she lashed out at the one she felt most responsible."

"But why?"

Tarn and Galthorn looked at each other for a moment. Tarn finally spoke: "While Brother Galthorn here was away, fetching you, Reneiver determined that he would go out and face the dragon himself. 'It isn't right,' he said, 'that we should live in mud burrows like rodents while that thing destroys our flocks and our herds!' Of course, even though he was surely the strongest man in the village, the dragon had little trouble with Reneiver." Tarn's face darkened, clouded by a memory. "What was most distressing, Master Davian, was the way the beast, ah, toyed with Reneiver, after… after he had been disabled."

Brother Galthorn added, in a low voice, "His screams were heard all through the night."

My nose and my aches suddenly became less significant. I have seen what dragons do with their prey. It was no wonder, then, that Lareina was upset. Listening to one's beloved beg for death is a horror that no one should suffer.

"Well. I am sorry for her loss," I said at last. "I hope this was the last dragon you will see, and the last time you will have need of me."

We bid each other good night. Tarn rejoined the celebration at the Merry Fisherman, while Brother Galthorn and I made our way through the town to the small rectory behind the church. As we walked, the fading sounds from the inn gave way to the typical sounds of the night—the chirping of insects and frogs, a soft splash in the river, the faint hooting of an owl preparing to hunt. It was peaceful, and we walked in silence, reluctant to disturb the serenity of the evening.

As we reached the church, Galthorn finally broke the silence. "Is it true, Master Davian, that the brothers of The Order are taken from their families when they are very young?"

"Yes. It is a necessary precaution."

"Precaution?"

"Brother Galthorn, you have seen only a very little of what I can do. We are trained from childhood to control our abilities, but those with the Gift display their abilities in infancy. Those who are not taken from their homes as infants can cause terrible harm without even being aware of what they are doing."

In the dim moonlight outside the rectory, the priest's sharply angled face looked as solemn as the stone monuments to the dead in the cemetery behind the church. "So you did not know your family?" he asked.

"I was not allowed to return to my family until I was twelve years old," I replied. "And then it was only for a short visit. My father was already dead."

"I am sorry."

"I had no memory of my family in any case. The time I spent there was very awkward, like visiting strangers. I have not seen them again."

Brother Galthorn's face was so sorrowful that I thought he would cry. Instead, he simply opened the door the rectory and went inside. He bade me good night; I retired to the guest room and attempted to ignore the pain from the battering inflicted by the dragon and the lovely young woman named Lareina. After what seemed like days of rolling from side to side, trying to find a comfortable position in which to lie, I finally drifted off to sleep.

CHAPTER FOUR

In my dreams, I see a woman. She is tall, or perhaps she seems tall because I am a child again. Her smile is sunshine and warmth, and she is beautiful. Not beautiful as I saw Lareina, but as one would see a mother, and I realize that she is the woman I saw for a brief time when I was young.

She is not as I remember in my waking hours, the woman I saw during that one brief visit when I was twelve years old, weary and broken by the unfair burdens of life, but alive and vibrant and waiting, arms outstretched, to offer me comfort and rest. Her eyes look down on me with a love so deep and selfless that my heart is filled beyond its capacity, and I begin to weep; and then I awaken, alone and saddened by the fading memory of what never was.

I wonder if my brothers in The Order suffer similar dreams.

The Order was summoned to our home when I was not yet six months old. Signs of my ability had begun to appear—metallic objects moving of their own accord, unexplained areas of heat and cold appearing and disappearing without cause. My parents, as most would, prayed to the Creator that there was another explanation, or that the manifestations would cease. They did not. I am told my father finally decided to contact The Order the night a roast bird suddenly burst into flame at dinner while I clapped my tiny hands and squealed with delight.

The brothers were kind, and I owe them my life. In times past, it was not uncommon for children with abilities like mine to be abandoned or killed outright. The Order gives a child with the Gift a home and the discipline necessary to live with his power.

Perhaps one child in one million has the Gift. On all of Saramond, then, there are no more than two hundred of The Order, as far as is known. All of us are male, though why this is so I do not know. There are many differences between men and women; I suppose this is another, albeit one that manifests itself in only a very few.

Infants adopted into The Order are watched around the clock when they are young. Only the experience of the elder members of The Order keeps the raw, undisciplined power of a babe with the Gift from injuring others or himself. In time, with discipline, the child begins to learn the extent and the limits of the Gift, and the responsibilities that accompany it.

* * *

The following morning broke bright and fair. I awoke at sunrise, partly from habit and partly because I could no longer lie comfortably on the many bruises I nursed. My shoulder felt a little better, but my nose was swollen and sore, and breathing through my nostrils was difficult. Desiring to stretch my limbs and perhaps work through the stiffness I felt, I resolved to take a walk along the river Cimlar. I dressed quickly and quietly, so as not to wake Brother Galthorn. The soft leather boots I favor made no sound on the stone floor of the rectory as I slipped out of doors.

The day promised to be warm, and the air was moist and heavy. I walked for some time, following the curves of the River Cimlar. The exercise worked the stiffness from my joints, and the pain began to fade a bit.

After walking for a time, I stopped to satisfy my thirst. A low spot on the bank provided a convenient place, and I knelt to drink from the river. The reflection that gazed back from the water was horrific—a lump on the bridge of my nose and darkened semi-circles below each eye. The marks of my first meeting with Lareina would be with me for some time.

My pace as I returned to Marthwee was leisurely. I was in no hurry to show my damaged face to the villagers, although, judging by the late hour at which the previous night's celebration finally expired, it might be some time before any of them appeared out of doors.

I was wrong. A soft splash from the river ahead brought me out of a reverie. There on the river's edge, illuminated by the morning sun, was Lareina, drawing water with a bucket. If it was possible, she was even more beautiful in the morning light than she had appeared the night before.

She was barefoot and wore a simple blue homespun dress, but surely no lady in all her finery at King Ednorwain's court was nobler in appearance or bearing than Lareina that morning. She set her filled bucket on the bank and pulled her long, dark hair behind her ears, lifted the hem of her dress to her knees, and waded a few steps into the clear water of the river.

I paused a moment, and then decided that I risked nothing by approaching her. She had already broken my nose; what more could she do?

Lareina started when she saw me on the trail beside the river, obviously as surprised as I had been to find someone else up and about so early. I will credit her this—she does not stay surprised for very long.

"What are you doing here, you fiend?" A night's sleep had not cooled her anger. "Do you mean to retaliate for last night?"

I moved a few paces closer, but I stayed beyond what I hoped was her throwing range. "No, lady, I could not sleep for the pain in my nose, and sought merely to stretch my legs and clear my head."

"What's in your head is clear enough," she snorted. "You followed me here to do me harm. Begone!"

"You wounded my pride last night. Today, you cut me. I mean you no harm, and I did not follow you here."

Lareina stared at me with brown eyes cloaked in mystery, trying to determine whether I was telling the truth. Slowly, she softened; and then she began to laugh.

"Do I amuse you, lady?" I asked.

"I am sorry," she said as she stepped out of the water. "But your appearance is rather comical."

I pursed my lips. "I am honored to serve some useful function for you, Lareina."

"Your eyes," she said. "The rings beneath them make you look like a bald treeurchin."

"The resemblance was clear enough when I looked into the water this morning."

"It is an improvement, Master Davian."

"Many thanks for your kind words, my lady."

"They were not intended to be kind, only truthful." She turned her back on me, and retrieving her bucket, she began to walk back to the village.

"I see now why Reneiver was so taken with you—your unmistakable charm." As soon as I said it, I regretted it.

Laneira spun and let fly with her bucket. Without a word, she turned and walked off, leaving me standing there, sodden and dripping.

* * *

Brother Galthorn was awake when I returned to the rectory. "Ah, there you are—Master Davian! You are soaked—and your eyes!"

"Yes," I said. "I had the good fortune to meet Lareina during my morning walk. And the rings under my eyes are part and parcel of the nose she so thoughtfully rearranged last night."

"Oh, dear," said Galthorn. "She is still angry, then."

"With my help," I admitted. "I was less than tactful."

"What happened?"

"I chose to insult her, and I used Reneiver's name to do it." Brother Galthorn's gaze was accusatory. He had no need to say a word. "I know, I know. It was inexcusable. Damned woman! Pardon me, brother."

"She has suffered a great deal, Master Davian. Her wound is fresh and deep."

"I know," I said. "My skill with women is likely the product of being raised by men who have lived nearly their entire lives apart from women. Excuse me, brother. I would like to change into dry clothing."

I retired to the guest room and retrieved a dry shirt and breeches from my pack. I removed my boots and decided to set them in the sun outside to dry. Returning to the middle room in the small, three-room rectory, I joined Brother Galthorn at the table for a simple meal.

"Brother Galthorn," I asked, between bites of sharp cheese, "Why did you ask about my childhood?"

He chewed thoughtfully before answering. "I, too, know nothing of my family."

"I know of my family. I just did not know them when I was a child," I said. "How is it that you do not know yours?"

"My parents were killed when I was an infant."

"I am sorry. How did it happen?"

"A dragon," he replied. "I was told it broke through the roof of our home and took them, leaving me behind. I was found later by neighbors and taken to the village church. The local priest and his wife took me in and raised me as their own."

"Hmm," I said. "Sadly, I have heard many such tales of children orphaned by the monsters."

"I imagine so," Brother Galthorn said. "Forgive me for casting a pall on our meal. My childhood was happy, and I learned early in life to give thanks to the Creator for all that He has done for me."

"When did you learn that the priest and his wife were not your true parents?"

Brother Galthorn looked at me steadily, with no trace of the uncertainty I had seen so often in recent days. "Well, that depends on how one defines his terms. To me, Athinaar and Elgiva were my true parents."

"Forgive me, Brother Galthorn," I said. "I did not mean…"

"No, no, I understand," he interrupted. "It is just that many do mean it in that sense. In my short time as a priest, I have already seen many 'true' parents who do not deserve that title."

"I have no doubt of that."

Galthorn took a drink of water and continued. "Well, it was obvious when I reached my twelfth year that I could not be the son of Athinaar. I was already a hand taller than he was and still growing."

I smiled. "That must have caused you to wonder."

"Only for a short while. My parents did not keep it from me for long after that."

"Who killed the dragon that killed your parents?"

Brother Galthorn frowned. "I do not know. I do not think Athinaar knew, either."

"No matter."

We ate in silence for a few moments, and then Brother Galthorn asked, "Master Davian, do you ever wonder how your life might have been different?"

"I do."

"And?"

"And I have come to the conclusion that since there is nothing I can do about it, so it is pointless to dwell on it."

"Hmm." The young priest chewed his bread slowly, occupied with his thoughts.

"Why do you ask, Brother Galthorn?"

"Well," he said, "I am told my father was a farmer. Sometimes I wonder how it might be to tend fields and livestock instead of people."

"In my travels, Brother Galthorn, I have found that all occupations have a certain amount of trouble and frustration; it is just that the nature of those irritations that are different. It is not necessarily easier to win over the mind of a goat than that of a sinner."

The young man smiled. "I don't know," he said. "There are some goats I've met that were less stubborn than some of the sinners in my parish—although I will deny saying so if you dare repeat that to anyone."

As we talked over our morning meal that day, I found myself warming to the priest. Brother Galthorn, for all the nervous energy and indecisiveness he had displayed in the first days of our acquaintance, was revealing himself to be a thoughtful and perceptive young man—one who might possess an inner strength that he, himself, was not aware of.

* * *

I had resolved to stay in Marthwee only one more day before returning to my home in Darnaatha. At Brother Galthorn's invitation, I attended a service in the small stone church that evening, given in thanks of the dragon's demise. The sanctuary, hushed and dimly lit, was full, with most of the adults in Marthwee packed into the small room. A number of them looked at me oddly, but it was to be expected. The blue and black under my eyes had not begun to fade, and by now the cause of my swollen, discolored nose was no secret in the village.

Lareina was there, too, with Tarn and Olgwin, her mother. She pointedly looked everywhere but at me.

It was a simple ceremony and subdued. Brother Galthorn preached a very short sermon, and a rather daring one considering that the dragon had very recently killed five of their number. In addition to thanking the Creator for delivering them from the dragon, the young priest boldly preached against the evils of sin, and how the dragon's appearance, if not a warning from the Creator, was certainly a reminder of how short a time one may have in this life.

Galthorn deserves credit for courage, if nothing else. The young man certainly took his job seriously. I do not believe that I would have had preached such a message to grieving friends, neighbors, and relations, hinting that their misbehavior might have prompted the visitation of the fell beast that devoured their loved ones. Not that Brother Galthorn said so, in so many words, but when emotions are high people tend to hear what they wish to hear.

I daresay that Brother Galthorn was not the most popular man in the village after the service. His forlorn expression as I met up with him outside the church indicated that at least one person in his parish had taken issue with his message.

"Beautiful evening, is it not?" I was in no hurry to broach the subject of the just-completed service, and the glorious orange and crimson sunset offered an excuse to talk about something else.

"It is, Master Davian, but I fear I have angered the entire village."

"Well, not quite, Brother Galthorn," I said. "For one thing, they were not all here."

He smiled ruefully. "But I spoke the truth."

"Ah! There you have hit upon the problem. Men who speak the truth are often the least popular. Especially when they are pointing out our faults."

The young man sighed, looking very like a scarecrow whose stuffing has half fallen out. "Well, I did what I am supposed to do."

"Brother Galthorn," I said, "I have traveled a great deal. It is my observation that the most popular priests—the ones with the grandest churches and the biggest waistlines—are the ones who make it their practice to say what people wish to hear. And what people wish to hear most is that they are not to blame."

The young man nodded sadly.

"All you can do is speak the truth and let the seeds fall where they may. Come," I said, taking his arm, "Let's have something to eat and perhaps that will help to lift your gloom."

A shout reached us from the center of the village. Someone was hailing me.

"Master Davian! I must speak with you!" A traveler on horseback brought his mount a magnificent white horse with a flowing gray mane, to a stop alongside us on the village's main street. The rider was a small man wearing a brown homespun shirt and leather breeches. His hair was short and thin, cropped nearly as close as my shaven head, which served to hide the fact that he was losing what little he had. He was rail thin, like Brother Galthorn, but with a pinched look to his face that was either due to the glare of the setting sun in his eyes or near-sightedness.

"I am Davian," I said. "What can I do for you?"

"I am called Fosdric," he said, eyeing me strangely. "I have ridden twelve days to find you, from the south. I was told—excuse me, Master Davian, but you don't look a thing like I imagined."

"I, ah, had an encounter."

"Ah," he said, knowingly. "Scars of battle, eh?"

"You might say that." From the corner of my eye, I detected Brother Galthorn suppressing a grin.

"Begging your pardon," Fosdric said, dismounting. He loosely tied the horse's bridle to a low branch of the cherry tree that grew beside the front door of Brother Galthorn's church. He was no taller than Tarn, the village headman, but looked as though he might be half Tarn's weight, soaking wet. "I come from Palthinoor district," he said. "About two days by horse from Stelnregon. That's about six days' ride from Darnaatha."

"I have been there," I said. "Why have you come so far to find me?" Fosdric's face was dirty and unshaven, and the fatigue showed in his eyes. His thin face, sharp nose, and weak chin gave him a decidedly rodent-like appearance.

"We have a problem," he said, "and we need your help."

"A dragon?"

"We… think so."

"What do you mean? Dragons are fairly easy to identify."

"Well—no one has actually seen it."

I raised an eyebrow and waited.

"You see, Master Davian," he said, stretching his arms behind his head, "There's patches of burnt grass, and some of the farmers is finding livestock killed and cut open."

"Not eaten?" asked Brother Galthorn.

"Forgive me, brother," I said. "Fosdric, this is Brother Galthorn, the priest here in Marthwee."

"Pleased to meet you, brother," said Fosdric. "No, not eaten, just cut open."

"That would be unusual for a dragon," I said. "They will sometimes cut open a victim before eating it, but they do not kill prey just to watch it die."

"Here's something even more peculiar—some of the animals' insides was missing, and there was very little blood spilled about."

"Hmm." I thought for a moment, and then asked, "About these burned places: Were there obvious targets of the beast's flame nearby—the remains of a house or a man, for instance?"

"No, not so we can tell," Fosdric answered. "Just big circles of burnt-up ground."

"Odd," I said. "And no one has seen anything?"

"Not a bloody thing—sorry, brother."

"No offense taken," said Brother Galthorn.

Something seemed amiss, beside the obvious fact that the dragon was acting unlike any I had encountered. "Fosdric, let me ask again: Why have you come so far to find me? Surely there are others of The Order between Palthinoor and Marthwee. I know there are. Would it not have been quicker to reach one of them?"

He seemed reluctant to answer. "Well, sir, that was our first thought," he said, slowly. "In fact, we spent about six or seven days calling on your brothers. Four of them, to be exact."

"And?" I was growing impatient; evening was falling and my empty stomach was reminding me that it was past time for the evening meal.

"And they, ah, were not available."

"Not available? There is no higher priority for a member of The Order than meeting the threat of a dragon. Who did you call— Eritan? Myath? Redakios? I know these men! I do not believe they would refuse to come."

"Well, Master Davian, they didn't exactly refuse."

"Well? What, then?"

Fosdric took a deep breath before answering. "Master Davian, every brother of The Order near Palthinoor district has gone stark, raving mad. Eritan, Myath, Redakios, and Halteor, too—they're all out of their minds."

That chilled me. One fear common to the brothers of The Order is the loss of sanity. The effort of keeping our abilities under control—or perhaps the abuse of those abilities—can cause one's mind to crack. It is a fate that affects too many born with the Gift.

Even so, for four of my brothers, all healthy, sober men, to cross the line into madness within so short a time was unsettling. Could this the work of the unseen dragon?

That, too, was a disquieting thought. As I have mentioned, we of The Order can sense the presence of a dragon, and they, in turn, can sense when we are near. If we now faced a dragon that could not only hide itself from us, but also drive us insane—I did not want to consider the implications. Nor did I relish facing this threat, especially when it appeared that there would be no one from The Order to give me aid.

Yet I could not refuse to go. The Order had to be informed, and I seemed to be closest Master to the problem. But The Order is situated in the distant west, among the mountains of the Kingdom of Loanda, a journey of several months, at least. With the incapacitation of the four brothers near Palthinoor district, there would be no help from The Order.

So I stood there, contemplating the situation with the weary, undersized messenger, and the apprehensive, accidental dragon-slayer of a priest, nursing a nose that had been broken by the most beautiful woman I had ever seen, and finding myself about to face a potentially lethal threat with no help in sight.

At that moment, in the dwindling golden twilight outside the rustic stone church in Marthwee, I had an epiphany: If the Creator existed, he surely possessed an odd sense of humor.

CHAPTER FIVE

I decided to rest as best I could that night and leave Marthwee in the morning. Fosdric tended to his horse and rejoined us for a meal at the rectory before retiring for the night.

The following morning opened with a reddening sky in the east, a sign, I feared, of things to come. Farmers needed the rain, of course, but as one who would be traveling for the better part of the next two or three weeks, I did not welcome it. More than that, the crimson sky seemed to warn of more bloodshed before the end of this journey. I hoped it would not be mine.

As usual, I rose at dawn and went for a walk to clear my head. Some of the minor aches I had suffered in the battle with Sennthurniss had faded, but my nose was still swollen and sore, in spite of the ice I regularly applied to it. I took my razor, one of the few objects of metal that I own, and shaved the stubble from my face and scalp, using the river for a mirror.

Contrary to popular belief, those of us in The Order who shave our heads attach no ritual significance to the practice. It is a simple matter of practicality. While I am able to safely deflect a dragon's flame, it may still pass close enough to ignite my hair. The last thing one needs while battling a dragon is to be distracted by one's head catching fire.

Brother Galthorn greeted me cheerfully as I returned to the rectory and entered the small center room. "Good morning, Master Davian! Did you sleep well?"

"I did not. My nose still hurts, and I could not relax for thinking of the journey ahead."

"I am sorry to hear that," he said breezily. "Maybe some breakfast will help." His good mood was not infectious.

"Well, the night's rest seems to have helped you, in any case," I said. "Will you be able to face your parishioners again, then?"

"Certainly," Brother Galthorn said, "Although I don't plan to for a while."

Seating myself at the rough wooden table in the center of the room, I asked, "What do you mean?"

Setting a plate of scrambled eggs, bread, and sliced cheese in front of me, he said, "I am coming with you."

I saw no useful purpose the young priest could serve in the weeks ahead. Before me lay hardship, the need to travel quickly and light, and most probably a violent confrontation in which he could only be a hindrance. Instead of expressing these thoughts to Brother Galthorn, however, I said only, "What?"

"I'm coming with you," he repeated. "You cannot be expected to face this challenge alone. And if this is a new type of dragon, the church must be informed. So, I will investigate and report to my bishop."

My jaw hung slack. "Brother Galthorn," I said, "This is not a pilgrimage I am about to undertake. If what Fosdric says is true, death or madness may wait at the end of this road. With all due respect, I do not see that you can be of any help to me."

"Certainly you can use someone to cook and maintain your gear, such as it is," he replied. "And it won't hurt to have someone to offer spiritual guidance, as well."

"Doesn't your parish need you?"

"I have already sent word to Brother Thiamos at Delvernon, just two hours walk upriver. He will see to the needs of the parish while we are away."

Fosdric entered the room, looking even smaller and more disheveled than the night before. "Good morning," he said, yawning.

"Good morning, Fosdric," said Brother Galthorn. "How do you like your eggs?"

"Eggs? Oh, bless you, brother," Fosdric said. "Until last night, I had nothing but jerky and stale biscuits for a week. I was forgetting what eggs looked like. Scrambled, please. Good morning, Master Davian—ain't you hungry?"

The food on my plate hadn't been touched. "I am, but we've been discussing whether Brother Galthorn will travel with us."

"Excellent idea," Fosdric said. "Especially if he cooks like this every morning."

"You understand," I said, "that we need to travel quickly, and that two will move faster than three."

"Ah," he replied, "But there is safety in numbers."

"I doubt we can meet anything I cannot handle—at least, not until we find this invisible dragon."

"No offense, Master Davian," Fosdric said, occupying the other chair at the table. "But I don't see any harm in letting Brother Galthorn come along with us. Hey—it might help to have somebody with the Creator's ear on our side."

Sighing, I finally began to eat the breakfast that Galthorn had prepared. The eggs were delicious. There was no denying that Brother Galthorn had a talent.

"So what of you, Fosdric?" I asked. "What is your calling in life?"

He eyed the food on my plate hungrily. "I, uh, I work with horses."

"Cavalry? I was not aware that King Ednorwain had units of horse stationed in Palthinoor district."

"He doesn't."

"Then I misunderstood."

"Hmm?" Fosdric was obviously famished, and the tantalizing aroma from Brother Galthorn's efforts over the hearth was all but making him drool. He was clearly having difficulty carrying on a conversation.

"What do you do, then?" I asked.

"I tend horses for the captain of the King's Guard in Stelnregon."

"A stable hand?"

"You might say that, yeah."

Brother Galthorn appeared with a plate full of eggs, bread, and cheese, and set it in front of his guest. Without a word, Fosdric attacked the food with the zest of a morning bird pouncing on the first venturesome worm of the day.

An undersized stable hand and an underfed priest—the prospects of this venture grew dimmer by the hour.

"How was your meal, Master Davian?" asked Brother Galthorn.

"Excellent, actually," I admitted. "What did you do to the eggs?"

Beaming, he said, "It's a secret I learned as a boy. A little salt and pepper, some grated cheese, and a pinch of an herb I will not reveal even on pain of death."

"My compliments, brother. Guard your secret well, and I guarantee you will be welcome at any parish in the land."

"So," he said, "When do we leave?"

"Fosdric and I will depart after he has finished his meal," I answered. "Brother Galthorn, your place is here."

"I wonder about that," he said.

"What do you mean?"

"I sometimes think I was assigned to Marthwee because the parishioners wanted an inexperienced priest who was easily dominated."

"So this is your first church, then?"

"Yes."

"And do they intimidate you?"

"Well…"

"And how will traveling with us to confront this dragon change things?"

"I don't know," he said, turning to collect his cooking utensils. "But I will go with you. Excuse me."

Brother Galthorn stepped outside, laden with the tools of his culinary trade. I heard the splash of water outside as he washed them clean.

Finally coming up for air, his plate emptied, Fosdric wiped his mouth with the back of his hand and belched. "I think he should come with us," he said quietly.

"Why?"

"Well, it's simple, isn't it?" He stopped, as though that answer sufficed to explain.

"Well?" My patience wore thin.

"It's like this, see: What kind of thing flies around leaving no tracks, excepting those burnt patches, cutting up cows and pigs and goats, and not a body sees it? Either it's a dragon, and you'll take care of it, or it's something else."

"Right. And?"

"Well, if it's something else, what else could it be?"

"I don't know."

"Right," he said. "And if it's like nothing else in the world, where did it come from?"

"I don't know."

"Exactly." Fosdric folded his arms and looked satisfied with himself. I, however, failed to see his point.

"Tell me plainly," I said, "Why this requires the services of Brother Galthorn."

"Like I said, it's simple," he said. "If this whatever-it-is can do things like nothing else in the world, then Brother Galthorn's training might be more helpful than yours."

I was aghast. "Are you saying you think this might be the work of demons? Or gods?"

"It may be, Master Davian, it may be," said Brother Galthorn from the doorway, carrying a dripping pan. He looked entirely too pleased at the prospect of a personal encounter with a physical incarnation of evil.

"You are both mad," I said. "I need some tea."

* * *

The two of them won out. I rationalized that I could find some way to keep Brother Galthorn away from danger once we found it. If nothing else, at least I would eat better than if he stayed behind in Marthwee.

We left after packing up such things as we would need—clothing, cooking gear, and the like—and loading them into packs on the back of Fosdric's horse, Aeryx. Heading south on the road to

Darnaatha, we were away just as the village was coming fully awake.

Since time was of the essence, I decided not to do more than leave hastily scribbled notes for Tarn and Panderthan thanking them for their hospitality and explaining the need for our sudden departure. I briefly considered stopping at Tarn's home anyway, just on the chance that I'd catch another glimpse of Lareina, but prudence triumphed over fancy.

We soon came to the field of my alleged victory over the dragon, which was marked by the charred remains of the unusable parts of the carcass. I asked Fosdric to bring Aeryx to a halt, and Brother Galthorn and I walked over to the field to examine the area for signs of the struggle. A large depressed area of flattened turf indicated the place where the dragon had come to ground. Some distance off to one side, still intact, was my long wooden spear.

Retrieving it, I said to Brother Galthorn, "Let us be on our way."

He said, "Isn't that remarkable? I would have thought that the spear would have broken under the dragon's weight."

"It would have, had it been stuck in the dragon when it hit."

"But… but I thought your spear brought it down."

"No, Brother Galthorn," I said, as we rejoined Fosdric at the road, "My throw with the spear was in desperation. I was only trying to get out of its way."

He knitted his brows in confusion. "But then—what killed the dragon?"

"You did."

"What?"

"Your shout, as you ran along the road," I said. "You distracted the beast in mid-flight, in the middle of its dive. It was so surprised by the sight of you running along the road, shouting at the top of your lungs, that it forgot itself just long enough to avoid the ground."

The young man stopped in his tracks, eyes wide, still uncomprehending.

"Simply put, brother," I said, "You startled the dragon, it slammed into the turf and most probably broke its neck."

Fosdric burst out with a guffaw and fell to his knees, laughing uncontrollably. Eyes tearing, he struggled to speak. "Oh! Oh! You mean… the priest… scared the dragon… to death! Oh, I'd have paid any price to see that!" And he collapsed again in a fit of hysterics.

Brother Galthorn was more embarrassed than anything. We waited several minutes while Fosdric brought his amusement under control, and then we continued on.

"Master Davian," Galthorn asked, "Why did you wish to retrieve your spear?"

"This is the memento I wish to keep from this encounter. It is a reminder in case I should get it into my head that I need not prepare to the fullest for my next meeting with a dragon," I said. "Besides, it makes a good walking staff."

* * *

Our walk during the rest of that day was uneventful. The red sky at dawn proved to be portentous, as the day grew steadily darker as we walked. Clouds rolled in from the west, and around midday a light rain began to fall. It was not enough to make travel difficult, but it served to dampen my already bleak spirit.

We stopped to eat our midday meal under a large oak tree that provided fair shelter from the drizzle. After half an hour, we moved on in under steadily increasing showers. Our hope was to travel as far as Elocin, the next town on the road, by nightfall. The inn at Elocin, the Court Jester, was spacious and comfortable; Brother Galthorn and I had stayed there the night before we arrived in Marthwee.

Our progress slowed as the afternoon wore on. Slowly, as the ground absorbed its fill of rainwater, the path we followed turned from hard-packed dirt to mud. The temperature began to drop as well, just enough to give us a slight chill. I was in a positively foul mood as darkness began to fall and we finally reached the outskirts of Elocin.

Finding the Court Jester easy enough. It was prominently located in the center of the village, and the sounds coming from within could be heard plainly all through the community. We wearily made our way through the muddy streets to the noisy, brightly lit inn. The proprietor, Bortz, a short, balding, heavy-set man with a squint to his eyes, greeted us with a smile as we opened the heavy wooden door and stepped inside, out of the rain. The scent of whatever simmered in the kitchen mingled with smoke from the hearth and several homemade pipes to draw us in with the promise of good food and fellowship.

"Greetings, travelers," he said, with a trace of lisp. "Come in and dry yourselves. Ah, Master Davian and Brother Galthorn! Welcome back! It is good to see you again so soon. Perhaps something to drive off the chill?"

"Thank you," I said, "Perhaps we will. We will also require lodging for the night and shelter for my friend's horse."

"Certainly, certainly," Bortz said, rubbing his hands together. "I am honored to have you here again, Master Davian. We have heard of your success with the dragon. Anything you need, Master Davian, just let me know. It's on the house."

"There is no need to do that, Bortz. We are happy to pay just like any other guest."

"Nonsense, nonsense. Nothing is too good for a brother of The Order and his friends. Please! You are my guests. I insist."

"But…"

"Now, Master Davian," Fosdric interrupted, "Don't insult the good man by refusing his hospitality." Turning to our host, he said, "Much obliged, good sir. Is there anything to eat?"

After calling a boy from the kitchen—his son, I assumed—to tend to Fosdric's horse, Bortz led us to a table in the expansive stone and timber main hall, where he soon had a flavorful meat and vegetable stew and freshly-baked bread set before us. His ale was cold—colder than when he poured it, of course—and it helped to wash down the meal very nicely. With a full belly and my clothing nearly dry, I finally began to relax.

As we finished our tankards of ale, Bortz appeared from the kitchen to offer refills, confirm our satisfaction with the meal, and ask about the events in the field outside Marthwee several days before.

"So, Master Davian," he said, settling next to Fosdric at the table, "How did it happen? I want to hear the details of the entire battle, from start to finish."

I cleared my throat. "Well, there really isn't much to tell."

Bortz chortled. "Ho, ho, a modest man if ever I saw one! Come now, let's have it, and don't leave anything out!"

"All right," I said. "As I approached the dragon, it threw a headless goat at me. I hit it between the eyes with a blast of heat. It took to the air and tried to cook me where I stood. I deflected the flame. Then—well, then Brother Galthorn came running down the road..."

"Just in time to see the dragon's end!" Galthorn said. "Master Davian was magnificent! He feigned weakness to draw the dragon into a fatal mistake, and the arrogant beast fell right into his trap. The monster, seven man-heights long if he was one, began a fearsome descent, faster than you can imagine, diving straight for Davian, intending to kill him with one swipe of its terrible claws. But Davian stood his ground, hunched and leaning against his wooden spear as though utterly exhausted. Down came the beast, hurtling toward its prey, gaining speed with each beat of its mighty wings, looking for all the world as though it had been flung from the sky by the Creator himself. And still Master Davian held firm—until the last possible moment, when it was too late for the dragon to alter its course. Then Davian pulled himself up and hurled his spear with all his might, straight and true, right at the onrushing demon's heart. The force of the dragon's downward flight drove the weapon home, and the creature crashed to the ground, killed instantly by the skill and daring of Master Davian."

I stared at Brother Galthorn in open-mouthed wonder. Fosdric hid his laughter behind a sudden and conveniently timed coughing fit.

"Absolutely remarkable!" Bortz exclaimed with delight. "That is the most amazing thing I have heard in my entire life!" I could not tell whether he was impressed by the fictional sequence of events related by Brother Galthorn or by the young priest's telling of the tale—which, truthfully, had been rather vivid.

"Remarkable!" Bortz said again, standing. "Well, if you gentlemen will excuse me, I need to attend to my other guests. See me when you are ready to retire and I'll show you to your room." The innkeeper began to make the rounds of the hall, talking with the groups of men as he went. As he moved from table to table, I began to feel the eyes of the other patrons on us. We had undoubtedly been noticed and marked as outsiders right from the start, but now, with my hungry belly and tired feet more or less satisfied, I took more notice of our surroundings.

The Court Jester was easily four times the size of the Merry Fisherman. It was a large rectangular building constructed on one level with a kitchen on one end, a large center hall, and a hallway dividing the far end into two rows of rooms for travelers—and those too tipsy after a night of Bortz's ale to walk home. Presently, there were two dozen customers at the inn, give or take a few. The more the townsfolk tried to pretend they were not looking at us, the more aware of it I became.

"It seems we are on display," I said quietly. "This is making me uncomfortable."

"You're a celebrity," Fosdric said. "Drink up and enjoy it." He stood and wandered toward the kitchen, in search of Bortz and another tankard of ale.

I shook my head. "Galthorn, why did you tell Bortz I killed the dragon? You and I know well that I did not."

Smiling, he said, "Truly, Master Davian, I doubt that the dragon would have thrown itself into the ground if I had run up to it without you there."

"No. That is true."

"So in a sense, my tale is true. Oh, embellished a bit, perhaps, but essentially true." He leaned across the table and spoke more quietly. "And I do not think it would do for the good people of Elocin to hear that you were not at the peak of your form. Especially not with those rough-looking characters back in the corner watching you so closely."

"Where?"

"Behind you, on your right. Four men sitting at a table in the corner."

Forcing myself to continue looking ahead at Brother Galthorn, I asked, "How long have they been watching us?"

"Since we arrived."

"Trying to judge how easily they might separate us from our belongings?"

"Perhaps. Or perhaps they admire your striking hairstyle."

I smiled. "That seems unlikely."

"I was trying to give the gentlemen the benefit of doubt."

"Admirable of you, brother. However, do not let good will for your fellow men blind you to their true intentions."

"Oh, I assure you that I do not. Remember, the Holy Book says we are to be as gentle as doves, but as wise as serpents."

"Wise advice," I said. "More practical than I have come to expect from the scriptures."

Brother Galthorn picked up his tankard and finished off the last of his ale. "Have you ever read the Holy Book?"

"Yes, but only a few sections," I said. "What I know of scripture is based on those occasions that I have heard it preached. No offense to your profession, brother, but your colleagues seem obsessed with personal sacrifice for the good of others. Usually as it relates to sacrificing one's finances in the collection plate."

"Yes, well, our livelihood depends on the generosity of our parishioners," he admitted. "Those funds provide for our needs and the upkeep of the church. And we are expected to use those funds to care for orphans and widows, too. There is never enough."

"People take care of themselves first, eh?"

"Yes." He nodded. "I can't blame them, really. After all, my goal is to shepherd them into eternity. That requires faith; most demand evidence they can see or touch. At least you, Master Davian, can point to a dead dragon at the end of a day."

The sound of on old bar room ditty, wildly off-key, came from the other side of the room. Fosdric, who had apparently drained another tankard or two of ale while Brother Galthorn and I talked, had burst into song. He walked across the floor toward us with the grace and precision of a bumblebee in flight on a windy day.

"...And they all called her Lil, just Lil!" Fosdric sang with enthusiasm, making up for his lack of tonality with sheer effort. His gait seemed to defy gravity. I marveled that anyone could lean so far from vertical without falling over. Collapsing onto the bench next to me, Fosdric swayed and grinned stupidly.

"Do you think it is wise," I said quietly, "to drink so heavily when far from home?"

Without losing his drunken appearance, Fosdric said under his breath, "You should watch your back, Master Davian."

"You noticed them too?" asked Brother Galthorn.

"I think you should help me to our room," said Fosdric.

Taking our cue, Galthorn and I picked up Fosdric by his elbows and, saying goodnight to Bortz, we maneuvered our charge down the hall to the room the innkeeper had prepared for us. A casual glance revealed that the four men in the corner were still watching us very carefully.

Once inside the room, Fosdric detached himself and seemed to instantly shake off the effects of the ale he'd consumed. "That is quite an act, Fosdric," I said. "Very convincing."

"Thank you, Master Davian," he said, bowing. "I was the toast of the city for my turn as Lavallior in *The Corridor of Horrors* last year during the Stelnregon summer festival."

Brother Galthorn laughed. "Delightful! I was completely taken in."

"Yes, yes," I said, irritated. "What about the men sitting in the corner?"

"Right," Fosdric said. "They was watching you."

"Yes. Brother Galthorn noticed that."

"That's all," he said. "I saw them watching you, and I didn't want them to think I saw them, so I played drunk."

"Clever work, Fosdric. You didn't, by chance, happen to overhear any of their conversation?"

"No. Why?"

"That might have been useful," I said. "Well, in any case, it helps to be reminded that one should always be on his guard when traveling. And now, gentlemen, I propose we secure the room and turn in for the night."

After examining the room and determining that the window and the hallway door were the only points of entry, we barred both, extinguished the candles and bade each other good night.

* * *

The day's walk through the rain and the mud, combined with the glasses of ale I consumed with dinner, helped to put me instantly into a deep sleep. So deep was my slumber that not even Fosdric's snoring, which Brother Galthorn assured me later was thunderous, was able to disturb me.

At some point during the night, however, I was roused from slumber by a shout from the direction of the door. "Hey! Hey! What's this, then?" It was Fosdric, and he was clearly agitated.

A scuffling noise was followed by a mumbling voice I could not understand. A crack of light seeped into the room through the doorway to the hall. Then the door closed, blocking the light, and all was still for a moment save for the heavy breathing of Fosdric coming from the floor in front of the door.

I sat up in the bed and felt around on the small table next to it until I found a candle. Focusing on it, I brought the wick to flame, and then looked toward the door.

"Fosdric," I said, "Are you all right? What happened?"

"Well," Fosdric said, as Brother Galthorn rose from a pallet on the floor to see to him, "I moved my bedroll over here in front of the door, just in case somebody paid us a visit in the night. And good thing, too, because somebody just did!"

"But how?" asked Brother Galthorn.

"Oh, there's lots of ways," said Fosdric as he stood. "Let's just see… here. See this?" He held a string in his hand that led over the top of the door. He gave it a jerk and pulled it inside.

"What is it?" Galthorn asked.

"Standard burgling equipment," Fosdric said, pulling the end of the string from the bar in the door. "Fish hook, lowered over the top of the door. Hook the bar, give a tug, and there you are—an open door."

"That was good thinking," I said, "positioning yourself near the door."

"Thank you, Master Davian," he said, bowing with mock humility. "Just common sense."

"Fosdric," Brother Galthorn said, "Just how do you know that this is standard equipment for burglars?"

Even in the dim light, I could see Fosdric redden. "I, ah, I've heard as such."

"I see," said the young priest, arms folded.

I saw, too, that the stable hand and part-time thespian just might be a man of diverse and useful talents.

CHAPTER SIX

The rest of the night passed without incident, although it was some time before the three of us were able to return to sleep. Morning came much earlier than usual, as much of my night was spent wondering what, exactly, the would-be burglar was after.

Most disturbing to me was the fact that I did not sense the approach of our uninvited guest. Those of us with the Gift can generally feel the presence of others nearby, even when unseen. I hear it as a sort of buzzing, not unlike that of a fly or mosquito, but inside my head, in the same way that I hear a dragon when it chooses to communicate.

The tankard of ale I consumed with the previous night's dinner was to blame, I decided, and I vowed to abstain from alcohol, at least for the rest of our journey.

I rose at dawn, finding the silence at the inn relaxing. Fosdric and Brother Galthorn were still asleep. Fosdric's snoring was finally stilled for a time as he had rolled onto his stomach sometime during the night.

The main hall at the inn was empty, and it seemed cold after the buzz of activity the night before. Curiously, the front door was unbarred. Even in a small village such as Elocin, that was unusual. I made a mental note to ask Bortz about it.

The ground outside was still wet from the rains the day before. Several sets of footprints were visible in the mud outside the door. There was no way to be sure, but my guess was that the men who had been so interested in me the night before were the same ones who paid a call on us in the dark of night. As tired as I was, I felt an early start was still our best course of action. Maybe we could put some distance between us and our would-be assailants before they rose for the day.

Returning to our room, I quietly roused my companions and shared my thoughts. They agreed, and we prepared to leave.

Bortz must have heard us moving about, because he was bustling about as we entered the hall. "Good morning, gentlemen! Did you sleep well?"

"Truthfully, no," I said. "We were disturbed by a visitor or visitors during the night."

"Rats?" Bortz asked with distaste. "I thought that good-for-nothing cat was getting lazy. I'll put him out as soon as I find him!"

I cut him off. "Human visitors. Someone tried to enter our room last night."

"Oh, no," he said. "I'm dreadfully sorry. Is there anything I can do for you?"

"Tell me," I replied, "Do you always leave your door unbarred at night?"

"Why, no, I—why do you ask?"

"Because it was unbarred this morning when I rose."

"That's strange," Bortz said. "I always bar the door at night. How can that be?"

"Explain it to him, Fosdric," I said. Fosdric took the innkeeper aside and began to explain the mechanics of how one might circumvent a barred door.

"Do you believe him?" asked Brother Galthorn.

I shook my head. "I don't know. He may have left the door unbarred with the idea of sharing in the profit. We cannot know for sure."

"I would like to believe he's an honest man," Galthorn said.

"As would I," I replied.

* * *

After a quick breakfast, we made our farewell to Bortz, who seemed genuinely sorry to see us go, and resumed our trek. Aeryx, Fosdric's horse, seemed none the worse for wear. The road, although wet, was firmer than it had been at the end of the previous day, and the skies, although cloudy, seemed to be clearing.

The terrain south of Elocin rose slowly for several hours, and then began a series of gentle undulations as we crossed a number of low hills. Progress was good, despite the hills. As the morning lengthened, the road continued to dry. The broken clouds kept the sun from growing too warm, and it was possible to look about as we walked to enjoy the greenery of the fertile countryside.

Elocin and the domains to the south are part of the Darnaatha district, a hilly agricultural area dotted with small farms and roamed by flocks of sheep. A temperate climate and ample rain in the spring and early summer assured a fair growing season and ample crops to feed the district, with enough of a surplus to allow for a healthy trade with surrounding areas for luxuries, such as jewelry and perfumes, and manufactured goods, tools, and metalwork; items not produced in any quantity locally. Surrounded by such a bounty, it was possible to forget for a time the trouble that called us afield.

At noon, we stopped at the base of a small hill. Fosdric watered Aeryx, and then joined Brother Galthorn and I for a meal of cold meat pies, a parting gift from Bortz. "Strange," Fosdric said, "Not much traffic on the road today."

Lost in my thoughts, I had not noticed. On reflection, however, I realized that the stable hand was right. "Nor did we see any travelers yesterday," I added.

"Is that unusual?" Brother Galthorn asked.

"How many did we encounter during our first trip along this road?"

"Quite a few, as I recall." Galthorn scratched his head.

"Indeed." An icy ball of dread began to form in the pit of my stomach.

"I thought perhaps that the traffic was simply thinner the further one traveled from Darnaatha," Galthorn said.

"That is true," I said. "Darnaatha is a city of nearly one hundred thousand, and there is nothing beyond Marthwee larger than five or six hundred people. The road is not heavily traveled this far from Darnaatha. Even so, we should have more company on the road."

"Maybe it's weather keeping them inside," Fosdric said.

"Possibly," I said. "But there should be traders and peddlers moving along the road, at least. They travel because they must, not for pleasure when the weather suits them."

"Hmm," said Brother Galthorn. "Perhaps we will see more traffic as we move along."

We talked and rested for about an hour, and then resumed our journey southward along the Darnaatha road.

* * *

The rest of the day passed uneventfully. Sunlight continued to break through the clouds occasionally, lifting our spirits and further aiding our travel as the puddles on the road dried to wet spots and began to disappear.

At dusk, we found a flat, shaded spot alongside the road to camp for the night. Taking Aeryx's lead, Fosdric wandered off to find a stream we knew to be nearby while Brother Galthorn and I collected deadwood to build a fire.

For a member of The Order, building a fire is child's play. In fact, for some of the brothers, too much of their play as children involved fire. That is one of the reasons that children with the Gift need to be in the care of elders. They must be surrounded by men who can sense, locate, and suppress spot fires in short order.

Focusing my mind on the tinder, I ignited the dry leaves and twigs, and Brother Galthorn and I settled to the ground to nurse the fire along. "Master Davian," Galthorn asked, as he chopped some vegetables from our pack into a pot, "Could you not just ignite a blaze and spare us the trouble of building up the fire from nothing?"

Smiling, I said, "I could, brother, but it is good for you to keep in practice against that day when I'm no longer here to do it for you."

The priest laughed softly. "Truly, though, could you ignite such a blaze with your mind?"

"I could, but I prefer not to use my abilities beyond what is truly necessary. Well, perhaps for a few small conveniences, such as igniting the tinder for a fire or heating a mug of water for tea."

"Why is that?"

"Every use of my ability requires physical energy, and I do not think it wise to drain myself physically for the sake of doing something that can be done easily enough in other ways." Shifting some larger sticks over the crackling flame, I added, "And I do not know what the long-term effects of my gift may be. Too many brothers of The Order lose their grip on reality before they die. Who knows but that the use of this power may cause one's mind to crack over time? No, brother, that is too great a price to pay for an instant meal."

Crackling leaves in the direction of the stream indicated Fosdric's return with Aeryx. "Ho!" he shouted.

"Ho, yourself," I said. "Why are you shouting?"

"It's simple, isn't it?" The little man stepped into view near the fire and looped Aeryx's lead over a low branch. "I don't want you blasting me by mistake, thinking I'm some bandit."

"Not likely. A bandit would have made less noise crashing through the forest."

"Ho, ho," Fosdric said. "How's that dinner coming along, Brother Galthorn?"

"I have finished with the vegetables. If you have the water, we can set the stew over the fire to cook."

The evening was pleasant. Skies had cleared, and the temperature was moderate. With luck, we might find enough dry leaves to prepare comfortable places to sleep for the night. Brother Galthorn's vegetable stew, although it was some time before it was ready to eat, was thoroughly enjoyable, and the water from the nearby stream was clear and cold. All in all, death and danger seemed very far indeed from our little pocket of forest just off the Darnaatha road.

As our fire dwindled, it was agreed that Brother Galthorn would take the first watch. Fosdric was to relieve him about midnight, and I would watch from the third hour until dawn. It meant a short night of sleep, but with a good day's travel we would arrive at Telthig, a village with a small but comfortable inn, by early afternoon. There would be time to sleep then.

* * *

Deep in the night, with the moons hidden by cloud, an unexpected noise roused me from sleep. Not knowing the hour, and not wishing to keep Fosdric awake longer than necessary, I began to sit up from my bed of leaves to ask him whether it was time to take my watch.

Too late, I sensed the presence of others in the woods around us. My cheek felt a sharp pain as though from the sting of a bee, and within moments the world began to spin with me at its axis, and I fell into the void.

Of the next several days, I remember little. There are vague memories of being carried and of hearing voices as I drifted in and out of consciousness. Even during those brief moments when I was somewhat aware of my surroundings, however, I was utterly incapable of moving or focusing my thoughts. I remember the words "Darnaatha" and "Order", and thinking that the road over which we traveled was exceptionally rough. I hoped that Fosdric and Brother Galthorn were still alive.

Hours or days later, I knew not which, I slowly came awake in darkness. Pressure across my eyes and temples suggested a blindfold. Experimenting with my stiff and aching limbs revealed that my wrists and ankles were bound. The unmistakable odor of urine assaulted my nose; whatever had been used to drug me had obviously relaxed the muscles that controlled my bladder. I was ashamed and angry. Breathing deeply, I began a relaxation exercise to conceal the fact that I was finally alert.

"Methinks he's coming awake, boys. Look sharp, now." The voice was gruff, and the accent indicated that the stranger was from far to the south. Reaching out with my mind, I tried to pinpoint his location.

"Look here, Master Wizard," the voice said, "Before you get any ideas about blasting away, you should know that my mates have got your friends far enough away you won't find 'em. Not quick enough, anyways, if anything happens to me, if you get my drift."

He paused, and I listened carefully with my ears and my mind. The only audible noises were the crackling of the fire and the chirping of night insects. I sensed Fosdric and Brother Galthorn, but not nearby. There were others, too, but I could not tell exactly how many. They were too close to Fosdric and Galthorn to differentiate between them.

"Do you believe me?"

"Yes." My voice was a croak, and I was extremely thirsty.

"Well, then, we have the beginning of an understanding." A rustle of leaves as Gruff shifted his weight. "So. You probably wonder why I dragged you here."

"Where?"

"Now, now," I heard. "All in good time, all in good time. What you need to know right now is that your friends have knives to their throats, and if anything surprises my friends what holds the knives, they have instructions to cut. Do you understand me?"

"Yes."

"Good. We're making progress, then. I was told your kind was smart. I'm glad they was right."

"Who are you?" I asked.

"My name? Not important." The leaves crackled as he shifted again. "If you want something to call me, try 'boss'."

"Right."

"Right, what?"

"Right, boss."

He laughed, a self-satisfied chortle that brought the blood to my cheeks. I forced myself to remember that losing my temper might cost Fosdric and Brother Galthorn their heads, and I cursed myself for allowing the young priest to travel with us. Gruff-voice and his companions obviously wanted me alive for some reason, but without the lives of Galthorn and Fosdric as bargaining chips, I would not have been taken and held against my will.

"See there," the voice continued, "That wasn't so hard, was it? Just remember that I'm the boss until I'm done with you. So don't get any ideas you forget to tell me about. Any surprises and your friends are dead."

"What do you want?" I asked. But instead of an answer, I heard a puff of air and felt another sting on my cheek, and once again the ground opened below me and pulled me down into nothingness.

* * *

Adrift on an ebony sea, I felt myself pushed and moved by forces I could not see or control. At first, there was only pitch, but gradually shapes and colors, swirling and blending, came into view. Unable to move, I watched helplessly as nightmare visions resolved and melted again before my eyes. Nowhere and everywhere, distinct and yet shapeless, time and dimension lost all meaning.

Slowly, I became aware of a sound in the distance. It grew slowly louder and more insistent. I reached for it, clung to it, willed it to approach; by locating it, I hoped I might free myself from the eternal darkness into which I'd fallen.

Maddeningly, it seemed an eternity as I searched for the sound. It beckoned persistently but allowed me to approach only slowly, as though afraid of being drawn into my hellish vision.

I clung to the sound as a drowning man clings to a slender bit of driftwood. Slowly, steadily, it grew in volume, until at last I was able to distinguish a voice, and then syllables, and finally words.

"Master Davian? Master Davian!" It was Brother Galthorn, calling from beyond the boundary of my unlit world.

The darkness around me began to evaporate, dissolving into an almost palpable film, opaque but resistant to my efforts to break through. Though light penetrated the barrier, my eyes still saw nothing.

"Master Davian! Please! Wake up!"

Try as I might, the veil would not lift—but neither would Brother Galthorn abandon me to the void.

"Davian, please! I do not know how long we—" I heard a muffled, heavy thud, and priest's voice was cut off in mid-sentence.

I found that I was able to open my eyes at last. It appeared that I was inside a covered wooden cart of the sort used by peddlers.

Still bound hand and foot, the ropes were rubbing my wrists raw. Through gaps in the slats along the side of the cart, I was able to see that we were in a town or village, and that the hour was either late or very early.

The twin doors at the back of the cart were pulled open and the unconscious Brother Galthorn was roughly bundled in next to me. The coppery scent of blood was in the air, but it was too dark to see exactly where Galthorn had been injured.

A voice next to the cart hissed, "That's what you'll get if you try to be cute. Got me?" It was Gruff. I assumed he was speaking to Fosdric.

The cart lurched and moved forward. A wave of nausea rolled over me and I tried to focus my eyes on a stationary object outside. My eyes found a tree and I clung to it for several minutes, breathing shallowly until the nausea passed. My head throbbed again. More than anything else, I prayed for the opportunity to someday inflict the substance with which I had been drugged on the men directing the cart.

Rolling to my side, I tried to examine Brother Galthorn to determine the extent of his injury. It was difficult to see in the dim light, and the priest's dark hair made it impossible to see the blood.

The cart stopped again. A scuffle erupted outside, but the noises quickly faded into the darkness. The driver of the cart dropped to the ground, and heavy footsteps marked his movements to the back of the wagon.

Creaking hinges; the doors swung open and outlined a large man with long hair tied at the back of his neck. I was unsure whether he knew I was awake, but apparently, he wasn't taking chances. "We have your little friend. Don't try anything or he's dead. You hear?"

I kept silent. That just seemed to irritate him.

"Hey, warlock," he said, a bit louder. "Get up. You can save your friend's life or get him killed. I don't care either way."

"What do you want?"

"Ah, good," he said. "You're awake. My mates have your little friend close by. They're watching us, see, and if something happens to me, they slit his throat. Understand?"

"What do you want?"

"My, but you're a tune with one note. All right, then, here it is: You're going to help us get rich."

"Why should I do that?"

The big man chuckled. "Why, it's simple, isn't it? You do what I say, or your friends get hurt. Do we understand each other?"

"Yes."

"Good, good. You're a smart man, warlock. I always thought your kind was smart."

"I'm not a warlock."

"Near enough," he said. "Come on now. Out you go." He grabbed my ankles and pulled me out of the cart, dropping me to the dirt. The fall, less than half a man-height, hurt my head tremendously. "Here." He cut through the ropes around my ankles. "Stand up." I struggled through the process of standing with my hands tied behind my back. Gruff made no effort to help.

"Now what?" I asked.

The big man laughed again, except with his eyes. They held a hardness that belied an inner determination to do anything to get what he wanted.

"My, you're curious, ain't ya? Well, remember what curiosity got the cat. You'll know when it's time for you to know. Now come with me."

"Who are you, and where are we?"

"I'm the boss, and I'll tell you where we are when we gets inside. Now move."

He stepped behind me and pushed between my shoulder blades, forcing me toward a modest thatched hovel just off the lane where the cart was parked. A small garden plot lay behind the building, and in the darkness, I could just make out similar dwellings, smoke rising from most of the stone chimneys, stretching away on either side.

My captor pounded three times on the wooden door as we arrived, and a thin, sad-eyed man opened it from within. "Ah, you're back, Elgyrn," he said.

"Shut up, fool," the big man said, clubbing the smaller man with a closed fist to the ear. "We don't need him learning our names. Bad enough he knows our faces." Grabbing my shirt with a meaty hand, he pulled me inside. Turning to the smaller man, he said, "There's a priest in back of the cart, sleeping. Carry him in."

Rubbing his ear, the smaller man asked, "Can't I just wake him and bring him?"

"Might not wake," Elgyrn said. "I had to persuade him to lie down."

The thin man made an "O" with his mouth and went outside.

"What is this about, Elgyrn?" I asked.

"I told you. You're going to make me rich." He pulled me by my shirt and threw me onto the dirt floor in front of the fireplace. A kettle boiled over the fire. I was hungry, but whatever was in that pot did not smell very appealing.

"You have said so." I waited, and the silence stretched. Elgyrn seemed in no hurry to share his thoughts on the matter.

From my position on the floor, I finally had an opportunity to assess my captor. Elgyrn was a big man, powerfully built, with a barrel chest and arms the size of young oaks. I would have wagered that he could crack coconuts with his meaty hands. His face had the rough and uneven look of clay that had been fired before the potter's work was done.

At length, the creaking door opened again and the smaller man, huffing and puffing under the weight of Brother Galthorn, staggered into the room.

With a sigh of relief, Elgyrn's assistant unloaded Brother Galthorn from his back. The priest tumbled like a rag doll to the floor and lay still.

"Whatever you did, Elgyrn, fixed him up a treat," the thin man said with a chuckle. Elgyrn only grunted, lost in his thoughts.

"If he dies, Elgyrn, you have no hold on me," I said.

"We still have your little friend."

"He can fend for himself. And the death you die will be particularly painful."

Elgyrn laughed, clearly prepared to call my bluff. "I know you better than you think, warlock. I don't think you will let a man die to save your own neck. If I thought so, you wouldn't be here."

He was right, but I had hoped he might believe otherwise.

Trying to ignore the agony in my head, I closed my eyes and forced myself to think. Elgyrn was dangerous and possibly desperate. Whatever he had planned, it was worth enough to gamble his life and the lives of his men that they could manipulate a brother of The Order. That was a feat not many would attempt. What, then, could require the unique skills we possess? Alas, the effects of the drug he had used made it impossible to think that far ahead.

"Bit of the morning after, eh, warlock?" Elgyrn chuckled. "Maybe we can spare some rum to clear your head. You—get him a drink."

The thin man slouched to a cupboard and pulled a bottle from within. His demeanor was that of a chastised schoolboy.

I normally do not indulge in hard spirits. It is unwise for members of The Order to befuddle one's senses. It does not happen often, but brothers have sometimes caused destruction on a truly spectacular scale when out of their minds with drink. However, I thought the rum might help relieve the hammering in my skull, and I was certainly of no use to Fosdric or Brother Galthorn in my present condition anyway.

The thin man brought a dirty, cracked mug filled with amber liquid to me. I took the mug and swallowed its contents as quickly as I could. The rum was cheap, and I grimaced as it burned a new, more direct path from my mouth to my gut. Elgyrn, watching me, had a hearty laugh at my expense once again. That was growing tiresome.

"I am losing patience, Elgyrn," I said. "You may push me to a point where I no longer care what happens to myself or anyone around me." The thin man edged away from me, but Elgyrn merely grunted without looking up and continued with his business at the rough wooden table.

The big man flattened a folded piece of paper with his filthy, ham-sized hands and began examining it. After a moment, he raised his eyes. "Come here, warlock," he said.

"Why?"

"Because if you don't, I'll beat the priest again. Come here."

Rising from the floor slowly to accommodate my stiff muscles, I shuffled across the room to the table. "What is it?"

"See this?" He tapped the paper.

"It appears to be a map."

"Very good, warlock. And this is our ticket to riches."

"Our ticket?"

Elgyrn grinned, gaps showing where several teeth had parted company with his smile. "My ticket, me and my mates. You, if you're good, you get to live."

"What does this map have to do with riches?"

"It so happens that this shows the insides of the dwelling of the king's tax collector for the district," Elgyrn said. "Including where he keeps the coin he's collected for the king—which I hear is there right now, waiting to be sent off to Ednorwain."

"So we are in Darnaatha? Are you mad? Are you not aware of the guards posted by the king to protect his money? King Ednorwain does not take lightly to thieves making off with his taxes." Then the pieces connected and I realized with a start why Elgyrn had kidnapped us.

For his plan to succeed, people would have to die. And he needed me to kill them.

CHAPTER SEVEN

The thought sent a chill down my spine. I have seen more than my share of death; such is the lot of brothers of The Order. However, most of the dead men I have seen were victims of dragons. My eyes have seen only a few killed by other men, but none have met their death at my hand.

This is part of the training for those of us in The Order. With the abilities we inherit, it would be child's play to take almost anything we wished from those around us. We cannot allow ourselves to succumb to this temptation, and we are trained from early childhood to understand the dangers of doing so. Many years ago, wiser men than I recognized that the survival of our kind depended on dedicating ourselves to service rather than conquest.

That is not to say that it has never happened. It is recorded in our histories that brothers of The Order have been tempted or coerced more than once to use their abilities for the oppression or domination of others. When this has happened, a deputation of elders was assembled and dispatched immediately to bring the rogue under control—sometimes with deadly force. When possible, restitution is made to those who have been harmed.

Our standing with the public is a thing we jealously protect. Despite our powers, we could not stand for long against armed, angry mobs. Although one of us may easily best an ordinary man, or even a company of men, a determined mob would eventually overwhelm even the strongest of us—although not before many had died.

If fear of The Order were to grow strong enough, no child born with the Gift would be allowed to live beyond infancy. Only the

Creator knows what toll the dragons would exact from mankind then.

And the brute, Elgyrn, meant to use me in a way that would surely ignite fear of The Order in the heart of Aerwald, a kingdom where our number have been welcomed as long as I can remember: He intended for me to kill anyone who stood between him and the gold in the king's treasury in the very city I called home.

Elgyrn laughed as he saw understanding dawn in my eyes. "So, warlock, you see why I need you?"

"I will not do it," I said.

"You will, or your friends die," he growled. "And not quickly, neither."

Time. I needed time to think, or time for Elgyrn to make a mistake. Unless I wanted Brother Galthorn and Fosdric to suffer more than they had already, I must cooperate with Elgyrn.

"Rest, now," Elgyrn continued. "'Tis morning, and we've naught to do until night."

"Is there a place I can wash?" I asked. "And perhaps you would allow me to walk home and retrieve a change of clothes. I would burn the ones I wear."

Again Elgyrn laughed. "You jest, warlock. You know Darnaatha better than I, and I don't trust you outside my sight. And I have no plans to leave the house in daylight."

Darnaatha had been my home these last five years. It is the largest city in the district that takes its name, and one of the largest cities in the kingdom of Aerwald. While I do not care for crowds, I find the presence of so many souls nearby reassuring for reasons I have not fully examined. Perhaps I prefer it because it is easier for one of my kind to be anonymous in a place of many souls than in a small village, such as Marthwee.

The city is located on a hill that commands the surrounding terrain for miles, ideally situated as a center of regional government. Many years ago, the first king of Aerwald, Wendorwyn, recognized its natural advantages and established it as a military command post. This of course went hand in glove with the collection of taxes. Where soldiers and government officials must gather, other industries take root to serve their needs, and so the city grew.

Darnaatha is not recognized for its contribution to the culture in terms of science or the arts, but it is a place where I can spend my days without being disturbed. Most of the city's residents are too engrossed in their own affairs, which usually involve extracting revenue from the surrounding district, to bother with me.

The king's tax collectors are busy men. Governing a kingdom requires a great deal of money. That money is kept inside a well-guarded storehouse and transferred to the king at regular intervals. If Elgyrn had done his research, the treasury was full and ready for plucking, like a ripened fruit on a low-hanging branch. One needed only a means to enter the building.

Which was, of course, why he needed me.

The day passed uneventfully and uncomfortably. My nose, which was still painful, had swollen again so that using it for breathing was impossible. My skin itched, and even through my swollen nose I was conscious of the stench of my clothing. I am somewhat ashamed to confess that I was almost more anxious to bathe and rid myself of my soiled garments than I was for the safety of Fosdric and Brother Galthorn.

The young priest eventually regained consciousness. Elgyrn gave me leave to tend to him as best I could, short of leaving the house and fetching a doctor. I used the rum to clean the wound on Brother Galthorn's head. From the size and shape of the contusion, it was clear that Elgyrn had used a club to persuade Brother Galthorn to cooperate. To his credit, Galthorn withstood my rough ministrations with stoic silence. The young man would suffer from the bruise for some time, but thankfully, his skull seemed to be still in one piece.

The house warmed during the heat of the day until the temperature inside grew oppressive, although I was able to moderate the effect somewhat. I sat close to Brother Galthorn and shifted some of the energy from the air around us to other parts of the room. Elgyrn stripped off his tunic and shirt and sweated profusely, but he refused to open the shutters to let the air circulate. The thin man left the house periodically—a prearranged signal to their conspirators outside, no doubt—and returned several times with his hair dripping wet, presumably from a well somewhere near the house.

Fosdric was kept outside and out of our sight. I sensed his presence, not far away, but Elgyrn shrewdly kept him far enough that I could not discern his location. Elgyrn was crude, but cunning; as long as Galthorn or Fosdric were held far enough away, I could not move against Elgyrn without the risk that they would suffer for it.

As the day wore on, Elgyrn grew more agitated. His manner clearly showed that the hour of action was approaching. He showed me the map of the king's treasury several times, repeatedly pointing out the locations of the guard posts inside and outside the building, and where we were likely to encounter locked doors. I listened with half an ear, more concerned with when or where I might have an opportunity to free us from Elgyrn's grasp and turn him over to the authorities.

The thin man hovered nervously about the small room, busying himself with some small task or another, preparing and eating a small meal from the pot over the fire, and more or less buzzing about like a fly, trying to find ways to vent his nervous energy.

Brother Galthorn slept the better part of the day. I had no knowledge of how our captors treated him while I was unconscious, but he appeared to be physically exhausted as well as suffering from the effects of the blow to his head.

At length, Elgyrn slapped his palms down on the scarred wood of the table and stood. The thin man started at the noise and spilled some of the gruel he had been eating while standing near the front door. Brother Galthorn, curled into a ball in the corner farthest from the hearth, slowly unwound and sat up, blinking sleep from his eyes.

"It's time, mates," Elgyrn said. "Time to go. Time to make our fortune. Time for you, warlock, to earn your keep."

Elgyrn nodded to the thin man, who dumped the remains of his meal onto the fire with a hiss. He pulled two strips of black cloth from his tunic.

"What's this?" I asked.

"Precaution," Elgyrn said. "No need for you to know exactly where we are until we get to where we're going." Thin Man tied the fabric around my head and over my eyes, applying just enough pressure to the bridge of my nose to be painful. He used the second piece of cloth to tie my hands behind my back.

A big hand in the middle of my back guided me out of the door and to the cart. "Get in," Elgyrn said. After fumbling for a moment to find a foothold, I pulled myself into the back of the cart and groped my way forward until I could turn around and sit. The cart creaked and swayed as Elgyrn climbed up to the driver's seat. With a lurch, the horse began to pull and we were underway.

I heard nothing from Brother Galthorn after my eyes were covered, and I sensed that he was not with us on the cart. It was to Elgyrn's advantage to keep us separated. Reaching with my mind, I detected Fosdric with at least two others moving as we moved, but not near enough to attempt to free the little man for fear of hurting him while disabling his guards.

We bumped through the streets of Darnaatha for many minutes. The evening air had cooled and the sounds on the freshening breeze indicated that a fair number of people had either moved outdoors to take advantage of the weather, or most of the homes in the city had shutters thrown open to let in the cooler air. The sounds of life reached us from all quarters; laughing, talking, the strumming of a lyre, a dog barking in the distance. Were I not bound, blind, filthy, and in a good deal of pain, it might have been a most enjoyable evening.

Elgyrn took the cart through a goodly number of turns. I do not know whether the turns were necessary or simply an attempt to mask the route to the king's treasury. As we moved, I sensed Fosdric and Brother Galthorn following close behind, but apart from one another.

The brutish Elgyrn had made another shrewd decision—since I first awakened, he'd kept the men holding Galthorn and Fosdric out of my sight. That made it difficult for me to identify their guards, and nearly impossible to locate them accurately. To free my companions, I must know where to focus my energies or I could harm them as easily as their captors. How much did Elgyrn know about the nature of the Gift?

At last, the cart creaked to a stop. It groaned and shook as Elgyrn dropped from the driver's position. I heard the back gates open, and Elgyrn said, "Out with you now."

Sliding forward, I had reached the edge of the cart's bed when a pair of large hands lifted me out of the cart and dropped me to the ground. Elgyrn was apparently growing impatient.

The ropes binding my hands were loosed, and then the blindfold was removed. The fading light of evening was a welcome change from the blindfold. Blinking as my eyes adjusted, I looked around to get my bearings. We stood in shadow between two small buildings overlooking Darnaatha's public square. The king's treasury dominated the side of the square to our right. The square itself was empty, save for two guards standing sentry outside the treasury. I sensed others higher up, and along the roofline I was just able to discern several archers outlined against the darkening sky.

Elgyrn had chosen the time of his attempted theft well. Both of Saramond's moons were hidden. The darkness would afford cover to those who wished to remain hidden from view.

The guards in front of the building were armed with spears, swords and daggers. Unlike some of the ceremonial buffoons who served as guards for the holders of lesser political offices, the men protecting the king's wealth were quite capable. The archers would be among the more accurate shots in the kingdom.

My mind searched the darkness around the outer edges of the square, hoping for a clue that would help me locate Brother Galthorn and Fosdric. The time fast approached when I would be forced to decide whether to harm the guards or try to disable Elgyrn and risk the lives of my companions.

"Not long now," Elgyrn said quietly. "Be ready, warlock, and move smartly when I say. My men are watching us close, and…"

"Yes, yes," I interrupted. "So you said." Galthorn and Fosdric were close, but Elgyrn had instructed his men well. They were out of sight and very close to their captors. Try as I might, I could not determine just where they stood in the darkness.

The sound of my voice may have carried to the guards in front of the treasury. They seemed to stand a bit straighter, listening into the darkness. Only voices in the distance and that barking dog, closer now, broke the silence.

Time stretched, crawling by with the patience of old men discussing weather. Finally, realizing that my attempts to find Galthorn and Fosdric were futile, I turned my attention to the guards before the entrance to the treasury. They were clad in armor. That was good; I might not be forced to kill them.

At length, the men on the roof disappeared from view. Elgyrn gripped my shoulder and hissed, "Now."

A changing of the guard. At least I need only worry about the men on the street. The two of us stepped into the square and approached the pair of guards standing at attention before the huge wooden doors that separated Elgyrn from his dreams of wealth. Which of us four, I wondered, would be alive to see the next day's sun?

The guards were posted on either side of the huge double doors. Torches cast a dancing yellow pool that extended down a low staircase and partway along a stone walk that extended out to the public square. A fence of wrought iron higher than a man surrounded the treasury, forcing us to approach the stair on the stone path.

The guards stiffened as Elgyrn and I stepped slowly from shadow into the shimmering pool of light. My clean-shaven head may have caused their anxiety, which I keenly sensed. Bare scalps most commonly belong to brothers of The Order.

The larger of the two directed his spear at us and issued a challenge. "Stop," he said in a deep voice that was rougher than a blacksmith's hands. "You have no business here."

Elgyrn responded as we continued our slow march up the walk. "Stand aside or die. I have a master of The Order here who'll do whatever it takes to get inside."

"Master Davian?" The guard on the right recognized me, but in the imperfect light of the torches, and with a helmet covering most of his head, I could not identify him.

"I have no quarrel with you," I said. "Please stand aside."

The larger guard spat and tightened his grip on the spear. "I knew The Order couldn't be trusted."

The smaller one—Penubo, I remembered—finally directed his spear at us as well. We had met two years earlier at some official function for which I'd been tasked with representing The Order. Fear showed plainly in the young man's eyes.

"Move or die!" Elgyrn stopped at the base of the staircase, about three man-heights from the gleaming points of the guards' spears—dangerously close for a man without an iron shield, unless one had a means of redirecting the path of a spear in mid-air. Elgyrn was betting his life on my ability to do just that, secured by his oath that Fosdric and Brother Galthorn would surely die if I failed to protect him from the guards.

My hatred of the vile man grew by the minute.

"We will not," the larger guard responded. He had little choice, actually. Treasury duty paid well, but the men assigned to it were expected to die before yielding their posts.

I was thankful for the torches. My abilities are not as strong after dark, especially when the moons are hidden, and the energy generated by the torches would be helpful.

Closing my eyes, I focused on the two guards. The energy from the torches seethed, flowing upward and outward, twin beacons shining brightly even behind the closed lids of my eyes.

With my mind, I turned the energy in the air around us to my will. Energy from the torches combined with the power that surrounds me every breathing moment, coming from beneath us, from the very heart of Saramond. Focusing on the guards, on their armor, I concentrated on the attraction that certain metals have for one another. With my mind, I twisted and pulled at the forces in the air as though it were taffy. The attraction between the guards' metal casings increased.

"What—?" The larger guard realized that something unusual was taking place.

"Don't play with them—finish them!" Elgyrn hissed.

Suddenly, Penubo gave a cry and dropped his spear as he and the larger guard half stumbled, half flew toward one another. With a metallic clank, the two were pulled together face to face, and they remained there, frozen. Though they struggled to move, to separate themselves from one another, their efforts were futile. Their armor might as well have been welded together.

"What are you doing?" Elgyrn demanded. "Kill them!"

"You need me to get into the treasury," I said evenly. "These men need not die for you to get there."

"They will know who I am!"

"You will be rich. Go somewhere else."

"Damn you, warlock! Kill them, or your friends die!"

"How long before the archers return to the roof? In the dark, their arrows might be on us before I see them." A lie, but worth risking.

Elgyrn glared, torn between the need to move quickly and his desire to eliminate witnesses to our crime. Snarling, he grabbed Penubo's fallen spear and turned to the helpless guards standing before us.

Before Elgyrn could act, I focused on the wooden handle of the spear and set it afire. The brute yelped and instantly dropped the weapon.

"Curse you, warlock, but I will kill you when this night is through!" Elgyrn angrily rubbed his singed hands together.

"Perhaps. But not now."

"Hey!" The larger guard had overcome his shock and realized that he could still sound an alarm even though he was unable to move. "Hey!"

I quickly crossed the three paces between us and clubbed the man on the top of his helmet with the side of my fist. "Silence," I said, quietly. "It it my wish that none of us is killed."

"You clean out the treasury and we're dead anyway," the guard said.

"The king cannot roast you alive where you stand. I can. Now, be silent."

He opened his mouth and inhaled, preparing to shout once again. "Hersig, please," Penubo said. "Don't."

"Thank you," I said. "Be reasonable and we may all live."

"The doors, warlock," Elgyrn growled. "Get us inside!"

"I don't suppose you have keys we can borrow?" I asked the guards. Hersig merely glared at me.

Leaving the guards, I mounted the three steps leading to the massive wooden doors. The rough timbers that had been used to fabricate the doors were thick and old. They would burn easily enough, but I had no desire to start a blaze that could spread to the other buildings on the square and perhaps to the rest of the city. The situation was bad enough without risking the deaths of thousands.

Placing my hands against the doors, I felt with my mind for metal inside. Sure enough, the hinges inside were of iron. Stronger and more durable than wood, but still vulnerable to the powers of the brothers of The Order. It required some effort, but I was able to force the hinges and the pins to repel one another. The torches outside dimmed as their heat was converted and redirected, but the pins, thankfully greased, worked free.

With a push, the double doors first bumped from their mountings to the ground, and then slowly toppled inward to hit the floor inside with an enormous crash.

Elgyrn glared at me with a fury that would have melted iron, if he'd had the Gift. The deafening noise was sure to attract attention. Better than burning down the city, I suppose, but now I had to make decisions very quickly or people would start to die. Perhaps beginning with me.

My plan was leaving much to be desired.

As I feared, the crash of the doors was answered by shouts from inside and behind the treasury. Elgyrn looked ready to explode. There was no turning back. Like me, he was now committed to playing this hand for whatever it was worth.

A dog began to bark close by, repeatedly, a loud, high-pitched yipping that sharpened the growing sense that everything was going very wrong. It seemed that even the animals were conspiring to summon help against us.

Elgyrn stormed past me into the treasury, cursing as he went. As he reached the fallen double doors, an arrow whistled past my ear. Blast! The archers had regained the roof and were trying to cut us down. Had we not been so close to the building, the first shot would have done exactly that.

When arrows are tipped with metal points, an experienced brother of The Order can sense their approach and flick them aside. If he faces an attacker armed with a bow, he can surround himself with a protective shroud that will deflect the arrows. This is tiring after awhile, but it is effective.

Sadly, the Gift is of little use if someone is intelligent enough to use a rock and a sling or fills his quiver with arrows tipped with stone. Yes, we can set the shafts alight in mid-air but that does not always alter their course.

As I moved to the relative safety of the massive arched door-way that once held the double doors, I heard my name above the ceaseless noise of that yipping dog.

"Master Davian!" I spun round. At the end of the stone path, just inside the circle of torchlight, was Fosdric. His arms waved madly, like a windmill in a gale. "Master Davian! This way!"

Looking over my shoulder, I saw Elgyrn stopped at the top of a stairway that led to an underground chamber where the money was counted and kept. There were guards in front of that door, who were no doubt charging up the stairway to investigate with weapons drawn.

Time to decide. I cast my die and bolted back outside. Elgyrn bellowed in rage behind me. Fosdric had already turned and run, and wisely so, because the archers on the roof had drawn on him as soon as he showed himself. Arrows littered the ground at the end of the stone walkway.

"I will return and free you!" I shouted as I passed the two guards, still locked together like sweethearts, and I bounded down the path toward the square.

As I ran, I threw up a protective screen behind myself and prayed that the archers had only metal-tipped arrows at their dis-posal. Either that was the case or their aim was poor, for you see I am still alive to tell the tale.

Fosdric proved to be deceptively fast. He gained the opposite side of the square before I was halfway across. Voices reached us from the darkness outside the square as others converged on the treasury to investigate the disturbance.

As I approached the building directly opposite the treasury on the far side of the square, Fosdric cried, "You better let the priest go! Master Davian is free and he's right behind me! If you harm the priest, you answer to an angry wizard! Your master is caught and there's no hope for you but to let the priest go and run for it!"

Fosdric had run into a passageway along the left side of the building I faced. Finding the passageway, I moved through it as quickly as I dared with my eyes still adjusting to the darkness. Light would have been helpful and easy enough to generate, but I was not inclined to reveal myself until I was out of sight of those the square.

Brother Galthorn and his captors were near. Fosdric could not see them, but I could sense them. Emerging from the passageway, I overtook Fosdric in a small courtyard. I clapped him heartily on the back—and was immediately set upon by a small white dog.

It would have been comical had not Brother Galthorn been in danger. The dog, a fluffy dustrag of indeterminate parentage, must have thought I was attacking Fosdric, for the cur leapt to his defense and clamped onto the left leg of my breeches. While he did me no harm, the distraction was irritating, and I shook my leg in a vain attempt to dislodge him.

"Hear me!" I cried. "I am Davian, a Third Level Master of The Order! Elgyrn is caught by the King's Guards, and you have naught to gain but your lives! Release the priest and live! Harm him and—yaagh!" The persistent little mutt had shifted his grip and gotten his teeth into the meat of my leg.

"Wolf! Stop it!" Fosdric grabbed the dog by the scruff of the neck and picked it up, holding it while it continued to growl in my direction.

There was no time to dally. I focused and brought a ball of light into being over my head, bright enough to dispel the darkness for ten or twelve man-heights in all directions. Shadows sharpened into human forms against the wall of a workshop at the back of the courtyard, huddled low against the wall to conceal themselves.

"You!" I walked toward the shapes and brought the light to bear directly over them. Three men, rough characters, crouching, surrounded a bound and gagged Brother Galthorn. The young priest was motionless and as limp as a child's rag doll. The faces of his captors were familiar, and it came to me in an instant: They were three of the men who had taken such an interest in us at the Court Jester in Elocin.

Before I could say another word, the little dog wormed free of Fosdric and charged Galthorn's captors at full speed, sounding a challenge with his piercing bark.

"Wolf! No!" Fosdric cried, but the dog paid no heed. He launched himself onto the nearest ruffian, a beefy man with an unshaven moon-shaped face, holding a knife half the length of his forearm. The utter folly of the little dog's assault must have startled the villain; rather than flicking away his diminutive attacker as he would lint from his shirtsleeve, the man lost his balance and toppled backwards, dropping his weapon with a clang as it hit the stones tiles of the courtyard.

With a moment's thought at the knife, I slid the blade across the ground and brought it to rest at Fosdric's feet. He immediately retrieved it while Wolf, growling and snapping, tried to find a clear path to his opponent's neck.

Brother Galthorn, seated between the other two, suddenly came to life, twisting and delivering a devastating smash with his elbow to the face of the man on his left. His captor howled in pain and collapsed, clutching his shattered nose. Galthorn, though bound, alertly rolled free of his captors.

Wolf, meanwhile, compensated for his meager size with sheer tenacity. Although he had not inflicted any real damage, his quick, sharp teeth prevented his foe from grabbing hold to throw him off. The little dog was keeping the largest of the three villains occupied all by himself.

Turning then to the last of Brother Galthorn's abductors, I focused the glowing light directly into his eyes, and said, "Now, then. Let us reason together." Fear was splashed across the man's gaunt face.

"Please, sir," he said—or began to say, as Fosdric cut him off by leaping in front of him and putting the oversized knife to his throat.

"Let me do it, Davian," Fosdric said. "Please? He deserves it after what they done. To a priest!" The man's eyes widened, realizing that his chances of escaping the courtyard were suddenly very small.

"No," I said. "The sheriff and the King's Guards will want these three, I think. Call off your dog, Fosdric. These men will give us no more trouble."

Indeed, they did not. One benefit of being a dragonslayer is that most men—not all, but most—think very carefully before giving me offense. Rarely am I forced to use my abilities against other men. The fear of what I *might* do is much worse, in truth, than what I am *willing* to do. Elgyrn was a rare man, one with a good understanding of my abilities and limitations. That, and his evil intentions, made him dangerous.

Fosdric managed, with effort, to pull Wolf off of his victim, who seemed grateful to be free of the determined little beast. We untied Brother Galthorn, who offered the strips of cloth with which he had been bound to the man whose nose he had broken. His victim accepted them gratefully and used the material to stanch the bleeding.

We walked slowly across the square. The fenced area in front of the treasury was ablaze with torches, and several dozen men milled about, most of them armed with swords. Several wore the uniform of King's Guards, and it's probable that some of those in plain clothes were also Guards who had not time to dress before rushing to the scene.

As we approached the stone path leading from the square to the treasury, a stern, flint-eyed man wearing the ornamented armor of the King's Guard ordered us to stop. "I am Caedwulf, captain of the King's Guard. Who are you and what is your business?" Archers along the roof of the building stood with their weapons drawn, ready for Caedwulf's order to bring us down where we stood.

"I am Master Davian of The Order," I said. Gesturing to the three being watched by Fosdric and Brother Galthorn, I added, "These three were partners of the man you captured inside the treasury."

"How do you know about that?" Caedwulf's eyes narrowed. He was about my height, but with a more powerful build. His dark hair fell to the broad shoulders of a man who wielded a sword often.

"It is difficult to explain."

"Try."

"In short, I was Elgyrn's unwilling accomplice."

The captain looked over his shoulder at the open doorway and the two guards, still fastened to one another, and then back at me. "So, you are responsible for that." It was a statement, not a question.

"Yes."

"Why, then, should I not take you into custody?"

I should have been more diplomatic, but it had been a long a trying day. I said, "Why do you think you can?"

Caedwulf's jaw tightened. Brother Galthorn touched my arm. "Patience, Master Davian. He is only doing his duty."

The priest was right. I sighed. "These men were holding my companions under threat of mortal harm if I did not do as Elgyrn wished. At the last moment, as we entered the building, Fosdric— Fosdric? Just how did you break free?"

"Wondered when you'd ask me that," the little man said, grinning. "All day, we was sitting outside that house you was in. There was two of them, watching over me all day. Well, the day gets hot, you see, so one of them says to the other…"

"Come to your point," Caedwulf said.

"I'm getting to it, captain," Fosdric said. "One says to the other, 'I'm going to nip off for a pint. Then once I get back, I'll watch over our goose while you gets a pint.' And the other one says, 'Mind you don't leave me here all alone the whole day, 'cause Elgyrn, he won't like it.' So…"

"The point," growled Caedwulf.

"So," Fosdric continued, unwilling to let an unappreciative audience ruin a good story, "I noticed this little fellow here, hanging about, looking hungry. Well, when my keeper wasn't looking, I slips him a little bit of the potato I saved from last night's supper."

"You carried a potato with you all day?" I asked.

"Never can tell," Fosdric said with a wink. "Anyway, I slips him some potato and a bit of bacon, and before you know it, he's my oldest chum. Followed us all the way through town to this place right here."

"And?" I was growing as impatient as Caedwulf.

"Well, next thing you know, old Wolf here sees my keeper push me around a bit, and he jumps on him. So I takes the chance to grab a rock and bash him—not that Wolf needed my help—and I ran to find Brother Galthorn, and then you."

"That was the dog I heard barking?" I asked.

"The same." Fosdric beamed with paternal pride, holding Wolf. The little dog growled at the man he had attacked.

"Where is that man, Fosdric?" I asked.

"Lying where I left him, I suppose, over there." He pointed off to the left of the treasury building. "We was in between those two buildings there, across the street."

The captain called two of his men and gave them instructions to search the area Fosdric had indicated. Turning back to us, he said, "We will, of course, investigate your story."

"Be my guest," Fosdric answered. "Pleased to be of service to his Majesty."

"Indeed. You, Master Davian," Caedwulf said, "What then? When Fosdric called to you, what then?"

"I left Elgyrn to the guards inside and followed Fosdric back across the square," I said. "I assumed that he had found Brother Galthorn."

"And had he?"

"We would not be here otherwise." I was growing weary, and I found that I wanted, more than anything, to be home and asleep.

"Be careful how you answer, Master Davian," the captain warned. "I do not know you. To my eye, it appears that my men interrupted a robbery between thieves who argued between themselves. Some were caught outright, and now you see an advantage in letting Elgyrn and these three bear the consequences for all of you."

This was growing tiresome. "One of us is a priest! Do you truly believe—"

"I do not know what to believe yet, Master Davian." The Guard's eyes, gray in the torchlight, seemed to miss nothing. He scanned the area around us, satisfying himself that his men were performing their duties as ordered.

Following his eyes, I saw that Penubo and Hersig were still fastened together in an undignified position. "Excuse me," I said to Caedwulf. "I promised these men I would free them when I returned."

A moment of concentration directed at the two men, and the forces holding their armor were neutralized. The two guards staggered as they struggled to regain balance. "Thank you, sir," Penubo said, but the larger man only glowered. Some of his comrades had made rather unkind comments that had reached his ears, and he was apparently one to hold a grudge.

"Continue, captain," I said to Caedwulf.

"Please do not leave Darnaatha without my approval. We will need your testimony at the inquest."

That was unwelcome news. "Excuse me, but who died?"

"Two of my men, at the hands of your partner, Elgyrn."

"Oh, no," I said. "Captain, I am truly sorry." I meant that. My decision to follow Fosdric had undoubtedly cost those men their lives.

But what else could I have done? Delaying long enough to disable Elgyrn might have meant the death of Brother Galthorn. I had gambled that the guards, with the advantage of numbers, would be more than a match for Elgyrn. But desperate men are not easily subdued. The young priest bowed his head and offered up a silent prayer. The three men with us, now closely watched by several other guards, looked even more dejected. Things would go worse for them since their leader had killed two of the King's Guards.

I cleared my throat. "I say again, Captain Caedwulf, that Elgyrn was is not my partner."

"So you say." He regarded me closely for a moment. "Just what are you doing here, Davian?"

"I thought I explained that."

"No, you have not. What are you doing in Darnaatha?"

"My home is here," I replied.

"I am aware of that," Caedwulf said, "but I also know you travel a great deal. Why have you returned?" His tone implied that he found life more pleasant when I was away.

"I have been requested for another mission. We were on our way from Marthwee, in the north. Fosdric here was sent to bring me back. We were ambushed at our camp three nights ago by Elgyrn and his men."

"We will get to the truth of that. What is this mission?"

"We leave in the morning for Stelnregon. We cannot stay for an inquest. There is a report of a dragon in Palthinoor district."

"This is news to me," Caedwulf said.

"It ain't for public knowledge, captain," Fosdric said.

Caedwulf stared at the diminutive horse-handler with a mixture of irritation and disbelief. "And how is it that you are privy to this information?"

"I was sent to fetch Davian," Fosdric said.

"By who?" Caedwulf asked.

"The captain of the Guards in Palthinoor district."

"Talliver?"

"Yes, sir," Fosdric said. He clearly enjoyed the attention.

"I know Talliver," the captain said. "Why would he send you instead of one of his own men on such a mission?"

"Well," said Fosdric, "I expect he needed someone he could trust to do the job."

"Mmph," Caedwulf grunted. "Try again. Why you?"

"All his men were already out chasing the thing."

Caedwulf raised an eyebrow. "And why," he asked, "Does the governor of Palthinoor district send all the way to Darnaatha for a brother of The Order?"

"I went to Marthwee," Fosdric said. "Davian was in Marthwee."

The torchlight shimmering off Caedwulf's angled face highlighted his growing impatience with Fosdric's incomplete answers.

"Captain," I said, "Apparently, every brother of The Order between here and Palthinoor has gone mad. The creature has somehow managed to travel unseen—no small thing for a dragon. It seems to have abilities that I do not understand."

Caedwulf considered that for a moment before reaching a decision. "Nor I," he said, "But I have my duty here. There will be an official inquiry into the deaths of my men. That must take priority."

"My word will have to suffice," I said. "I was not a willing participant in the events here tonight. I could have killed your men, but I did not. I tried to find a way to get through this without bloodshed. The loss of your men is grievous, and again I say I am truly sorry. But you have the men responsible in custody, and I must leave in the morning. If a dragon is truly capable of moving about unseen, it is a danger far greater than Elgyrn. Or me, for that matter. And if, somehow, it is responsible for the sudden madness that has disabled those charged with protecting the kingdom from dragons, then delaying me may cost many more lives than were lost here tonight."

"Davian," Caedwulf responded, "I find it difficult to believe that the man who pushed in those doors with his mind can be forced to do anything against his will."

"It is not so hard to believe," Brother Galthorn interjected. "There are men such as Elgyrn who will stop at nothing to get what they want. Such a man has an advantage, because he is not constrained by conscience, morality, or decency. I am thankful, captain, as you should be, that Master Davian is not such a man."

CHAPTER EIGHT

Captain Caedwulf's curiosity about our presence at the king's treasury during the attempted theft was eventually satisfied—or at least satisfied enough that we were allowed to leave instead of escorted to accommodations in a dungeon, to await the proceedings of the inquest and perhaps a criminal trial. While Caedwulf might have discounted Fosdric's dramatic tale of the events of the previous days, he was less inclined to disbelieve a priest. And since Brother Galthorn corroborated Fosdric's account in all but the most florid details, Caedwulf finally concluded that we were telling the truth.

My companions had somehow managed to secure my belongings during our period of captivity, for which I was grateful. Only my dragonspear, which had been left at the site of our camp the night we were overtaken, would need to be replaced. That was done easily enough, as I had several in reserve at my home.

All in all, aside from the unfortunate guards who had perished defending the king's treasury, our greatest loss was the time that had been stolen by Elgyrn and his band; three days had passed since our journey to Stelnregon was interrupted. We could afford no further delay in tracking the invisible dragon that Fosdric had fetched me to confront.

We left Elgyrn and his lackeys to the King's Guard. I was glad to be rid of them, and relieved that I had not been forced to choose between killing the guards and allowing Elgyrn's men to kill Fosdric and Brother Galthorn. I learned that my traveling companions had not been blindfolded during our captivity, which meant that Elgyrn had not been concerned that they would later identify him to authorities. He had never intended to let them live, regardless of whether I cooperated.

My home in Darnaatha was not far from the treasury. After we retrieved our items from the hovel where Brother Galthorn and I had spent the day, we proceeded to my own. It is a modest dwelling on the outskirts of the city, not very different from Brother Galthorn's small rectory. The stone building is roofed with thatch, and incorporates three rooms—the front room, which doubles as kitchen and living area; my sleeping chamber behind it; and a small reading room attached to the back of my bed room, almost as an afterthought. The rooms are small and sparsely furnished. As I travel a great deal, I want no abundance of personal belongings to attract unwanted guests while I am away.

My first order of duty was to clean myself. Several days of lying unconscious in the same clothing had made me rather offensive to others, especially since it is impossible to control one's bladder while in a drug-induced sleep.

As soon as we entered my home, it was clear that it had not been vacant during the nine days I had been away. Someone had made use of the premises for at least one day; there was ash in the hearth that had not been there when I left Darnaatha with Brother Galthorn for the journey to Marthwee.

Nothing seemed to be missing, although it appeared that whoever had called had rummaged through my meager possessions. Perhaps they were found unworthy of stealing, or perhaps, as seemed likely, the culprits were Elgyrn and his cohorts, now in the custody of the King's Guards.

Making my way through the house to my reading room, I noticed that the books I keep were slightly out of place, as though they had been read and replaced in different positions on their shelf. Most of the books relate to The Order, dealing with history or techniques for controlling the Gift. No doubt this was the source of Elgyrn's information about the nature of my abilities, which allowed him to develop a strategy for using it to his advantage.

As disturbing as the intrusion was, I was not especially upset. One is truly secure only when one can bar his door from within. A house that sits empty for many days at a time is a temptation for those who prefer taking from others to earning their own bread. Until such a time as I choose to employ a guard when I am away, I prefer to leave little to attract a thief. That and my reputation are usually enough.

My occupation and its frequent journeys are also reasons that I have yet to take a wife. It seems unjust to ask a woman to bind herself to me when I am called to go where I am needed, usually with little notice and always with the possibility that I may not return.

I might add, at the risk of seeming immodest, that the air of danger and adventure that cleaves to brothers of The Order is a strong attraction to many women. Female companionship is not something for which I would lack, if I chose. In my younger days, I was foolish enough to believe that my appearance or charm had some bearing on my appeal, and I indulged my desires more often than I care to admit. I am older now, and I daresay a bit wiser. Many, perhaps even most, of those women were attracted not to me, but to what I represent: escape from the boredom of a simple life. There is a sharp contrast between the lives of the men they have known all their lives and the life they imagine I lead, and some women find the allure of the unknown irresistible.

Wisdom comes with age. True happiness is not to be found in brief encounters with women with whom I would not share my life, and so now I refrain from such entanglements. Those experiences, I now understand, were less about romance than they were a temporary stilling of self-doubt.

Besides, I must confess, that I have also learned that a jealous man can be more dangerous than a full-grown dragon. Dragons are far more powerful than men, but it is nigh impossible for a dragon to surprise a brother of The Order. Men can be stealthy; dragons cannot.

Which is why an invisible dragon might be a threat heretofore unknown. The questions were these: Could I sense this creature at a distance, like a normal dragon? And was it responsible for the insanity that disabled my brothers in The Order?

It was late when we finally reached my dwelling and there was no food in the house. At that hour, no respectable inn would be serving, so our night promised to be a hungry one. Still, none of us complained, as we were thankful to have survived Elgyrn's plot with nothing worse than aches and bruises. Brother Galthorn, thankfully, seemed no worse for the blow to his head, and Fosdric, it seemed, had either behaved himself during his time in captivity or was quite good at rolling with a punch, because he seemed to have come through our ordeal without any visible bruises. After my initial inspection of the house, I collected several buckets of water from the well outside and filled a large tub in which to bathe.

"Uh, won't that water be a bit chilly? Wait—forget I asked," Fosdric said.

Indeed, I am glad he did, for my desire to wash was so great that I had almost forgotten to warm the water. It was quickly done, and the water was pleasantly warm when I slipped into the tub.

I am no fanatic when it comes to cleanliness, but I welcomed the opportunity to scrub the film of sweat and filth that had accumulated while I was subject to Elgyrn's wishes. As natural as it is for me to moderate extreme temperatures, I sometimes forget the feeling of dried sweat on my skin. The bath revived and relaxed me, and I was prepared for a long night of blissful sleep when I rejoined Fosdric and Brother Galthorn inside the house. Even the ache of my broken nose had faded enough that it would not keep me from my rest.

The light from the two lamps I possessed flickered and danced along the stone walls of my modest abode. Fosdric was playing with Wolf, who had attached himself to the diminutive stable hand by using a ragged piece of cloth as a tug-of-war rope. Showing none of the fatigue I felt, the little dog bit and pulled on the cloth as though the fate of the kingdom depended on it. Releasing his hold, Fosdric laughed as the pocket-sized mongrel enthusiastically shook the very life from the rag. "Good boy! That's a good dog!" Wolf happily wagged his longhaired tail in response to Fosdric's praise even as he continued to growl and bite his "prey."

Brother Galthorn clapped his hands in appreciation. "You've found quite a friend, Fosdric," he said. "I, for one, am glad that he's on our side!"

"Let us see whether he feels it is necessary to announce his presence to the world while we are trying to sleep," I said.

"He's all right, he is," Fosdric said. "Wolf here is a world-class, champion watchdog. He'll only bark when there's danger nearby, you wait and see." The little dog stopped biting the rag and yipped, tail wagging in agreement.

"Why did you choose to call him 'Wolf'?" asked Brother Galthorn,

"Well, it's simple, isn't it? He thinks he is one, so that's what his name is."

"Oh, very true," Brother Galthorn said. "He surely proved himself tonight."

Beaming, Fosdric produced a small crust of bread that he tossed to Wolf. The little dog caught it in mid air and swallowed it after two quick bites. "Well, gents," Fosdric said, "That's it for the food. We'll have to tough it out for the night."

* * *

As I'd feared, early the next morning, a high-pitched series of barks, so closely spaced that they sounded like one long howl, jolted me from a sound sleep.

The rosy glow on the wall of my sleeping chamber indicated that the morning was still young. From the front room, Wolf let loose with another series of barks. Wiping sleep from my eyes, I rose to see what was disturbing Fosdric's little watchdog.

"Shut up, Wolf," his master said sleepily. "I'm still sleeping."

The little white dog stood in front of the door and barked again, one piercing staccato yelp.

"Outside?" I asked. Barking happily, Wolf began jumping and turning circles in front of the door. Clearly, someone had trained this dog at some point. "What say you, Fosdric?"

"Let him out. He'll come back." Fosdric, lying on the floor in front of the glowing hearth, rolled over and went back to sleep.

Sighing, I went to the door—and noticed with a start that it was no longer barred. Looking about, I saw that Brother Galthorn was not in the house, and I relaxed. I opened the door and Wolf darted outside, right into the path of Brother Galthorn. The young man was laden with the makings of a hearty breakfast, apparently having made a journey to the farmer's market in the city square.

"Good morning, Master Davian," he said. "A fine day, is it not?"

"I have yet to see enough of it to know."

Galthorn smiled. "Could you hold the door, please? My hands are quite full."

"So I see. Thank you for taking this upon yourself, Brother Galthorn. If you had waited a bit, we might have offered some help."

"It was no trouble," Brother Galthorn said, negotiating the doorway. "I always rise early, and I thought we might need some nourishment."

"Very true." I was famished.

Brother Galthorn laid out a treasure upon the table near the hearth. The priest had found the local farmer's market and obviously persuaded one or more to do business at an hour when they are usually still in the process of opening their stalls. I added some wood to the fire, and then nudged Fosdric with my foot. "I am sorry to disturb you, Fosdric, but to eat we must build up the fire. It will soon be too hot for you to lie there comfortably." On cue, Wolf trotted over and happily began to lick Fosdric's face.

"Pthah!" Fosdric sputtered, swiping at his face. "All right, all right! I'm moving!"

Brother Galthorn set to work, and soon the air inside my home was filled with the savory aroma of ham, eggs, and the herb tea I favor. "I am sorry," he said, "that we do not have time to wait for bread dough to rise. I purchased a loaf at the market, but I daresay I could have baked better." He looked about for a moment, and then added, "And, of course, a properly equipped kitchen."

"Why, Brother Galthorn," Fosdric said, "You are a positively smashing homemaker. You'll make someone a wonderful wife someday, you will."

"Thank you, Fosdric," the priest responded, as he scooped fried eggs and ham from a pan onto plates, "As long as that was not intended as a proposal of marriage."

"I make no promises," Fosdric said, "The more you cook like this, the better you look."

Grinning, Galthorn ferried the heavily-laden plates to the table, already set with cheese, bread, and tea. After seating himself, the priest led us in a brief prayer of thanks for our food, and we began to eat.

"Seriously, now, Brother Galthorn," I said, "Where did you come by such skill as a cook?"

Galthorn swallowed a bit of cheese. "Candidates for the priesthood are commonly assigned to cook for the elders at the monastery. Kitchen duty is also assigned to those who are disobedient or a bit slow in their lessons." He grinned shyly. "Let us just say that I have a great deal of experience in the preparation of food."

"Were you disobedient or slow?" asked Fosdric, flipping a scrap of ham to Wolf, who caught the tidbit in midair.

"Some of both, or so thought the abbot," Galthorn replied. "I suppose I asked too many questions. It was assumed that I asked because I didn't learn, or because I did not want to learn."

"Speaking of questions," I said, "There is one I've been meaning to ask."

"Yes?"

"In Marthwee, you preached to your parish that the appearance of the dragon might have been a warning or judgment from the Creator."

"Yes, that's right."

"Yet, I have observed, as I am sure you have, that often those most blessed with wealth or power are the least deserving of those gifts. And conversely, tragedies often befall good people or young children. What messages would the Creator be sending then?"

Brother Galthorn chewed slowly, pondering. At last, he said, "Perhaps I should have phrased my message more carefully. What I meant was this: We cannot know when ill tidings may befall us, so it is best not to wait until it is too late to repent and make one's peace with the Creator. Better to do it now, before the dragon, metaphorically speaking, is already upon you."

"That is not at all the way it sounded, sitting in your church that morning."

"I know." He sighed. "My sermons sometimes lack tact."

"I don't know, Brother," Fosdric said. "Seems to me you need to rile them up or scare them once in awhile."

"Why?"

"Well, that's simple, isn't it?" Fosdric paused to set his nearly-empty plate on the floor for Wolf. "If you don't give them a jolt every now and again, they fall asleep on you. That's why, when we do a play—did I mention that I was the toast of Stelnregon after my role in *The Butcher's Wife* in last year's outdoor summer theater?—we always have plenty of laughs and fight scenes. You have to keep the people awake."

"Spiritually speaking," Brother Galthorn said.

"Oh, right, of course," said Fosdric.

"Hmm. Thank you, Fosdric," said Brother Galthorn.

"Gentlemen," I said, finishing the last of my eggs, "As enjoyable as this has been, I fear it may be the last restful meal we have for some time."

Fosdric groaned. "There you go again. Is every one of you in The Order so sour?"

"We need to be on our way," I said. "There is no point to stepping softly around the truth."

"Thank the Creator you ain't a priest," Fosdric snorted. "You'd have them snoring or rioting, one or the other."

* * *

Brother Galthorn suggested we rest a day before continuing on to Stelnregon. While we would have benefited from the extra time to heal our bruises, to say nothing of Brother Galthorn's skill over the hearth, each day's delay might mean lives lost and property destroyed. Stelnregon was still ten days' journey by foot, which, despite recovering Aeryx after our affair with Elgyrn, was to be our mode of transport. Horses were in short supply, aside from those employed by the King's Guards.

So after cleaning the cookware used in our morning meal, we made preparations to leave. I prepared a pack with my bedroll, clothing, razor, and assorted herbs of medicinal value. I also filled a small pouch with a quantity of gold and silver coins from a compartment secreted beneath a floorboard in my sleeping chamber. It was, I judged, sufficient to address any emergency we might encounter—any that could be solved through barter or exchange, at any rate.

For a brief moment I considered taking my entire savings, thinking that it was folly to leave it behind when I might never return to reclaim it. Instead, I pushed the thought from my mind, returned the pouch in its nook, replaced the floorboard, and went about completing my preparations to face the invisible dragon.

CHAPTER NINE

The tantalizing scent of the fried ham we'd eaten for our morning meal was still strong as we embarked. It must have been potent to penetrate my healing nose. Truly, Brother Galthorn was a worker of small miracles.

The sun was brilliant in the morning sky as we reached the main road that led to Stelnregon. It promised another sultry day. Although I can keep myself comfortable even on the hottest day, I felt awkward about doing so while my companions suffered. Besides, I do not have the stamina to control temperatures in multiple pockets of air for hours on end.

Fosdric's new best friend, Wolf, had decided to join us for the journey. The piffling pup was content, securely tucked into a makeshift sling on Aeryx's back. He seemed to be the only one among us eager to be on our way.

"Why is it," Brother Galthorn asked Fosdric, "Wolf is allowed to ride while we must walk?"

"We have a long ways to go," Fosdric replied. "It's not good for the pads on his feet to walk that far."

"So, just as we grow weary and need rest," I said, "He will need to be exercised to stretch his unused legs."

"Leave it to you to find the stone in every cherry," Fosdric snorted.

Brother Galthorn laughed. "You must admit, Master Davian, that Wolf's bark may prove more valuable than a true wolf's bite."

"If he chooses to use it when strangers approach," I said. "Especially at night. I grant you that."

* * *

Once away from Darnaatha, we made respectable time. Between the natural cheerfulness of Brother Galthorn and the ready wit of Fosdric, my gloom began to lift. The young cleric possessed a remarkable ability to tolerate the irreverent worldview of our traveling companion. For all of his candor when speaking from the pulpit, Brother Galthorn's approach was much more gentle in person.

However, try as I might to enjoy the brilliant blue sky, the gentle morning breeze, and the relaxed demeanor of my companions, I could not escape the sense that this unseen foe must possess some heretofore unknown power. Not only did it move about the countryside undetected, but, if Fosdric was to be believed, the brothers of The Order in the district had all lost their minds simultaneously upon the arrival of the invisible dragon. Such thoughts filled me with a deep foreboding I could not dispel.

"Fosdric," I said at last, "Tell me again about the brothers who were summoned before you were sent to find me."

"Not much to tell," he replied. "They all looked the same when they was found. Staring at nothing. Drooling like village idiots."

"They said nothing? No clue as to what caused their madness?"

"Not that I know," he said. "'Course, I only saw Myath, but it was like he was lost inside himself somewhere."

Myath was an elder of The Order, a man who had seen many summers and faced the fires of many dragons. He was well known for his simple, almost pauperish lifestyle, not what one would expect from a man to whom thousands—perhaps tens of thousands—owed their very lives. To me, Myath embodied the very ideals of The Order: Service, sacrifice, and humility. Losing him was a blow not just to The Order, but to the world at large.

"No, wait," Fosdric continued. "Now that I think on it, he did say something. But it was so queer, I didn't think on it again until now."

"What was it?" His narrow face had the sorrowful appearance of one who bears ill tidings, but I had no patience for his reluctance. "Out with it!"

"He said, 'radiant'."

"Radiant?"

"Yah. Radiant. That one word."

"That's all? Nothing more?"

Fosdric shrugged. "It's just—well…"

I glowered, too irritated to speak.

"Well, he kept saying it, over and over. He wouldn't stop."

The thought of a brilliant mind, reduced to repeating a single word was greatly distressing. If this unknown force could enfeeble a man with an unsurpassed mastery of The Gift such as Myath, how could I hope to encounter this enemy and come through it unharmed? I did not relish living out my days as a mental invalid.

* * *

It was on the third day after leaving Darnaatha that we saw the dragon. Evening it was, and perhaps fatigue after a day's journey had dulled my senses. We had just settled on a suitable resting place for the night in a secluded hollow after a day of hard travel over rough country. It had been a day of climbing and descending endless hills and valleys south of Darnaatha under a close, gray sky. None of the hills were physically daunting, but the cumulative effect over the course of a day was tiring. By evening, finding the level grassy area, hidden from the road by a stand of brush and mature oaks, seemed like a gift from the Creator.

Whatever the reason, the beast was nearly upon us before I was aware of its approach. In fact, it was only when the little dog, Wolf, freed from his perch on Aeryx's back, began to run in frenzied circles, barking furiously at the sky, that I noticed anything amiss. The shadow of the beast swept silently across our small band so quickly that I would have missed it had I looked away for even a moment.

Suddenly alert, I finally felt the beast's presence. "Dragon! Down!" I hissed to my companions. They complied at once. Fosdric alertly scooped Wolf into his arms and muzzled the dog with his tunic. Despite the cover provided by the trees, advertising our position was ill advised in the extreme.

The sense I had was of a young dragon, but strong; perhaps one that had recently reached adulthood. If so, it would be a difficult foe in terms of physical ability, but likely inexperienced with my kind. I hoped it was so. When confronting a beast of such raw power, one learns quickly to be thankful for any advantage.

After a moment, however, I realized that the beast had taken absolutely no notice of our presence. With my mind, I felt the creature sail southward, in the direction of our destination, Stelnregon.

Something else: The mind of the dragon seemed bent on a single objective, but what it was I could not tell. Never before had I sensed another mind, dragon or human, so narrowly focused. Perhaps that was why I had not felt its approach.

I waited a short time before venturing out of the trees toward the road to confirm with my eyes what my inner senses had reported. There, in the distance, was an irregular blot against the fading orange light of the evening sky, growing smaller as I watched.

Brother Galthorn soon appeared at my side. "Why did it not stop?"

Shaking my head slightly, I turned back toward our little camp. "Be glad that it did not."

"Master Davian," Galthorn said, "I understood that brothers of The Order and dragons can sense one another, even at great distances." The young priest followed as we picked our way through the brush that ringed our resting place for the night. "Why did it not take notice of us?"

Fosdric threw a small stick for Wolf to retrieve and then turned to us. He was more direct. "Why you didn't feel that beast? We was nearly dragon feed!"

"I don't know," I confessed. "It was over us before I was aware of it."

"Oh, that's fine, that is!" Fosdric snorted. "We could be filling a worm's belly before we can say a last farewell!"

"The dragon was acting strangely," I said. "Its mind was almost hidden—consumed by a single thought. I have never known a dragon so completely absorbed by one task."

"What task?" Galthorn asked.

"I could not tell."

Growling happily, Wolf burst into our clearing, wagging his tail and dragging a stick at least twice as long as himself. Fosdric laughed and knelt to accept the gift. "Well," he said over his shoulder, "At least he weren't thinking about us."

Brother Galthorn wore a pensive expression. "One single thought, you say?"

"So it seemed."

"Like Myath."

In truth, that gave me a chill. A man's mind, reduced to a single word endlessly repeated; a dragon's mind, focused with needle-like precision one reaching one goal, even to the point of ignoring a mortal enemy in its path.

What in the Creator's name awaited us in Stelnregon?

* * *

My thoughts kept me awake long into the night. Disturbing visions of orange flame sheeting out of a darkened sky and a lifetime lost within the confines of my mind stood between me and rest. Before the night was half over, my head began to throb and I decided that sleep was impossible.

Tossing aside my cloak, I pulled on my boots, rose, and added some fuel to our dying fire. Brother Galthorn and Fosdric were fast asleep, trusting, no doubt, in Wolf's senses, rather than mine, to warn of approaching guests. I decided to walk for a bit, hoping that the cool night air might clear my mind and help me to sleep.

I made my way to the road, thinking again about the danger that lay before us. Why would this invisible dragon choose to cut open livestock it did not eat? Fosdric had not mentioned any animals missing, only mutilated. Surely a farmer with a dead, mutilated animal would not fail to notice another animal that had disappeared. But the point was this—dragons, while sometimes taking cruel pleasure in the manner of killing men, do not cut open cows or pigs just to watch them expire.

The night was dark, but I focused enough energy to cast a soft glow on the road ahead. A fall in the dark would not do. Difficulties enough lie ahead without adding to them through carelessness.

Crickets chirped softly in the darkness and an owl hooted somewhere in the distance. My thoughts drifted peacefully as I wandered along the road, touching lightly on one thought and then another, never threading together more than two that were related. No sign or sense of anyone nearby, except my two slumbering companions, intruded into my reverie.

Nothing except—

An angry sun burned into my eyes and I had to shield them with my hand. I lay on my back, dazed, in what seemed to be a grassy field. Shapes hovered over me and it was all I could do to discern them. Gradually, with effort, I recognized the faces of Fosdric and Brother Galthorn.

"Where am I?" My dehydrated tongue felt as though it was covered with a dragon's hide.

Brother Galthorn brought a waterskin to my lips and I drank. "There, now," he said. "We found you walking the road several hours ago as though in a trance. It was very strange."

"Your eyes were closed," Fosdric added.

I took another pull from the skin before speaking. "How far from our camp are we?"

"About three miles, wouldn't you say, Fosdric?" Brother Galthorn answered. Fosdric nodded in agreement.

"Three miles," I repeated. "Yet, my last memory is just after setting foot on the road. It could not have been even a quarter of an hour—no more than half a mile, surely! Are you saying I walked nearly three miles with my eyes closed?"

"Well," Brother Galthorn said, "We cannot say, but your eyes were most certainly closed when we found you."

"Which raises another question. How did you find me?"

"Wolf," Fosdric said. He whistled and a small, furred face thrust itself upside down into my field of vision. The little dog barked sharply, as though commanding me to stand.

"Wolf saw you was missing," Fosdric continued. "He got to fussing and growling until he got Brother Galthorn and me out of bed. I tried to quiet him down, but he just ran and barked until we followed him. And he kept on doing that until we followed him out to the road, and then until we caught up to you." Fosdric beamed like a new father. Tired of waiting for me to rise, Wolf barked again and then scampered off into the grass in search of more excitement.

I lifted myself to one elbow, groaning. The ache in my head had not dissipated. In fact, it had grown worse since the night. A memento from the battle with Sennthurniss, I thought, or perhaps the substance Elgyrn used to render me helpless. There was nothing to do for it, however, and lying in a field certainly wasn't going to improve my condition. Slowly, I rose to my feet and looked about.

The road lay just a few man-heights away. The sun was still fairly low in the sky, which meant that we could still manage nearly a full day's travel, even allowing for time to return to camp to collect our belongings. As fatigued as we were from having our rest interrupted during the night, we had no choice. Whatever waited in Palthinoor district required our immediate attention.

CHAPTER TEN

Our travel that day did not cover as much distance as we would have liked. We were weary from our travel during the night, and I found that the dull ache between my eyes was slowly growing more insistent.

Even Fosdric was not his usual cheery self. In the short time that I had known him, the little man had been a non-stop font of song and conversation, which often served to lift our spirits and relieve the tedium of a long day's journey. But this day Fosdric kept to himself, and so our gloomy, haggard band slowly made its way closer to Stelnregon.

The monotony was unbroken. We met no travelers on the road, either coming from or going to Stelnregon. Indeed, as we had noticed as early as our second day of travel, between Elocin and Darnaatha, the road was strangely empty.

Merchants normally ply the roads between the larger cities during the summer and fall months when travel is easiest. After the spring thaw, when the roads have dried enough to permit travel, the wagons of traders are as thick as mosquitoes on the Darnaatha road. Today, again, we saw none, and I took it as an ill omen. Itinerant merchants are often the first to learn of news from afar, especially if it affects business. Reports of bandits, wars, and dragons spread quickly along the roads, faster, it seems, than the merchants who travel them.

At length, Brother Galthorn, walking beside me, asked, "Why is your mood so grim, Davian?"

"The quiet," I said. "It is unnatural."

"Indeed," he agreed. "I have never gone so long without hearing Fosdric's voice." Fosdric, walking on the other side of Aeryx, snorted.

"You misunderstand," I said. "No other travelers on the road. It is never like this at this time of year."

"No birds, neither," Fosdric said. "Where's the birds?"

We walked on a few paces without speaking. He was right— the birds were silent, too. In fact, there were no animal sounds at all, so far as I could tell. Even Wolf, I realized, had been strangely quiet. It was as if all Creation was trying to hide from something, all except we three fools, a burdened horse, and a small white dog. Were we mad for choosing to confront an enemy that moved at will, unseen, leaving only scorched earth and mutilated animals as evidence of its passing? What in the name of the Creator were we doing?

Suddenly, a crushing pain, as though a steel spike had been driven through my temples, drove me to my knees. My dragon-spear dropped to the dust. Through a roar of meaningless noise, I heard faint voices that seemed to come from a great distance. Swirling, nauseating colors ebbed and flowed through my field of vision, fascinating and terrifying all at once. The voices continued a conversation using words whose meanings were hidden from me. Slowly, maddeningly, the voices grew louder, piercing the din, growing more distinct, more clear, yet still twisted and confused. I strained to hear, listening for a phrase, a word I could discern, something that might help me understand the agony in my head…

A stinging slap across my left cheek brought me back to the world. I was still kneeling in the road, and the rumpled form of Fosdric took shape before me. His eyes were on mine and he was clearly worried. Brother Galthorn stood behind Fosdric, a mirror image of concern. I turned at a sound; little Wolf stared at me and growled, keeping Aeryx's legs between us.

I slumped forward and would have fallen if Fosdric had not jumped forward to catch my shoulders. "Master Davian, are you all right?" Brother Galthorn asked.

"In a moment," I said. "Please, let me sit a moment." The ground beneath me spun as though the world itself was trying to throw me off, and my legs were unable to support my weight. I wanted to close my eyes and rest, but I feared that doing so would drag me down into that swirling vortex of noise and color again.

"One second, we're walking along," Fosdric said, "And the next, boom! You're on your knees, swaying back and forth like a daisy in the breeze!"

"Fosdric, please," said Brother Galthorn. "Davian, are you all right?"

"Did you hear them?" I asked.

My two companions looked at each other for a moment. One did not need the Gift to hear their thoughts. *Myath—he's losing his mind just like Myath.*

"Voices," I continued. "I heard voices. Strange. I couldn't understand them. Too noisy—or a foreign tongue. Not dragons. Not enough—" The memory of swirling colors danced again in my mind, and I closed my eyes and shook my head to clear my thoughts. "Well, at least the pain is gone," I lied, although it had subsided. "Shall we continue?"

"I say we stop here for the night," Fosdric said.

"No," I snapped, struggling to my feet. "I feel fine. We have hours of light before nightfall."

"Fosdric is right," said Brother Galthorn as he helped me stand. "Whatever caused your faint today and the journey in your sleep last night, some rest would do you good. It would do all of us good."

"Amen, brother," Fosdric said, as he began unpacking our cooking gear from the bundle he'd removed from Aeryx's back. "I'm all in from chasing our sleepwalking wizard last night."

"I am not a wizard," I objected, looking for a more comfortable place to sit down again. Brother Galthorn had my arm, and he guided me to a lush patch of turf by the side of the road.

"Might as well be," Fosdric grumbled. "Can't understand a bloody thing you do."

"Fosdric," chided Brother Galthorn.

Turning from his task, the little man said, "What? Our best chance if we find this thing we're looking for is him. Now he's cracking like ice on a summer day. And you and me is skating on that ice, brother."

"Please, not now, Fosdric," Brother Galthorn said.

"When, then? We need to figure out what we're doing before we meet this thing or we might as well cash it in now and save it the trouble. Or better, maybe we just turn tail and head for the North Country, as fast as we can run. Take our wizard here some-place he can rest for a nice long time. Maybe that dragon lives, but so do we. Let someone else deal with it, eh?"

"Perhaps he is right," I said. At the moment, I felt incapable of dealing with Fosdric's dog, much less a dragon.

Brother Galthorn helped me sit and then turned back to Fosdric. "No," he said evenly. "The dragon has to be met, invisible or no. We will help Davian in any way we can, and with the Creator's help, we will defeat it."

Fosdric sighed. "You've got faith, I give you that, brother," he said, returning to the job of setting up our crude camp. "Either that, or you're as crazy as he is."

* * *

Lengthening shadows heralded the end of the day. Fosdric and Wolf had somehow managed to catch a rabbit, and the scent of Brother Galthorn's stew simmering over a small fire was enticing. My newly awakened hunger served to revive me, oddly enough, my senses sharpened by aroma of cooking meat. Standing and stretching, I noticed that Fosdric was observing me out of the corner of his eye while he tried to interest Wolf in a game of fetch the stick.

"Are you better, then?" he asked.

"Yes, thank you. A bit fatigued, but my head is clear."

He picked up the stick at his feet and pitched it back toward the road. "That's good." Fosdric kept his eyes on the little dog who watched the flight of the stick without the slightest hint of interest.

"Fosdric, I am all right."

"Right."

"I feel fine."

"For now." The fading sun in the west cast an orange glow upward from the horizon. The color was not unlike that which emanated from the snout of a dragon in battle.

"That is true," I admitted. "I do not know why I have acted so strangely of late. It may be the thing we seek—the thing that seems to have overwhelmed Myath and the others. Or it may be some consequence of the experience with Elgyrn."

"It doesn't matter, does it?" Fosdric said, throwing the stick again. "What matters is me and the priest ain't got a chance if you're off your nut when we meet the dragon."

"You don't have to come," I said. "I am used to facing these things alone."

Fosdric snorted. "Ah, you don't know where it is. You need me to take you to it."

"I have been in Palthinoor district before."

"Not lately."

"Has it changed that much in fifteen years?"

"That's not it," he said, facing me. "The district is big. I'm thinking you'll want to go to where the beast left his marks straight off. You could be weeks finding them."

"And you know where they are."

"Yah," he said, returning his attention to Wolf, now curled up at his feet. Fosdric bent over to scratch the dog behind his ears. The fuzzy white tail thumped the ground happily.

"How is that?"

"Eh?"

"How do you come by that knowledge?"

"King's men, bringing horses back," Fosdric said. "They talk, I listen."

Brother Galthorn interrupted. "Dinner is served," he said, taking his cooking pot from the fire and spooning his stew into three—no, four bowls.

"Are we having company?" I asked.

"Hm?"

"There are four bowls."

"Ah, yes," said Brother Galthorn. "The fourth is for Wolf." Responding to his name, the little dog trotted up and stood expectantly, tail wagging. "Patience, Wolf. It's still hot."

I rolled my eyes and took a bowl from Brother Galthorn. Clearly, the dwarfish mutt had won the priest over to his side as well. Fair enough, I thought. As long as he ate what was offered and did not come to expect to be served first.

* * *

The night passed uneventfully. As fatigued as we were, we dropped off to sleep soon after nightfall. As it was during the day, the quiet was unnerving. The usual cacophony of night creatures was absent, as though even the insects were afraid to make themselves known. The uncommon stillness should have been peaceful, but it served only to set us more on edge. The only sounds to pierce the darkness as I slowly drifted off to slumber were the crackle of the dying fire, and Wolf whimpering softly in his sleep.

I dreamed. Not the recurring dream of the woman I never knew; this was a dream different from any I had ever had.

Floating: I floated above a luminous sphere, unable to move. No, I was unable to move in a way that was familiar to me. Winds buffeted me, stronger than any I had ever felt, yet I paid them no heed and I was not pushed out of my course.

For I was moving. The sphere moved below me, rotating slowly. Colors were brilliant, nearly blinding in their radiance. Blues, greens, grays, and scattered tufts of white, and the blues, where I saw them, seemed to shimmer. It was intensely, awe-inspiringly beautiful. Never before had I seen a sight so lovely, a jewel whose value was beyond measure. I was entranced, content to drift and marvel at the wonders passing before my eyes. Strangely, I found that the miraculous sphere remained visible even when I attempted to close my eyes, as though my eyelids had somehow been made transparent.

Slowly, I became aware of brighter points of light dotting the surface of the sphere. Here a small one; there, a larger one, burning brightly, moving slowly across the surface. Without warning,

I was dazzled by a flash of light, painfully bright. Instantly, I was hurled at the sphere as if flung by an enormous trebuchet. The surface surged upward to meet me and I cried out—and found to my dismay that I had no voice.

Darkness enveloped me and I was numb, without sense or sensation. No sound or feeling pierced the veil that separated me from the living, for I was convinced that I had died. Surely this was what the dead experience when they first depart their mortal shells. To my surprise, I felt no remorse or regret for a life ended too soon, mistakes made, or things left undone. I felt nothing. Nothing at all.

That was odd, I thought, and I pondered why it was so. The fear of death is surely one of the strongest emotions in men. The newly dead must at least echo the feelings of the living, but my heart was numb. All I felt was a passing clinical curiosity.

Was life so empty for me that I cared not whether I lived or died? It was true that my life was lonelier than most, but I was not without companionship, and there are some I consider friends. Yet the thought of leaving those friends behind as I embarked on another journey, a solitary journey of the spirit, did not sadden me as I would have expected. For some unknown reason, it was simply another fact to consider and file.

Perhaps if I had the strength of Brother Galthorn's faith I would have felt joy at passing through to another level of consciousness, confirmation of our faith in an afterlife; eager for my imminent arrival in the presence of the Creator, to spend my days in the eternal company of the righteous dead; or, conversely, terror at the thought of my impending condemnation to the never-ending torment reserved for those who failed to heed the warning of the Creator's servants during their mortal days.

I felt none of those things. No sadness nor joy nor fear. It was as though I had turned to stone.

The wind resumed its assault, blowing and buffeting me with renewed vigor. Though I could no longer see or hear, I sensed my body being shaken from head to foot by, by…

By Fosdric, who had hold of my shoulders and was trying to rouse me from sleep.

"Master Davian! Please, get up!" Fosdric's eyes showed concern; clearly he had been trying to wake me for some time.

"What is wrong?" I asked. I took several deep breaths as I tried to clear my head.

"You were sleeping so deep, I thought we'd never get you up." Fosdric stood and turned back to the fire. "Come on, now, we've got your tea for you."

The scent of the bitter brew helped to bring me to my feet. The deep sleep had not refreshed me, and my legs were a bit unsteady as I stood and stretched.

The tea helped. I drank it as quickly as I could and immediately poured a second cup. The liquid warmth spread through my entire being, and I began to take notice of my surroundings.

Shadows told me that the sun was higher in the sky than I would have liked. "Fosdric," I asked, "How long have you been awake this morning?"

"A few hours," he said. "We thought you needed the sleep." He peered at me clinically, as though he were assessing the condition of a horse. "You were having some awful dreams."

"Hmm? How do you know?"

"You was thrashing about like a hooked fish," Fosdric said. "Isn't that right, brother?"

"Well, yes," Brother Galthorn agreed. "I was worried. You seemed very agitated—at least for a while. Then you became very still."

"My dream was unsettling," I said.

"Everything about you is unsettled," grumbled Fosdric. I chose to ignore him. There was no point in responding. Besides, he was right.

CHAPTER ELEVEN

A cold breakfast awaited me, as Brother Galthorn and Fosdric had been awake for quite some time. The provender, a hash of potatoes, rabbit, onions, and some of Brother Galthorn's secret herbs, was no doubt better when hot, but it was still most satisfying.

"Galthorn," I said, "Kindly forget every reason I ever gave for you not to accompany us." The young priest blushed at the compliment.

Since Fosdric and Brother Galthorn had already prepared themselves for departure, we were soon away after I finished my meal. The morning did little to improve our flagging spirits. As before, the expected sounds of life were absent. The morning sun was quickly hidden from us by an ominous sheaf of dark gray clouds, and the low drumbeat of distant thunder sounded a menacing cadence for our footsteps.

At least the pain in my head had gone. Better, the nearly constant throbbing in my nose had at last subsided to a barely noticeable ache, except on those occasions when I absent-mindedly applied pressure to it.

As we walked, the sky grew darker. It seemed fitting, if not overtly portentous. If the Creator had chosen to test our resolve, He was doing a fine job. The humid air was still and stifling. Looking to the west across a broad plain, distant lightning sputtered and flashed from low clouds that seemed to meet the horizon, almost as though they were rising from the bowels of the world to confront us.

An electrical storm. Perhaps the only thing on Saramond I dread.

"Brother Galthorn," I said. "There is something I need to tell you."

"Yes?"

"I should not be outside if that storm crosses our path."

He looked at me, puzzled.

"The lightning," I explained. "It affects me in unpredictable ways."

"Wait a minute," Fosdric said, stopping in his track. "What do you mean, 'unpredictable'?"

"Fosdric, have you ever seen someone in the midst of a delusional episode?"

"Delusional? You mean, seeing things what ain't there, and the like?"

"Yes," I said. "And have you ever seen anyone have a seizure?"

"I have," said Brother Galthorn. "One of my parishioners fell down and began frothing at the mouth during a service a few months ago. A few of the older folk thought he was possessed by an evil spirit."

"Was he?" asked Fosdric.

"Oh, no," the priest said. "I have seen such things. Demons are real, you can be sure, but old Wolgrym has suffered these seizures for many years."

"So," Fosdric turned to me, scowling, "You'll be doing that, too?"

"Possibly," I answered. "I don't know. As I said, the effect is unpredictable."

Brother Galthorn suddenly grasped the implications, and he was plainly worried. "What does this…I mean, how does your… uh, do you…"

"Do I use my power during these episodes?" I finished for him. "Yes. I very well might."

"Oh, this is just fine!" Fosdric exploded. "And you was waiting for a convenient time to tell us, I suppose? Like maybe two seconds before you blasted us to jelly? Thank you very much!"

"Fosdric! I'm sure Master Davian won't do anything to harm us." Brother Galthorn was nothing if not an optimist.

"Actually, brother," I said, "Fosdric is right to be concerned. If the storm is severe, you two should take Aeryx and put distance between us until it passes."

Fosdric turned and stomped away down the road, too angry to speak. Brother Galthorn looked at me with sorrowful expression. "I am sorry," he said.

"No need. I should have told you. My mind was on the invisible threat we seek." Brother Galthorn picked up Aeryx's lead from where Fosdric had dropped it and we resumed our progress toward Stelnregon.

"How do you normally prepare for electrical storms?" Galthorn asked.

"I stay in a room excavated beneath my home," I said. "It has a stout wooden door above it. Keeping a good deal of wood between myself and the storm seems to minimize its effect."

Over his shoulder, I heard Fosdric say, "Try to blast me and I'll introduce you to some wood, I promise you."

* * *

Near midday, as we searched for a place to rest and prepare a simple meal, the downpour that had threatened all morning finally made good on its promise. It came upon us suddenly. One moment there was only a sudden breeze bearing the scent of rain, but before we could enjoy the respite from the oppressive humidity, wet, angry missiles began hurtling from the sky. Within seconds, sheets of rain soaked us through and commenced to turning the hard-packed road into a rapidly liquefying muck.

"Well, this is fine," Fosdric muttered. "Just fine."

"Oh, you grouse," said Brother Galthorn. "This is just what the vegetation needs. I give thanks for it."

"Bleeding farmer." Fosdric continued to grumble as we struggled to lead Aeryx off the road to a small stand of trees that offered some hope of shelter. "Keep your bleeding plants and herbs and flowers…"

A flash turned everything painfully white. A moment later, a deafening crack was followed by the pungent scent of air split by the power of the Creator Himself. I turned to find Fosdric and Galthorn, to assure myself that they were unhurt. Instead, I saw a great white dragon being led on a tether by two bent and misshapen things. Horrible they were, once men but human no longer, with grotesque faces lifted from the demented nightmares of a demon's tortured sleep.

Surely these cursed beings had been vomited forth from the very bowels of hell. My most vivid childhood imaginings had never conceived of anything like the fell brutes that stood before me.

They looked on me with neither hatred nor contempt, but with fear. For though they had somehow tamed the white dragon, and no doubt planned to loose it in the hope that it would strike me down, they sensed that I, Master Davian of The Order, was possessed of a power greater than any they had ever known.

"What have you done with my friends?" I cried. "Answer quickly or forfeit your lives!"

The hideous things stared at me, too terrified to speak. The dragon fought against his tether, anxious to take to flight and begin the battle that could only end in death for one of us. And still the rain continued to fall in powerful waves, washing over me in a refreshing, cleansing torrent. I felt strong. No, *mighty*—mightier than any who had ever trod the soil of Saramond. With one motion, I stripped off my shirt and stood before them, a commanding presence, prepared to incinerate all three unholy things right where they stood.

"No answer, eh? You will pay dearly for your insolence! I am Master Davian, a third-level Brother of The Order. Prepare to meet your gods!"

The taller of the two abominations suddenly knelt in a pose that can only be described as penitent, that of a supplicant in prayer. As it did, it dropped the dragon's tether and the huge white beast bounded away into the driving rain. Coward! No matter. I would find it and finish it soon enough.

The creature kneeling before me appeared so wretched, and the action seemed so foreign to such a monster, that I was taken aback, unsure of what to do. Could such a beast know of the Creator? Would the Creator hear the prayer of one so foul?

While I contemplated these theological questions, another flash of lightning struck close by, blinding me for a moment and rocking me with the blast. The energy loosed by the strike fed my own, and I knew that I possessed the power to defeat any foe, and more. Indeed, so alive did I feel that it came to me that I might conquer all the world, holding Saramond in my grasp as a child might hold a fig. No army in the field could stand before the awesome power of Master—no, the Lord Davian!

A gale howled around me and I blinked hard to clear the rain from my eyes. One of the ogres was gone! The penitent one still knelt before me, praying in some twisted tongue to its evil god, but the shorter one was nowhere to be seen.

I spun around, sensing a presence behind me. Curse the lightning! The fury of the storm had overwhelmed my senses. The little one had used my moment of confusion to circle behind me. There! I met its gaze. Its beady, rat-like eyes glittered with panic as I prepared to delete it from this plane of existence. The rock it carried in its claw dropped harmlessly to the rain-slicked turf as it cowered, awaiting the end.

"Prepare to die, foul beast!" I cried, and I gathered my strength to strike.

Another flash! But it was not lightning this time, for I heard no crash of thunder. No, this flash was visible to me alone. The taller creature, the one that had knelt in despair, had treacherously leapt upon me as soon as I turned, and I was bested, felled by my carelessness and foolish bravado.

I fell heavily to my knees. Vision failed and the world contracted to a single point before my eyes. Desperately, I tried to summon the energy to retaliate, but it was of no use. I was finished.

Collapsing to the cool, wet grass, my final thought as I lay dying was regret; regret that I did not strike when I first had the chance.

* * *

My very next thought was great surprise. So convinced had I been of my imminent death that the sensation of gentle rain falling on my face came as a shock. Briefly, I gave thanks to the Creator for sparing my life. I must confess, to my shame, that prayer was not something to which I was accustomed, and I marveled that the Creator would answer such a prayer as might have come to me unknowingly in my dying moments.

The dragon! Remembering it with a start, I opened my eyes and leapt to my feet, searching all about for the terrible white beast that had allowed itself to be led on a tether. As I reached my feet, however, my sense of balance failed and I tumbled roughly to the sod.

I struggled to stand again, but this time I was conscious of a sharp pain in the back of my head, as though someone had pushed a fireplace poker through my skull and into my brain.

A hand grabbed my elbow, and another took hold of my shoulder. "Master Davian! Are you all right?" It was Brother Galthorn, his voice full of concern as he helped me rise.

"Galthorn! Where is Fosdric? Is he safe?"

"Here," Fosdric answered, standing under a nearby oak tree. "No thanks to you." He looked as though he was eyeing a snake and trying to decide whether it was venomous. The little dog, Wolf, sat timidly at his feet, watching me carefully. That was a most uncharacteristic position; either he'd been was intimidated by the storm, or he was, like his master, unsure of my intentions.

The little man was soaked through, his thinning hair plastered weakly against his head. Brother Galthorn, at my side, was just as wet, looking as though he had just completed a baptismal service in the River Cimlar. He led me toward the tree where Fosdric stood.

"Are you yourself again? Or do I have to get another rock?" Fosdric asked.

"Rock?"

Brother Galthorn interrupted, "Yes, and I'm terribly sorry. I had to hit you with a rock before you could do something to Fosdric. I'm sorry."

"You…hit me with a rock?" That certainly explained the pain, which, I discovered, radiated from a prominent lump on the back of my head that hadn't been there that morning.

"Yeah, and it was the nick of time, too," Fosdric said. "You was winding up to blast me off the face of the world."

The pieces came together all at once. It had been a fairly straightforward delusion, but why I had seen my companions as ogres and Aeryx as a dragon, I do not know.

"Oh, no," I groaned, rubbing my eyes. "No, no, no."

"Oh, yes," Fosdric said. "You nearly done us in. I tried to get a jump on you, but you turned 'round before I could knock you out. If Brother Galthorn here hadn't jumped quick as lightning, I'd be fit for burying and that's all. If there'd even been enough left of me to bury."

Standing there in the steady drizzle, disheveled and embarrassed, Brother Galthorn looked as much like a farmer's scarecrow as any man I have seen before or since. "I am truly sorry, Davian," he said.

"There is no need," I said. "It is I who must apologize to both of you. Without your quick action, brother, Fosdric would be dead. I was preparing to incinerate him just as you hit me. And it was only dropping to your knees that saved you."

The young priest was pale. "H-how… What do you mean?"

"I saw the two of you as hideous, deformed monsters—demons, leading a great white dragon on a tether. When you dropped to your knees in prayer, it was so unexpected and bizarre that I was frozen in place."

To my surprise, Fosdric suddenly exploded in laughter. "I thought beating the dragon was a miracle!" he choked. "And now he goes and bests a brother of The Order! Hoo, hoo, hee! They'll never believe it back home! The priest who takes on dragons and wizards, and lives to tell!" Then Fosdric was overcome, and he collapsed into convulsions of laughter under the tree.

Neither Brother Galthorn nor I shared Fosdric's appreciation for the humor he found in their brush with death. Galthorn was still shaken, but not so much by the prospect of meeting the Creator, I think. I truly believe he was mortified that he was capable of violence against a fellow man.

For my part, I was ashamed that I had nearly killed my companions, whether I was in my right mind or no. I had placed the two of them in mortal danger—which, I realized with a start, might still be present.

"How is the weather? Has the lightning passed?" Only a prickling sensation on my arms and scalp remained from the tremendous surge in power I felt during the height of the storm, but I did not want to repeat the confrontation they had just survived. If there was any lingering chance I would harm Galthorn or Fosdric, I wanted to be away from them as quickly as possible while I still saw them as men.

"Yes," said Brother Galthorn. "It is only a light rain now, and that seems to be lifting."

Indeed, the drizzle had lessened even in the short time since I had awakened from the blow to my head. "That is good news, anyway," I said.

"Never you worry," said Fosdric, who had quieted from guffaws to snorts and snuffles. "If the lightning was still around, the good brother would have bashed you again." And that sent him into a new fit of giggles. "Brother Galthorn, wizard tamer! Ha, ha, hee, hee, hee!"

Brother Galthorn and I settled next to Fosdric and Wolf under the oak to wait out the rest of the rain. Aeryx stood nearby, stoically waiting to resume the journey. Wolf, apparently satisfied that I was no longer a threat, grabbed the sleeve of Fosdric's shirt and initiated a tug-of-war.

Looking out through the endless gray mist, I tried to imagine what we might confront next. In the span of a fortnight, I had nearly been crushed by a falling dragon; a beautiful woman had broken my nose; I had been drugged, abducted, and forced to commit a crime; my mind showed signs of failing; and now, I had nearly killed my companions, and in turn, had been knocked senseless by a rock-wielding priest.

Somehow, it seemed that whatever lie ahead could not possibly be worse.

CHAPTER TWELVE

The three of us and the little dog, Wolf, sat under the oak tree, wet and staring at the gloomy, steadily falling drizzle for what seemed like hours. It was not, of course, but time is elastic, slowing and stretching when our experiences are the least enjoyable. It certainly was not the way I would have created the world had it been left to me. Be that as it may, the early afternoon of that day seemed to extend into eternity.

Finally I stirred and asked, "Fosdric? Truly now, what is your reason for being here?"

He was sitting with his knees pulled up under his chin. "If you was mucking stables all day, wouldn't you grab a chance for a little action?"

"Yes, perhaps," I allowed. "But this? Leading a Master of The Order to meet a dragon no one can see?"

Fosdric sighed, staring straight ahead. "Aye, well, it seemed like a better idea at the time."

"Now Fosdric," Brother Galthorn said, "You must admit that this has been quite an adventure so far."

"Right," Fosdric said. "Something to tell the grandkids about. If I live."

Galthorn leaned forward, his thin face turned to face Fosdric. "Sometimes the things we must do require that we forget about ourselves. The man who loves others first will himself be most loved."

"Bah," said Fosdric.

"It's true," insisted the priest. "Those who put themselves last are first in the heart of the Creator."

"I thought he helped them what help themselves," Fosdric retorted.

Brother Galthorn's brows furrowed. "That is not in the Holy Book," he said. "Service to your fellow man is the highest form of love. The Creator honors that above all else."

"Maybe in your world, brother," said Fosdric. "But in the real world a man has to look out for himself. 'Cause nobody else will."

The young priest smiled. "If you truly believed that, Fosdric, you would not be here now."

Fosdric just snorted, hunched his shoulders, drew his knees up under his chin, and stared out at the rain.

* * *

Some time later, the rain slackened enough that we decided to resume our journey. Although the drizzle continued to fall, further delay gained us nothing. We were already soaked, and there were still hours before nightfall.

At least moving served to get our blood moving again, and I no longer had to expend energy to keep us from getting chilled. The low, gray skies were in keeping with our spirits, although the storm had left a fresh, crisp scent in the air. Though our feet splashed through muddy pools and sank into the softened surface of the road, the cleaner feel to the air had an invigorating effect. I looked forward to stopping for the night when we might strip off our wet clothing and allow them to dry before a crackling fire.

The balance of that day, and the next, and the one after that, were blessedly uneventful. Though the clouds remained with us for the next two days, the sun reappeared on the third. The warmth was welcome, as was its effect on the sodden Darnaatha road. Were it not for the disquieting absence of the travelers one would expect at this season, we might have enjoyed ourselves.

The proprietor of the small inn that housed us the fourth night from Darnaatha was overjoyed at our arrival. The sudden and unexpected disappearance of traffic from the road had not only hurt his business, it had become difficult to replenish the supplies he needed to run a proper inn. The innkeeper told us that we were the first guests he'd had in nearly two weeks. Though he apologized for a few shortages in his menu offerings, we took no notice as we were thankful to sleep indoors on dry bedding for a change.

The sunny days stimulated an improvement in our spirits. Fosdric, I think, had come to believe that I was not going to accidentally roast him during the night. Perhaps his good cheer was the result of a better night's sleep.

Brother Galthorn, for his part, was never outwardly disheartened, but his youthful face clearly reflected the influence of sunshine and blue skies. This day was one of those in which the world around us was so glorious that it was difficult to feel discouraged, even by the prospect of facing an invisible foe of unknown power.

About the middle of our sixth day, we crossed the border into Palthinoor district. The guardhouse was deserted. This was unexpected. I had hoped we might learn something about the state of affairs from the King's Guard stationed there.

The borders of the four districts within the kingdom of Aerwald are open to one another. Guards are posted at the borders along the main roads only to monitor traffic. Rumors of taxing travelers between the regions had so far been only that, but a good king—and Ednorwain seemed to be good, at least as far as efficient rule was concerned—must stay informed of the comings and goings within his domain. His guards would not abandon their post without good reason.

We ate a cold lunch of jerked meat and hard biscuits in the deserted guardhouse. There was little talk between us; Fosdric, too, seemed to understand that the guards' absence was unusual. Brother Galthorn tried to engage us in conversation, but after several vain attempts, his cheerful mood cracked in frustration.

"Well, then," he said, "What next? Will you tell me, or must I guess?"

Fosdric was first to answer. "Oh, sorry there, brother. My mind's just turning over a problem here, and I always go quiet when I think."

"My apologies, Galthorn," I said, swallowing the last of a biscuit. "The empty guardhouse disturbs me."

"Why is that?"

"There are always guards posted at the borders between the districts," I said. "Monitoring the traffic. Basic administration of the kingdom."

Fosdric, tossing a scrap of jerky to Wolf, added, "Aye, and they keep an eye out for blokes wanted by the sheriff."

Brother Galthorn raised an eyebrow at Fosdric, who didn't notice. "Yes. Well, what do you think would cause the guards to abandon their post? Could they be chasing a wanted man?"

"Nah," Fosdric said. "They'd leave at least one of them here."

"What do you think, Davian?" Galthorn asked.

"Fosdric is right," I said. "It probably means that the guards were badly needed elsewhere."

Galthorn frowned, deep in thought. "What would draw them away?"

Fosdric and I just looked at Galthorn. It only took a moment for him to catch up to our thoughts. "Ah. The dragon. Uh, is this a bad sign?"

"Yes," I said. "It is." I stood and stretched, working the tension out of my shoulders. "We had best move along. It appears we will learn nothing until we reach Stelnregon."

* * *

The afternoon, though sunny and pleasant otherwise, was heavy with a sense of foreboding. If anything, Fosdric and I were even quieter than at lunch. We learned, however, that Brother Galthorn responded to anxiety with a non-stop stream of chatter.

The terrain south of the border between Palthinoor and Darnaatha districts was marked by a series of low hills, which gradually increased in height as we got closer to the city of Stelnregon. The landscape forced the road into numerous twists and turns to navigate the hills, and the open prairie south of Darnaatha was replaced by thick stands of deciduous forest. This was no difficulty to travelers on foot, but it did prevent us from seeing more than a half a mile down the road most of the time. Under normal circumstances this was of no consequence, but now, with our desire to know what was happening ahead, it was frustrating.

At the time, I imagined that it was Brother Galthorn's never-ending monologue that caused my temples to throb again that afternoon. As we moved further into the district, the pain between my eyes returned. I said nothing to my companions, but Fosdric, ever alert, stole glances at me from time to time. Perhaps the discomfort showed in my face, but if Fosdric noticed anything amiss, he said nothing.

We soon had other things to consider. About mid-afternoon, we stumbled onto the remains of a dragon.

Its presence was heralded by its stench. As we approached the crest of a small hill, an overpowering odor of death washed over us, stopping us in our tracks.

"Whoa!" Fosdric held Aeryx's lead and half-stooped, breathing through his mouth while his stomach settled. Aeryx nickered fretfully; he had picked up the scent, and perhaps knew better than we its meaning.

"What is that?" Brother Galthorn's voice was muffled as he spoke through the sleeve of his robe, which he pressed tightly over his nose and mouth.

"Something big," said Fosdric, panting.

"Or many things," I said, pressing on to the top of the hill. Wolf, in his sling across Aeryx's back, began to bark. There, halfway down the slope, among a small stand of ash and maple just to the left of the road, was a dragon. Judging by the stench, and the wilted leaves on the broken branches littering the ground nearby, the monster had been dead for several days at least.

A buzzing noise reached our ears as we stood there trying to retain our last meal. At first I thought it might be a hive of bees, but I quickly realized that the sound was that of the scavenger insects always present for a carrion feast. Sure enough, a closer look showed the carcass had drawn to itself an enormous swarm of flies.

"Master Davian," Brother Galthorn gasped, "What is it?"

"It is a dragon," I replied dryly. "That would seem to be obvious."

"Yes," he said, "But why is it lying there that way?"

"Because, brother, it is dead." I should not have been so impatient with the young man, but with my head aching and my stomach lurching, I had little patience for questions.

"Yes," he persisted, "But why would so much of it be lying there?"

That was a good question. For reasons that were nauseatingly obvious at that moment, a dragon's carcass is usually attended to right away. After a dead dragon is butchered for its meat, hide, and bones, the offal is burned straightaway. Flies are nuisance enough without offering them enough feed for generations. A dragon left to rot can be a public health emergency.

Besides, the value of a dragon's remains is so great that this beast simply should not have been there in that condition. A single dragon can nearly lift an entire village out of poverty. People will pay dearly for clothing or tools made from dragon's hide or bone, not to mention the multitude of potions and folk remedies produced from various parts of a dragon's anatomy. In my travels, I have seen everything from headache powders to hair-restorer to cures for obesity derived from bits of slain dragon. Quackery, all of it, but highly profitable. It is small recompense for the devastation a dragon can inflict, however, so one cannot blame the survivors of a dragon's attack for using the beast's remains to rebuild their homes and lives.

The odds favored the probability that someone had seen this dragon fall. The monsters do not typically die of old age or natural causes. They are cursedly resilient; I do not know of a single disease that afflicts them. No, when a dragon dies, it is usually in combat, and a dragon in combat makes enough noise that it is difficult to ignore.

Brother Galthorn, still gasping for breath, asked, "Do you think this is the dragon we were looking for?"

Fosdric and I answered simultaneously, "No."

"Why do you say that?"

Stifling my gag reflex and taking quick, shallow breaths, I said, "Because this dragon would not be left to rot if the danger were past."

We were very near the fallen creature, close enough to give it a fair visual examination. "Look here," Fosdric said, pointing to the dragon's midsection. His eyes watered and he held a rather unsanitary rag over his nose and mouth. "What do you make of that?"

A neat incision had been made across the dragon's powerful chest, a thin, straight line slicing diagonally from a point near the beast's left foreleg to the bottom of the ribcage on its right side. The cut, as nearly as we could see, had severed hide, muscle, sinew, and bone as neatly as a razor slicing through a sheet of paper.

"What could have done that?" Brother Galthorn's eyes were wide in fascinated horror.

"Another dragon?" Fosdric offered.

"No," I said. "The cut is too clean. Another dragon would not have had the time to cut a line so, so..."

"Precisely?" Fosdric finished my sentence.

"Precisely. Thank you. Besides, a slash from a dragon's claw would leave a ragged wound." I stepped closer to the carcass now, my headache and the overpowering stink nearly forgotten as I tried to make sense of the puzzle before us. Surely no man had inflicted this wound. No weapon on all of Saramond could slice so neatly through the armored hide of a dragon. Looking more closely, and swatting flies away from my face, I noticed something else.

"Fosdric, do you see this?" I pointed at the incision.

"Yeah," came his muffled reply.

"Do the edges of the cut appear burned to you?"

The little man leaned closer, squinting. He nodded. "Looks like it's been cauterized, even," he said, before retreating to find air not quite as affected by the dragon's unbearable stench.

Circling the remains, I searched for other signs of battle. I found none, on the creature or on the ground nearby. The branches seem to have been broken off the trees when the dragon fell to ground.

"Uh, begging pardon, Davian," Fosdric said from upwind. "But how long do you plan to stare at the beast?"

"I'm sorry, Fosdric," I said. "It is a bit ripe, I know."

"That's all right," he said. "It's just that I'd like to keep my lunch where it is, if you don't mind."

"I understand. It's just that I—where is Brother Galthorn?"

Before Fosdric could respond, a wet cough from the weeds along the far side of the road answered my question. "Just...just a minute," came a weak voice. After another fit of coughing followed by seemingly endless spitting, an unsteady Brother Galthorn rose into view among the greenery on the roadside. He was as pale as the inside of a potato.

"By the Creator's beard, Davian," Fosdric said. "Let's put some air between us and that stinking monster!"

"Agreed. Are you all right, brother?"

The young man nodded and began to follow us downhill, his thin face taut with the effort of holding his rebellious stomach under control.

"What do you think killed it, then?" Fosdric asked.

"I have no idea," I said. "But whoever wields a weapon that can take a dragon out of the sky this way could be a powerful friend."

"Or," Fosdric said, "The worst enemy we ever seen."

CHAPTER THIRTEEN

A renewed sense of urgency spurred us onward, both from a desire to learn who or what and felled the dragon and the need to flush the rotting beast's disgusting odor from memory as quickly as possible.

We walked silently for a time, considering the implications of the dragon's demise. At length, Fosdric, still walking ahead of Aeryx, said, "Davian, did you see anything else about that beast that struck you funny?"

"Well," I said, "Besides the wound, no."

"There were no scavengers," said Brother Galthorn, now nearly returned to his normal coloring.

"Exactly," said Fosdric.

They were right. I should have seen it. A carcass that size would normally attract ravens, wild dogs, or rats—something larger than flies, at any rate. And yet, there had been no sign of any. In fact, the only animal larger than an insect we'd seen in days, besides Aeryx and Wolf, was the dragon lying dead behind us.

The pain in my head returned suddenly, and with a vengeance. I stopped in my tracks for a moment and rubbed my temples to try to ease the pain in my head. My companions stopped as well, and I heard Fosdric sigh.

"It's starting again, ain't it?" he asked.

"I'm all right," I said.

"Sure you are," he said. "And tonight we'll find you halfway to Stelnregon, or you'll be roasting us in our sleep. I'm not going to—"

Fosdric was interrupted by Brother Galthorn's shout: "Dragon!"

Cursing myself for missing the approach of yet another dragon, I yelled, "Behind me!" Which, in retrospect, was ridiculous, as I had yet to spot the beast.

Fosdric and Brother Galthorn leapt into action immediately. Fosdric pulled Aeryx's lead and Galthorn ran alongside the big horse, speaking quickly but calmly into his ear to calm him while they guided him toward a nearby stand of oak and maple. Poor cover, but better than none.

The dragon was on us almost immediately. From behind us it came, flying six or seven man-heights over the road and moving quickly. I whirled to face it, readying my spear and gathering my strength. My hope was that the beast would focus on me, at least long enough for my companions to reach the trees. My ability to focus or deflect energy weakens with distance, and it occurred to me suddenly that my friends might have been safer close behind me.

Behind me, Fosdric and Galthorn had almost reached the trees and were coaxing Aeryx off the road. Barking wildly, Wolf struggled to free himself from his sling on Aeryx's back. Galthorn grabbed the little dog and darted out of sight into the woods.

The dragon loomed large. It showed no sign of slowing, apparently counting on having caught me unprepared. I steeled myself for its attack. But something was amiss. With surprise, I realized that this dragon, like the one that caught us unawares five days earlier, was not interested in us at all.

I crouched as the dragon swooped past, the downdraft from its massive leathery wings kicking up dust and pebbles around me. Squinting to keep debris from my eyes, I turned and watched as the behemoth, oblivious to my presence, continued its flight in the direction of Stelnregon.

"What in the bloody hell?" Fosdric's voice came from the direction of an ancient oak, big enough that a man's arms would not encompass the trunk.

"Stay there!" I shouted. While I didn't believe the creature was coming back, it is never wise to bet one's life on predicting a dragon's behavior.

Some minutes passed in which the only sounds were a few muffled "woofs" from behind the oak. I reached with my mind but felt nothing. The dragon had gone.

"You can come out," I called. "It is gone."

Brother Galthorn, carrying Wolf, was the first to emerge from the trees. "What happened? Did you chase it away?"

I shook my head. "I do not know."

"Like the other one, eh?" Fosdric led Aeryx from the trees and back to the road.

"Yes. It was as though we didn't exist."

Galthorn finally decided to let the squirming dog run free, and he bent down to set Wolf on the road. As he straightened up, he asked, "What does this mean, Davian?"

"I haven't a clue."

Wolf scampered a short distance back along the road in the direction from which we'd come. He stopped and stood, tail rigid, and barked repeatedly in the direction of the trees. His piercing yelp quickly reminded me of my headache, and I rubbed my temples again.

Fosdric sighed, and I knew he was watching. "I am fine, Fosdric."

"Right."

"Well, then," Brother Galthorn interjected, "Shall we be off?"

"Yes, if you can draw Wolf away from whatever he's found."

"Wolf!" Fosdric's call was a command, and the little dog scurried to obey. His master scooped him up, tucked him back into his sling, and gave Aeryx's lead a tug to start us on our way.

* * *

We made camp that night in a small clearing just off the road. The ground was flat and dry, and a small stream nearby provided cool, clear water. The ache in my head had subsided somewhat, but I still took the opportunity to freeze a small quantity of water and apply it to the back of my neck. That eased the pain a bit more, and I was able to relax for the first time since we left the guardhouse at the border.

The episode with the dragon had weighed on our minds the rest of that afternoon. I could make no sense of it. Never had I heard of dragons behaving as these had. There was no one from The Order near enough to consult; as you may have guessed, we can communicate with one another over some distance when necessary. I searched far ahead of us for the presence of one of my brothers, but I sensed no one. Without more information, then, there was nothing for it but to press on. The animals, Wolf and Aeryx, were skittish, but I considered that only natural, as they were still the only animals about. They must have sensed whatever had driven the normally abundant wildlife into hiding.

Our evening meal, at least, was pleasant. Brother Galthorn worked another small miracle with a few vegetables and the last of the dried beef we had purchased at the inn a few nights before. As luck would have it, a dense patch of wild blueberries was nearby, which made for an unexpected treat.

"Ah, that's more like it," Fosdric said, reclining against a fallen log after dinner. The setting sun and flickering fire cast reddish-orange highlights across his face. "I got to say, brother, them berries has to be one of the Creator's best ideas." He closed his eyes in contentment, at peace with the world. Wolf, who had eaten nearly half of Fosdric's stew, curled up next to his master and instantly fell asleep.

The young priest, busily cleaning the cooking gear, smiled. "You know, Fosdric, all of creation was part of His design for—"

I waved him quiet. Fosdric's breathing had already slowed to a gentle snore.

* * *

Clouds greeted us on awakening, but at least the pain in my head was gone. That was a good omen, I thought, and I quickly set about preparing my gear for the day. We hoped to make it as far as Naribor, a village just one day's travel from Stelnregon. The inn there would provide us with better lodging than we had endured in recent days, and perhaps we would get some news of what lay ahead.

"I am sorry we do not have more to break our fast," Brother Galthorn said. "All we have left are blueberries."

"Fine with me," Fosdric said, scooping a double handful from the bowl Brother Galthorn offered.

"I just hope they agree with me," I said. "It has been a long time since I have eaten blueberries, and so many in so short of time could be, ah, inconvenient."

"I know," Galthorn said. "I am sorry."

"For what? It isn't your fault that the game around here has disappeared. You can't cook what we can't see, brother."

"We should eat well tonight," he said.

"Amen to that, brother," Fosdric said, around a mouthful of berries. "The Happy Traveler knows how to set a board. Old Wigard there is a master, he is. Mmm, I can almost smell the mutton now."

"Well," I said, "Let's get moving so we get there before he closes the kitchen. Are you ready, Fosdric?"

"Mm hmm." The little man snapped his fingers, bringing Wolf at a run. Scooping him up, Fosdric carried him to Aeryx to secure him in his sling for the day's journey.

A light breeze picked up late in the morning, not unpleasant, but a bit unusual. It came from the northwest, behind us, while the clouds overhead continued their natural slow march from west to east.

Sure enough, as I had feared, eating an entire meal of fresh fruit had its consequences. By midday, both Brother Galthorn and I were in need of frequent stops along the road. Somehow, Fosdric seemed immune to the laxative effect of the berries. To his credit, he managed to refrain from making light of our trial, taking advantage of the interruptions to tend to Aeryx and play with Wolf.

If there was any benefit to our condition, it was that neither of us were inclined to complain that we had no food for our midday meal.

The frequent stops impeded our progress and made me irritable. The delays caused by Elgyrn and my lapses into insanity had already cost us valuable time, and it was impossible to know what devilry might have been prevented had we arrived sooner in Palthinoor district.

The day ground slowly on. Between the turmoil in my gut and the thick cloud cover, I was a less than an ideal traveling companion.

It became clear by mid-afternoon that we would not reach Naribor until after sundown. Though food was still far from my thoughts, Fosdric, the only one among us whose appetite was still healthy, would be in a fix if we arrived at the Happy Traveler too late for a hot meal. At length, Fosdric's patience began to wear thin. While he said nothing, the set of his jaw as I announced my need for yet another stop made clear his frustration at the delay in reaching his next meal.

We finally reached the outskirts of Naribor shortly after dusk. I was thirsty and near exhaustion, and the haggard look on Brother Galthorn's face indicated that he felt no better. At least my appetite had finally been restored and my stomach seemed to have returned to normal. Perhaps it was only that there was nothing left to expel.

Naribor is essentially a suburb of Stelnregon, one of the small villages of farmers who till the fields surrounding the district's capital. Stelnregon sits on the shore of the Southern Sea, but the lands along and beyond the hills that flank the shore are fertile and well-watered. As the lowlands grew prosperous from its natural deep-water port, the hill country nearby prospered as a source of vegetable and dairy products for those along the sea.

As we approached the village, it was soon apparent that things were not as they should be. We saw no smoke from the small, thatched-roof dwellings, no lights in the windows, and no sound of human habitation. What's more, I sensed no one with my mind save those with whom I traveled.

Brother Galthorn put the obvious into words. "It's rather dark," he said.

"I don't like it," Fosdric said.

"It's been abandoned," I said.

"What?" Brother Galthorn was incredulous. "Why would they do that?"

"So's we can't get a decent supper," Fosdric grumbled. "I'm for searching the inn and cooking up whatever we find."

"Oh, we can't do that," Galthorn said. "That would be stealing."

"Bah!"

"We can leave compensation for the owner," I said. "It would be as though he had served us himself."

"Yah," Fosdric said. "Except we do all the work."

That settled, we ventured into the village. Fosdric led the way, as he had visited the Happy Traveler more than once during his years in Stelnregon.

An ominous feeling pressed down upon us as we entered Naribor. Unlike Marthwee, which was almost as quiet when Brother Galthorn and I arrived there three weeks earlier, I was able to sense the presence of no one at all in Naribor.

The soft padding of our feet and the gentle rhythm of Aeryx's hooves were the only sounds to break the ghostly stillness. As if by unspoken agreement, we moved slowly and quietly through the main street, loath to announce our presence. Our eyes examined every doorway, every window, for a sign of life. We found none.

As we neared some of the hovels, it became clear that the citizens of Naribor had left their homes in haste. The doors of most of the homes were ajar, and some of the inhabitants had been in the midst of preparing meals, which were abandoned unfinished or left over the cooking fire to burn. The crisis must have occurred at the dinner hour. Spoiled, half-eaten meals in several homes testified to the panic that must have gripped the village.

"What do you think, hey?" Fosdric asked, as we examined the moldy remains in a cooking pot.

"Were it not for the open doors, one would almost think they had vanished into thin air," I said, returning an overturned chair to its place by a crude wooden table. "This food has been here for days, at least."

"Um, almost three weeks, I think," Brother Galthorn said from the doorway of the hut.

"Eh?" Fosdric said.

"Well, with that much mold, it has to be two weeks or more," the priest explained. "When I was a candidate at the monastery, we sometimes had food that spoiled. And I, uh, well, it was usually my job to clean up such accidents."

"So this was abandoned just after you came through, Fosdric," I said.

"Yah."

"And the food left out to spoil in place. No mice, rats, or treeurchins availed themselves of the banquet?"

"No flies, neither," observed Fosdric. "This is peculiar, and no mistake."

"Was there any hint of anything amiss when you were here?"

"Nope," Fosdric said. "Business as usual. Wolf! Quiet!" The little white dog had been in the street, barking at something in the direction from which we'd come. On hearing his master's call, he obediently scurried around Brother Galthorn and into the hut, seeking Fosdric's approval. Fosdric bent and gave Wolf's ears a scratch.

"Well, gentlemen," I said, "Let's get to the inn and see whether there is any unspoiled food in the village."

* * *

The Happy Traveler, in more joyful times, was a cheerful place. We found wood and lamps and soon had the inn ablaze with light. An inspection of the kitchen revealed some edible vegetables, and some of the smoked meat in the larder seemed safe enough, so Brother Galthorn set about preparing a meal.

The inn was larger than one would expect for such a small village because Naribor was usually the first stop on the route travelers follow when journeying north or west from Stelnregon. It was larger than the Court Jester in Elocin, at least ten man-heights across. The main hall was neat and clean, except for several weeks of accumulated dust. There must have been few guests at the inn at the time of the innkeeper's departure, since it seemed unlikely that he would have taken any more time to clean before abandoning the village than had his fellow citizens.

Fosdric and I spent some time examining the rooms and the innkeeper's quarters, which were situated on opposite sides of the main hall, looking for any clues that might explain the sudden evacuation of Naribor. The scene was the same as throughout the village—some spoiled, uneaten food in the innkeeper's room, some personal belongings left behind in the guest rooms, and no signs of life.

The smell of vegetables being sautéed brought us back to the kitchen. "That has a powerful healing effect, Brother Galthorn," I said. "How are you feeling?"

"Quite well, thank you," he said. "I think the danger has passed."

"Or you've passed it," Fosdric said, chuckling. Brother Galthorn smiled good-naturedly.

"How much longer, do you think, before dinner?" I asked.

"Oh," Galthorn said, "Not more than half an hour, surely."

"All right. Fosdric, let us take one more look outside to be sure we're truly alone in this place."

The wind outside had picked up a bit since our arrival in Naribor, still blowing from the northwest. It dawned on me then that the breeze had been at our backs all day. That's unusual so close to the sea. Normally, winds blow inland from the sea during the day, and from land out to sea as temperatures fall after sunset.

Fosdric followed me through the inn's front door and we stood in the street for a moment, giving our eyes time to adjust to the darkness. The air was cooler, and a hint of rain was in the air. That was true to form; expecting dry weather to follow us for our entire journey was unreasonable, I know, but I still did not welcome another day's walk in the rain.

"That's queer," Fosdric said.

"What's that?"

"You wouldn't think to see sunset this late."

"What?"

"Over there," he pointed. The road through Naribor was a straight line that bisected the village, roughly pointing northwest toward Darnaatha and southeast toward Stelnregon. Silhouetting the trees that lined the road past the outskirts of the village, I saw an orange glow that leapt upward from the horizon.

"Fosdric," I said, my stomach suddenly feeling much as it had earlier in the day, "You would not see a sunset in the southeastern sky at any hour."

"Eh? Oh, damn! You're right!"

Just then, Brother Galthorn emerged through the doorway. "Hello! Dinner is in the pot, and—" Turning to peer at the heavenly glow that had captivated Fosdric and me, he asked, "What is that?"

"Pray that I am wrong, brother," I said, staring at the southeastern sky, "But I think that is the devastation of Stelnregon."

CHAPTER FOURTEEN

The three of us stared silently at the angry incandescence along the horizon for a long time. The color was almost that of a normal sunset, but the inconstant glow bloomed and faded again and again as we watched.

The northwest breeze now made sense. Air rushes into a fire, feeding it, and judging by the glow, which had grown to color a third of the southeastern sky, this fire was very large indeed. Its energy was a crackling buzz in my mind, even at the distance of a day's travel.

"What shall we do?" asked Brother Galthorn. The priest stared at the phosphorescent sky, his young face contorted with anguish. His long, thin fingers anxiously twisted and pulled at the sleeves of his robe.

"Pray, brother," Fosdric said quietly. "That's your line. I don't see there's much else to be done."

Galthorn grabbed my shoulder. "Master Davian, isn't there something you can do?" The young man's distress was palpable, like the hot bitterness of the herbal tea I favor.

"Fosdric is right," I said, "There is nothing we can do."

"But—"

"No. One of us riding hard might reach the city in an hour or two. But which of us is up to it? Is Aeryx fit for such a ride after a day's travel? And what would we do when we arrived?"

"Could you not stop the fire?"

"Brother Galthorn," I said, "My abilities do not include creating or absorbing energy. Once a fire begins, I can guide it, focus it. If the fire is small enough, I can even direct it, turn it back upon itself, perhaps even save some lives. But this—" I gestured toward the glowing sky, "This is immense. Containing it would require an incredible amount of effort. The combined powers of a dozen Masters might not be enough to bring it under control. And right now, I am exhausted, hungry, and ill-prepared to fight the thing that may have started the blaze."

His eyes grew wide. In his desperate desire to help those undoubtedly suffering and dying tonight in Stelnregon, he had not considered that the dragon we sought might be responsible for their misery.

"But," he said, chin trembling, "Is there nothing—?" His voice trailed away to a whisper.

"Not tonight," I said.

His hand fell from my shoulder. I turned away. The young man's pain was palpable, and it took several deep breaths to bring my own emotions into check. From the size of the fire, the loss of life in Stelnregon would be unimaginable. But there was nothing for it but to gather our strength and press on in the morning.

And even though the final leg of our journey would be mostly downhill, as we descended to the sea, it promised to be more arduous than we'd hoped. If the fire still burned, we could be walking into an inferno. The added stress of the heat and keeping Aeryx calm would leave us drained by the time we arrived.

Fosdric stood a few paces aside, staring at the ground. A few stars peered through a gauzy layer of clouds or smoke overhead, dispassionately watching our drama unfold below. Cold, staring eyes from across the vast reaches of heaven, watching without comment or care. *Creator, can you see us? Some assistance would be welcome.*

"Come, brother," I said, turning to the young man. "Let us eat, and then rest as we may. There will be plenty for us to do tomorrow."

"No," Galthorn said.

"Aw, come on, brother," Fosdric said. "You're not doing any good standing around out here. You need to eat something."

"I will be in shortly," Brother Galthorn said. "Go on and start without me."

"Wait," I said. "You're not thinking of riding Aeryx to Stelnregon yourself."

"No," he replied. "Just a few minutes alone. Please."

Fosdric and I said no more, but left the young man there outside the inn, standing in the reflected glow of what might be the loss of thousands of homes and untold lives. With subtle orange highlights playing across his thin, sharply angled features, Brother Galthorn seemed more a statue than a man, frozen in place, eyes fixed in the direction of a scene we dared not imagine.

* * *

The meal Brother Galthorn had prepared was no doubt excellent, but I do not think Fosdric or I tasted much of it. Our thoughts were directed toward the burning city and the carnage we feared awaited our arrival the following day.

Stelnregon was an ancient city, as I have mentioned. As with many old cities, the dwellings are too close together, are often of poor construction, and, thanks to the forested hills north of the city, usually built of wood. Under normal circumstances, almost anything might touch off a fire that could quickly spread out of control. However, the abandonment of Naribor, the absence of travelers along the Darnaatha road, and the disappearance of every wild creature larger than an insect indicated a more sinister cause.

Fosdric and I finished our meal in silence. Brother Galthorn did not rejoin us. As we returned our plates to the inn's kitchen, Fosdric said, "Why don't you check on the brother, hey? I'll look in on Aeryx."

"Good idea." I moved the stewpot a bit further from the cooking fire to keep it from burning and then headed outside.

The glow on the southeast horizon was as bright as before, an orange hue that would have been beautiful except for what it represented. The priest, however, was nowhere in sight.

"Brother Galthorn!" I called. There was no sound except the faint murmur of the breeze as it hurried past the inn to feed the fires at Stelnregon. Reaching with my inner senses, I listened for the buzz of his mind, although the static crackle of the distant fire made discerning his presence difficult.

A quiet woof from behind and a soft bump against my leg—Wolf's nose—announced the presence of Fosdric's dog. "Hello, Wolf," I said. "What are you doing here? Where is Fosdric?" He simply stared at me, mouth open and tail wagging. I tried again: "Where is Brother Galthorn?"

At the mention of the priest's name, Wolf began barking, a series of rapid, high-pitched yips, accompanied by a series of counterclockwise spins. He looked like a miniature folk dancer from the eastern wilds.

"Where is he, then? Where is Brother Galthorn?" Wolf trotted a few steps toward the side of the inn, the side facing Stelnregon. Then he turned around and barked again.

"I'm coming, I'm coming." The dog scampered around the corner of the inn and was lost behind its whitewashed wall. He barked twice more, as if to give me a fix on his position.

Wolf barked again as I came around the corner, wagging his curly tail in pride. "Good boy," I said, and I bent to scratch behind his ears. "Thank you, Wolf." Brother Galthorn was on his knees, leaning against the wall in a position of prayer. He was fast asleep where he knelt.

"Brother Galthorn," I said, touching his shoulder.

"Huh!" Galthorn started at my touch. In spinning to face me, he lost his balance and flopped to the ground like a rag doll.

"Come inside, brother. Eat something. You were asleep."

"Yes, all right," he said thickly as he struggled to his feet. "I was—I was just, um, praying, and I—"

"This has been a very long day," I finished. "And I expect a longer one tomorrow. Let us gather our strength while we may." I took his shoulder and guided him toward the front door of the inn.

"That is what I was doing," the priest said.

"Perhaps the Creator's response was to put you to sleep," I said. "That may be what you need most." We slowly walked back into the inn, stopping only to call Wolf, who was barking into the darkness. Perhaps the unnatural stillness of the abandoned village had worn his nerves thin, too.

Fosdric and I managed to convince Brother Galthorn to take some food before sending him off to bed in one of the guest rooms. As tired as I was, I brewed a cup of tea. We needed to plan the coming day and I needed to clear my head. Returning to the main hall, I chose a seat near the fireplace, sipped the bitter brew, and stared at the cold ashes.

"Could be rough tomorrow." Fosdric joined me after banking the hearth fire in the kitchen.

"Yes."

"No telling what we'll find in Stelnregon."

I sighed. "The fire feels big."

"You can feel it?" he asked, eyebrows raised.

I nodded.

Fosdric whistled. "I'd 'a not guessed that."

"Heat is just another form of the energy that's all around us. I've always felt it. I don't know what it's like not to feel it."

"So," he said, leaning forward in his chair, "You can…feel… things besides heat and the like?"

I leaned back and considered the stable hand. This was the first time he had asked about the Gift. "There is an energy that comes from within Saramond. It ebbs and flows with the passing of the moons across the sky. Fire has it, thunderstorms—"

"Yah, I know."

"I am sorry," I said. "Thunderstorms, certain metals, dragons, of course. Even people."

"People?"

"A quiet buzz up here." I tapped my temple. "Everyone has it."

He frowned. "Can you tell what I'm thinking?"

"No," I said. "Only dragons." That was not entirely true, of course. Brothers of The Order can communicate with one another without speaking. That is a closely guarded secret, however, and it has served more than one of us well in an emergency.

"Well." Fosdric clapped his hands to his knees. Wolf, who had slipped into the room and was lying quietly at his feet, looked up at his master expectantly, awaiting his next move.

"Where do we go tomorrow, Fosdric?"

"What do you mean?"

"Where would we be most likely to find a remnant of the local government in a time of crisis?"

The little man crossed his legs, leaned back and stroked his chin. "Well," he said, "With the city probably a mess, I expect they'd get up to Tyngstaal Castle. It's on a hill, open ground on all sides, a moat around it—I don't see how a fire could burn all the way up to the castle."

Tyngstaal Castle was an impressive structure. It had been more than ten years since last I'd seen it. Built about three hundred years ago by a security-minded nobleman, it had withstood three sieges by large and determined military forces during the years of civil turmoil that led to the birth of the kingdom of Aerwald. The slopes of the hills leading up to the castle had been clear-cut to give archers on the walls clear fields of fire in all directions. The moat was wide and deep, which kept ladders and engineers away from the walls, but might serve during a fire in the city below to keep the castle from catching, as long as those within the walls were diligent about stamping out embers borne by the wind.

It might also provide refuge to some of the thousands now surely fleeing for their lives.

"Well," I said, "Unless we see a better option when we reach Stelnregon tomorrow, we will make for Tyngstaal." I splashed the dregs from the mug of tea into the fireplace and rose from my chair, intending to bid Fosdric good night.

At that moment, however, Wolf leapt to his feet, and with catlike quickness darted down the hall toward the guest rooms, barking furiously. Fosdric and I stared at each other stupidly for several seconds before following at a run.

The little dog stood outside the room Brother Galthorn had chosen and barked at the door with such intensity that he literally hopped. Fosdric reached the door first and called, "Brother Galthorn! Are you all right?"

A quiet voice from behind the wooden door answered, "I believe so."

Without waiting to consider Galthorn's response, Fosdric threw his shoulder against the door and jumped into the room. Wolf followed without missing a beat in his incessant barking. I followed and immediately overran Fosdric, who had stopped un-expectedly about two paces into the room.

The two of us tumbled spectacularly in a spray of limbs, com-ing to rest after overturning a small table set next to the bed. From my vantage point on the floor, around the table resting on my head, I could see Brother Galthorn sitting up in the bed, staring unblinkingly across the room, and Wolf hop-barking in the same direction. Pushing the table aside and sitting up, I saw the cause for Wolf's alarm: A man stood in the far corner of the room. He pointed a metallic device in our direction.

At least, he appeared to be a man. He had two legs, two arms, a torso, and a head, roughly the same size and shape as a man's, but it was hard to categorize the creature as a man. He wore a garment made from a silver fabric of some sort that covered his entire body, except for his round face. His eyes were large and wide open, and they flicked from Galthorn, to Fosdric, to me; but in truth, he seemed most intimidated by Wolf.

Considering our less than heroic entrance, I was not surprised.

For a long moment, no one moved except for the valiant Wolf, who continued to bark without pause. The stranger's gloved hand shook slightly as he held the device pointed at us. "Wolf," Fosdric said softly, "Wolf, hush. There's a good boy."

The little dog obediently stopped barking. He moved slowly to Fosdric, facing the stranger and growling, the fur standing at at-tention on the back of his neck. Fosdric, still on all fours after our uncoordinated entrance, slowly reached out and stroked the little dog's back, trying to calm him. Or perhaps he was trying to calm the stranger by quieting Wolf. A wise move, in either case.

The object in the stranger's hand was dull gray, roughly the size and shape of a cylinder the length of his forearm. A smaller cylinder extruded from the end nearest us, and there was a small handle beneath where he gripped the object. The stranger's index finger rested on what appeared to be a small lever, which no doubt released whatever was inside. From the stranger's demeanor, it was a good guess that the device in his hand was a weapon.

Whatever he was, the stranger was not an impressive speci-men of it. If he was a man, he was rather doughy—thick about the middle, with a weak chin that barely anchored a pale, round, perspiring face. He had the look of one who was normally attended by servants, for he surely did not work to earn his bread. And he was certainly no warrior. One accustomed to combat would have had a steadier hand.

"Now, sir," Fosdric said, "We don't have no quarrel with you. So, how about you put down that thing and we have a nice, friendly chat? I'm sure there's some ale around, and you look like you could use a drink. Eh?"

The stranger's wide eyes showed no sign that he understood a word Fosdric had said.

"M-maybe he's deaf," stuttered Brother Galthorn.

"I do not think he understands our language," I said. "His dress marks him as a stranger."

"I've never seen the like," agreed Fosdric. Wolf growled low in his throat. He had clearly made up his mind about the intruder.

Fosdric tried again, this time pantomiming along with his words. "Do you want something to drink?"

Comprehension dawned, and the stranger slowly nodded.

"Follow us," Fosdric said, pointing out through the open door. "The kitchen is that way."

The stranger thought for a moment, and then gestured with the device. He wanted us to walk in front of him. Until we knew what that gray metallic cylinder did, or how vulnerable he might be to my abilities, it seemed wise to try to reason with him. Whoever and whatever he was, it seemed unlikely that he could be responsible for the firestorm in Stelnregon.

Moving slowly, so as not to further alarm our nervous guest, Fosdric picked up Wolf, who was still growling, and led Brother Galthorn and me, in that order, into the hallway and toward the kitchen.

The hallway entered the main hall of the inn at one end of the wall, so that one had to turn to the right to make for the kitchen. I heard the clatter of Wolf's nails hitting the floor as Fosdric disappeared around the corner. Brother Galthorn, several paces ahead of me, stepped into the hall, glanced to his right, stopped and turned around to face me.

"Down," he said.

"What?"

"Down," he repeated, his wide eyes flicking quickly to the left.

Sensing a surge of emotion from Fosdric, even though I could not see him, I threw myself to the floor just as the little man swung a piece of timber the length of his arm at the stranger's head. The log rushed past my ear, and before the stranger could react, the wood connected with a muffled thud.

I rolled to my feet and turned, expecting to see the stranger crumple and fall. Instead, he stood still, dazed, with his left hand clamped to the side of his head. The device in his right hand, forgotten, slipped from his fingers. Before it hit the floor, I seized it with my mind and pulled it to myself.

"Aiee!" The silver-clad stranger's first word to us was a cry of anguish—not from the blow to his head, it seemed, but at the loss of his weapon.

Trying to remember how the stranger had held the thing, I pointed it at him and waved it toward the chair next to the great stone fireplace. A tingling sensation spread through my arm as I held the device, and a buzz of energy emanated from it, a sound unlike any I had ever heard or sensed. Clearly, this was something new.

"Now," I said, "We shall see what this intrusion is about. Please sit down." I waved the thing again to indicate where I wanted him to sit.

The stranger moved stiffly, his eyes fixed on the device in my hand. His journey of perhaps half a dozen paces seemed to last half the night. As he sat, it became obvious to us that he was trembling.

"*Purdoil derkable frommin kazzon?*"

Now, these were not the stranger's precise words. To be honest, I do not remember what he said. I write this nonsense only to convey my first impression of the Outsiders' Tongue.

Fosdric and Brother Galthorn were obviously as confused as I. We looked at each other blankly, without a clue as to what the odd creature wanted. Wolf, who had followed us from Brother Galthorn's room, stood just beyond the stranger's reach and continued to growl deep in his throat.

The stranger repeated his words, more excitedly. Fosdric responded by pushing him into the chair.

"Now, then," Fosdric said, "What's the meaning of you barging in on poor Brother Galthorn here, and scaring him half to death, eh?"

"I wasn't that scared," the priest muttered.

The stranger continued to stare at the device in my hand with such obvious terror that I began to feel uneasy. Perhaps the destructive power of the weapon was far greater than we could imagine.

Well, there was only one way to find out, I reasoned.

"Let us see what this does," I said. Pointing the thing at the hearth, I prepared to pull the small lever with my finger.

The stranger screamed and tried to jump up from the chair, babbling in his strange tongue. Instead, he managed to tangle his feet and pitched face forward to the stone floor of the inn, shouting a steady stream of gibberish all the while.

Suddenly, I heard a frantic voice inside my mind, painfully loud: *"...kill us all! Blasted ignorant backwards savage—"*

Startled, the weapon fell from my grip and I staggered back with my hands to my head. The stranger seized the opportunity and tried to scrabble across the floor to retrieve his fallen device. Fosdric, still holding the branch, leapt to intercept him and raised the makeshift club to deliver a blow.

Before I had time to consider my reaction, I thought at the stranger, *Stop!*

Almost instantly, the stranger clapped his hands to the sides of his head. Since he had been trying to crawl, more or less, this caused him to once again fall face-first to the floor.

For a long moment, no one moved. The stranger, halfway between the chair and the weapon, raised himself to his knees and stared down at what appeared to be a decorative patch on the breast of his odd silver garment. Then, slowly, he looked up at me. Fosdric stood over the odd creature, the branch raised over his head, ready to strike. I shook my head slightly at Fosdric's unspoken question. We stood still, waiting to see what the stranger would do.

Slowly, he reached down to the patch, tapped it with a gloved finger and spoke to me. I did not understand the words he spoke, but in my mind I heard, *"Can you understand me?"*

I nodded. Brother Galthorn and Fosdric stared at me, mouths open.

The stranger, eyes fixed on mine, spoke again. *"Was it you who told me to stop?"*

I nodded again. The stranger's eyes grew wide, and then he began to laugh—although I must confess that at first, I did not quite recognize it as such.

Fosdric finally lowered the branch. He walked to where I stood, bent over and traded his club for the stranger's device. "We should be more careful with this, eh?" He turned and pointed it at the stranger.

The stranger's laughter stopped. *"Please tell him to be very careful with that! It can destroy the entire building if he pushes the (word)!"* The last syllables were in the stranger's tongue, but I understood his meaning. His eyes conveyed sheer terror.

"Fosdric," I said, slowly, "I think that device is more powerful than we think."

"Eh?"

"Do not to touch anything on it," I said. "He says it can destroy the building around us."

"Oh." Fosdric slowly turned and carried the device to a table along the back wall of the room. He gently set the device down on the table, and then he recovered his club from the floor and took up a position near the stranger's chair. "I'll stick with this, hey?"

Focusing on the stranger, I thought, *How did you hear me?* As before, the stranger winced and clapped his hands over the places his ears should have been.

"Please! Not so loud," I heard.

"Excuse me, Master Davian," said Brother Galthorn, quietly. "Are you talking to—it?"

"I think so."

"Is it a Messenger?" The young priest's eyes were full of fear and hope.

"I do not think so," I said. "Would we have been able to over-power a Messenger?"

Galthorn frowned. "It is not recorded in the Holy Book that a man was ever able to subdue one of the heavenly host."

"Please," said the stranger, *"May I get up? This position is uncomfortable."*

Yes, I thought. *But move slowly, and please return to that chair.*
"Agreed."

"Fosdric," I said aloud, "He is going to stand, but only to re-turn to the chair."

Fosdric lifted an eyebrow, but kept his gaze locked on the stranger. Our guest slowly lifted himself to his feet, returned to the chair and sat down.

I am Master Davian, I thought. *I am a Third Level Master of The Order. Who are you?*

"I am Commander Orson of the ship 'Explorer'," he answered. Brother Galthorn and Fosdric were puzzled. They heard only the stranger's words, which were unintelligible. To help them at least follow the thread of the conversation, I spoke my thoughts aloud.

"How can you hear my thoughts?" I asked.

"Apparently, my (word) is picking up the (word) generated by your thoughts," he said. *"And the amazing thing is that your thoughts are translated into my language! And you are receiving the transmission from my (word) in your tongue! This is fantas-tic!"*

"Yes, wonderful," I said. "But how can you hear them?"

"I just told you," Orson replied. *"Your thoughts are being (word) as (word) waves that my (word) is receiving and translat-ing."*

"Do you hear me inside your head?"

The stranger laughed again. *"No, no. There are small speak-ers inside my hood, near my ears."* He pointed to the sides of his head; apparently his ears were in roughly the same place as they would be on any normal man.

"Speakers?" An image of small creatures whispering into Commander Orson's ears came into my mind. My confusion must have showed.

"*Yes, speakers—oh. A speaker is a device that reproduces sounds that are created somewhere else.*"

"I see," I said, though truly I did not.

"*And you are hearing my translated words in your mind.*"

"Of course," I said.

The stranger laughed again, obviously delighted. "*Fantastic! Your mind is an organic (word), sending and receiving (word) (word)!*"

"It is not so strange," I said. "It is the same as talking with dragons."

Commander Orson started, and his face paled. That was easy enough to interpret—he looked as though he had been punched in his ample belly.

"What is it?" I asked.

"*Are you one of them?*"

"One of who?"

"*One who controls the dragons?*"

"What do you mean? No one controls dragons. They can only be killed. That is what I do."

He breathed an audible sigh. "*Thank the Creator.*"

"You are a follower of the Creator?" At those words, Brother Galthorn gaped, eyes wide.

"He *is* a Messenger!" the priest said, in awe.

"No, he ain't," Fosdric said.

"*It is an expression, a figure of speech,*" said Orson.

"Brother Galthorn is a priest," I said, gesturing to the young friar. "He is wrestling with the idea that you are a Messenger from the Creator."

Orson laughed again, but weakly. "*No, I am not a (word). But if there is a Creator, you really need Him now.*"

"What do you mean?"

The stranger leaned forward and massaged his forehead with the fingers of his right hand, as though suffering from a headache. "*Did you see the orange glow on the horizon, in that direction?*" Without looking up, he pointed to the southeast with his other hand.

"Yes," I said. "We believe it is a large fire in a nearby city."

Orson looked up. If the expressions of his people matched ours, then his look can only be described as somber. *"I know it is."*

"How do you know this?"

"Because," he said, sitting up straight, *"I've seen the man who commands the dragons. And he wants to rule your world."*

CHAPTER FIFTEEN

Fosdric and Brother Galthorn sat, glassy-eyed and staring. My head spun with the implications of what I had just shared with them: Someone had found a way to command dragons to do his bidding, and he was apparently bent on conquest. And that man, according to Orson, had begun with the destruction of Stelnregon.

"These are ill tidings, if true," I said to Orson.

The stranger, who had been sitting with his head in his hands, looked up, ashen-faced. *"I swear to you, it's true."*

Fosdric, now holding Wolf in his lap, roused himself. "Ask him where he's from." I repeated his question to Fosdric.

Orson's answer made no sense: *"I was part of an expedition to explore your world."*

I asked, "What do you mean, 'our world'?"

The round man sighed. *"I am from a world that is farther away than you can imagine."*

"I do not understand," I said. "I am familiar with all of the lands of Saramond, though I have not traveled to them all."

"No, no. My world circles one of the stars you see at night."

"What's he saying?" asked Fosdric.

"He said he comes from one of the stars we see at night."

"He's a Messenger!" exclaimed Brother Galthorn.

"No, he ain't," said Fosdric. "If he's a Messenger, how is it I got the drop on him with my club?"

"You didn't hurt him," countered the priest.

Brother Galthorn had a point. Other than dropping his weapon, Orson showed no ill effects from the blow to his head.

"Orson," I said, "Are you hurt? Fosdric dealt you rather a sturdy blow."

"Oh, no," he said. *"My suit protects me from sudden impacts like that."*

"Why did you drop your weapon?"

"My suit goes rigid on impact," Orson said. *"Safety device. I guess the (word) slipped out of my hand when my fingers went stiff."*

"Mmph," I grunted. "Your suit has Brother Galthorn half-convinced that you are a Messenger."

Orson shook his head. *"No, I'm afraid not."*

"We are having difficulty understanding how you came from a star," I said. "Please explain."

"We built ships that sail the emptiness between the stars," he said. *"We detected extremely high readings of (word) coming from your world, more than what we'd expect from a star alone. So we decided to sail here to explore."*

I repeated his words to my companions. Fosdric nodded; Brother Galthorn was still perplexed, unsure of whether Orson was a divine being or not.

"Where's his crew, then?" Fosdric asked. I relayed his question to Orson.

He grimaced. *"The levels of (word) were much higher than we expected. When we tried to land, our instruments were nearly useless. We lost control of our landing craft and crashed near here."*

"I am sorry," I said. "Were you the only survivor?" Fosdric registered surprise at my question. Brother Galthorn bowed his head.

"Oh, we all survived the crash," Orson said. *"But I might be only one left."*

"What do you mean?"

"Almost as soon as we got out of the craft to inspect the damage, one of those—excuse me, do you have anything to drink?" Orson began to shake again.

"Water?"

"No, no," he said, shaking his head. Apparently, that bit of body language is universal. *"I mean something to drink."*

"Ah," I said, catching his meaning. "Fosdric, are there any spirits left in the inn?"

"The ale's turned," said Fosdric, standing. "But we might find a spot of rum somewhere. Come on, Wolf." He set the little dog on the floor, and the two of them made for the kitchen.

Ignoring Brother Galthorn's disapproving frown, I returned my attention to our guest. "You were saying?"

"One of those monsters jumped us," Orson continued. *"It was enormous! I opened the hatch, and there it was!"*

"A dragon?"

"We've heard of creatures like this on my world, but I thought they were mythical," he said. *"Make-believe. Bedtime stories to scare naughty children."* Orson began to tremble, and the horror in his eyes made it plain that it had been his first encounter with a dragon.

He was lucky. Most people do not live to meet a second.

Brother Galthorn, trying to follow the thread of the conversation, asked, "Do they not have dragons on his world?"

"Brother Galthorn wants to know if you truly come from a world without dragons."

"No! I mean, yes!" His shaking was now so pronounced I marveled that he kept his balance in the chair. *"We have big animals, yes, but nothing that size that can fly! How can anything that big fly? Or shoot flame? How is that possible? That's not physically possible!"* His eyes focused elsewhere, some unseen point in space somewhere beyond me. He truly seemed puzzled.

I turned to Brother Galthorn. "You understood?" He nodded, still unsure of what to make of our guest.

"Orson," I said, "Dragons have always been with us. They have always been able to fly and breathe flame. We learn to live with them, and there are those of us who have the ability to kill them."

"You?" he asked, incredulously. There might have been something like fear in his face—fear of me.

I nodded. "Yes, and others like me."

"How?"

"Never mind." Caution seemed prudent. There was no need to disclose my capabilities yet. "What happened to separate you from your crew?"

Orson took a deep breath before speaking, his trembling slowly subsiding. *"Like I said, I opened the hatch, and the dragon was right outside, coming right for us. I shouted something, I don't remember what, and I tried to jump back inside to close the hatch. I—"*

"Success!" Fosdric emerged from the kitchen with a bottle in one hand and several mugs in the other. Wolf tapped along behind, happily wagging his tail.

Commander Orson looked expectantly at Fosdric.

"What is it then, Fosdric?" asked Brother Galthorn.

"Rum," he said cheerily. "Good stuff, too." With a dramatic flair, Fosdric deposited three mugs on a table and poured a generous splash of amber liquid from the half-filled bottle into each one. He turned and handed one to Orson with a slight bow, as if he were the proprietor of the inn.

"Davian?" Fosdric offered a mug to me.

"No, thank you," I said. "Bad idea."

Fosdric shrugged nonchalantly and offered the mug to Brother Galthorn. The priest accepted it warily.

"Well, gentlemen," Fosdric said, lifting his glass in a toast, "Down the hatch."

Fosdric drained his mug in two swallows, and followed it with a satisfied exhalation of the fumes, which no doubt carried halfway to Stelnregon. Brother Galthorn continued to eye his glass with suspicion, lifting it to his nose and wrinkling it in distaste.

Our pudgy guest, after a moment's hesitation, lifted the mug with one hand and dipped a gloved finger from his other into the mug. As Fosdric, Galthorn, and I watched, perplexed, Commander Orson sat with his finger in his rum, unmoving, as though he was listening to something. At length he nodded, withdrew his finger, lifted the mug to his lips and drank. Immediately, he was seized by such a fit of coughing and sputtering that I thought he had accidentally inhaled the potent liquid.

"Orson," I said, "Are you all right?"

"I'm good," he gasped. *"Fine."* He looked up, blinking tears from eyes filled with sorrow. *"You know you're the first people I've talked to in over a week?"*

"Did I tell you?" Fosdric said. "Good stuff, eh?"

"Fosdric," Brother Galthorn said, holding out his mug, "You had better have this."

"Oh, come on, brother. A little nip never hurt anybody."

"Oh, no," Brother Galthorn protested. "I couldn't."

Commander Orson reached out his hand to Brother Galthorn, who slowly handed his mug to the stranger. Without hesitation, Orson tilted back his head and downed the rum with two loud gulps.

"Hoo hah," Orson wheezed. That needed no translation.

A hammer blow of pain exploded between my eyes. Staggered, I fell to my knees, an explosion of stars clouding my vision. Brother Galthorn jumped to my side.

"Master Davian? Master Davian?"

"All right, all right," I squeezed out. In truth, I felt as though I'd been hit across my forehead with a red-hot iron bar. My eyes were tightly clenched against the pain.

"Here, brother," I heard Fosdric say. "Davian, drink this."

Without questioning, I took the cup he offered and took a drink. I was fairly certain I had swallowed molten metal. I coughed. My gut was on fire, and it spread through my entire body.

"Better, eh?" Fosdric asked.

"Yes," I said, with wonder. "Yes, it is. A little."

"What's wrong?" Orson asked.

"Headache," I said. Communicating with Orson, which had not bothered me to that point, aggravated the pain behind my eyes. I took another pull on the rum. This swallow went down more smoothly. My head felt better.

"A sharp, stabbing pain between your eyes?" Orson asked. He suddenly seemed worried.

"Yes. How did you guess?"

Commander Orson jumped from the chair, and Fosdric quickly reached for his makeshift club. *"No, no, wait! I think we're in big—"*

Wolf's frantic barking interrupted him. The little dog spun in counterclockwise circles, half leaping into the air as he barked. The last time he'd done that—

With a heart-stopping whoosh and a rush of air, the roof of the inn erupted in flame.

Orson slapped the emblem on his chest and shouted something, a single word. He must have deactivated his communicating device, for I did not hear him inside my head. From the mask of terror upon his face, however, it was not difficult to guess his meaning.

"Dragon!" shouted Fosdric.

"Really!" I yelled. I should not have been so curt, but I was angry that another of the accursed beasts had caught me off my guard. This was a disturbing and dangerous trend. A mighty bellow echoed through the inn, masking for a moment the angry crackling of the fire overhead, and then another patch of the roof exploded in flame. Brother Galthorn responded, somewhat predictably, by dropping to his knees in prayer.

"Pray outside, brother," I shouted as I yanked him to his feet. We needed to escape the inn before the burning roof collapsed.

"This way!" Fosdric shouted, making for the back door. He was right. I finally caught a sense of the dragon's presence, and it was somewhere outside the front wall.

This dragon, like the one that overflew us, seemed bent on a single task. Its thoughts were very faint, like a narrow shaft of light directed away from us. It knew where we were, however, and it meant to do us harm.

We burst through the back door as water bursts through a weakened dam: Fosdric first, followed by Wolf, Brother Galthorn, and me. We quickly dashed into the thick wood behind the inn, picking our way around the mature oaks and maples by the light of the flames leaping from the thatched roof of the Happy Traveler. It was only after we had put several dozen man-heights between the inn and ourselves that I realized Commander Orson was not with us.

"Stop!" I said. "Hold a moment. "Stay here and stay down. I have to get Orson."

"I will come with you," said Galthorn.

"No!"

"But—"

"No! Galthorn, your heart is true, and I value that—and you—most highly. But we have had this discussion once already. Leave the dragon to the dragonslayer! Pray over there—from cover!"

The young man nodded and sought out a large oak tree. Fosdric was already hidden and doing a fine job of keeping Wolf muzzled.

Turning back to the inferno that was the inn, I slowly moved closer, watching for Orson while I felt for the dragon with my mind. It was not as easy as it should have been. I vowed to discover how the beasts were concealing themselves once this disorganized adventure was behind us.

The monster was still in front of the burning hulk of the inn. Another blast of flame billowed over the roof. There was still no sign of Commander Orson.

Moving to my left to gain a better vantage point, I finally saw the dragon for the first time. It was another that had only recently reached maturity, a beast with the size of an adult but probably not the wisdom or experience of an elder. It seemed oblivious to my presence, though I did not know why. Dragons and Masters are as visible to one another as a bonfire to an owl on a moonless night. This one, however, seemed to be searching for something and paying no attention to me.

For a brief moment, the dragon's complete disregard for the presence of a Third Level Master of The Order stung my pride. I quickly stifled that useless emotion. In my business, the proud often become the dead.

Movement in front of me attracted the dragon's attention. Backlit by the burning inn, it was a moment before I realized what my eyes beheld. Orson had emerged from the building, stumbling and falling through the doorway as he escaped the flames.

It was another moment before I understood why he was falling: He was almost completely nude. Orson had been removing his outer garment as he ran, and his feet had snarled in the leggings.

Suddenly, my head exploded with a blast of sound. It was loud, painfully loud, blocking out all other sound and thought. Falling to my knees, I clapped my hands over my ears—and found to my distress that the sound came from Orson's communication device, for the high-pitched screech was inside my head.

Clearly, the dragon heard it, too, because it leapt into the air at once, enraged, its attention focused on the source of the deafening noise. I tried to call out to Orson, to warn him, but the sound was so completely overwhelming that I was helpless, unable even to speak.

With horror, immobilized by the head-shattering cacophony, I watched helplessly what was sure to be the end of the strange man from the sky. Commander Orson struggled to his feet, finally freeing himself from the entangling garment. I noticed with detachment that Orson appeared to have led an easy life, because he was certainly not in fighting condition.

That mattered not to the dragon, which bore down on him in a fury. Driven to near madness by the unending shriek from Orson's device, the beast swooped down, intending to put an end to the noise and the one who had inflicted it upon him.

Orson struggled to rise, and I saw now why he was so clumsy in his movements—he had removed his garment with one hand while cradling his weapon in the other. Orson must have run for the weapon while Fosdric, Brother Galthorn, and I ran for the door.

A powerful rush of air, the downdraft from the dragon's wings, alerted Orson to the peril descending on him, like a mouse sensing not a moment too soon that a hawk is almost upon him. He screamed and turned to run, but he somehow intertwined his feet in the exposed root of a nearby tree. With another shriek, Commander Orson pitched forward, face down in the dirt as the dragon plunged with its claws extended for the kill.

As Orson hit the ground, the impact must have triggered his weapon. A thin beam of impossibly bright light erupted from the end he had earlier pointed at us. The beam was projected upward, into the path of the dragon. The creature may have taken no notice of it, or if it had, it regarded the beam as of no consequence.

That was its fatal mistake.

As the dragon plunged into the beam, an impossible thing happened: The huge beast was cut into halves as neatly as a woodman's knife parts a rabbit's fur.

There was smoke, an angry sizzle, and high-pitched squeals that may have been the dragon's death-scream, or perhaps bursts of steam as the beam of light encountered the foul creature's inner juices. It was all over in a second, and two gigantic slices of surprisingly dead dragon crashed to the ground on either side of the quivering Commander Orson.

It was some moments later that Orson finally stirred and lifted his head from beneath his arms. All the while I was in agony, hoping against hope that somehow, something would put an end to the piercing trill that threatened to turn my mind into pudding. Once Orson realized that the dragon was well and truly dead, he slowly got up and walked over to his discarded coverall. After fiddling with it for a few seconds, the mind-rending shriek suddenly ceased, and I collapsed into a heap, relishing the stillness in my mind.

The quiet did not last for very long. "Master Davian! Master Davian!" Brother Galthorn came panting after a full gallop through the thicket, disentangling himself from a small shrub that grabbed at his robe. "Master Davian, are you all right? Is the dragon dead?"

"Yes," I said wearily, raising myself to my knees, "and yes. Commander Orson dispatched the dragon."

Brother Galthorn looked around for Orson, found him, and then quickly averted his eyes. I glanced at Orson and saw that he was still struggling to squeeze himself back into his silver suit.

"Here, now, brother!" Fosdric and Wolf arrived less out of breath, having chosen a more cautious approach than had Galthorn to the entangling underbrush. "Oh, it's you, Davian. Is it gone?"

"Dead," I replied, nodding at the still smoking remains.

"Creator be praised!" breathed Galthorn.

"What in the name of—Davian, how on Saramond did you do that?" Fosdric asked.

"I didn't," I said. "It was Orson."

Fosdric stared at the strange man from the stars, unbelieving. "He used his, uh, thing, then, did he?"

Nodding, I struggled to my feet. My head felt as though a dragon was inside demanding to be set free.

"Davian," Galthorn said, still averting his eyes from the pudgy stranger, "Why did Commander Orson remove his clothing?"

"I have not had the opportunity to ask him."

"Could stand a little exercise," Fosdric observed.

"Fosdric, be kind," Brother Galthorn said, gently scolding.

A crackle of sound burst upon my consciousness and I heard Orson's voice in my head. *"Davian? Can you hear me?"*

I thought in his direction as I answered. "I can, although I am pleasantly surprised that I am not deaf. Or dead."

The rounded form of Commander Orson, now fully dressed again, appeared in my field of view. *"You—oh, sorry! I completely forgot you'd hear it, too!"*

"What exactly were you trying to do?" I asked.

"Well, I thought I'd distract or confuse it with a distress beacon," he said, wiping his forehead with the back of his hand. *"And then, while it was busy trying to get into the building, I'd shoot it from the trees over there."*

"Shoot it? With your device?" I nodded at the metallic device in his hand.

"Yes," Orson said. *"But the roof started to fall in on me, so I had to get out of the building sooner than I thought. And then the dragon found me sooner than I thought."* He paused and looked at us sheepishly. *"I guess I didn't exactly impress anyone with my tactics."*

"Your plan was interesting," I said, "In theory."

"But my execution wasn't great."

"We are all alive and unhurt. That is what is important."

Orson grinned, his gap-toothed smile like that of a young boy. Regarding the fallen beast, he said, *"That makes two dragons for me now."*

I gaped at the pudgy man. "So, you brought down the dragon we found just inside the border of Palthinoor district?"

Orson frowned, confused.

"It had a sharp wound across its abdomen, here." I marked the location a slashing motion across my chest.

The commander nodded. *"I don't think it expected the weapon. It came at me slow. I had a lot of time to shoot."*

"Well done," I said, "But please—the next time we encounter a dragon, let me contend with it."

Orson's smile disappeared. *"Can you really kill these things?"* He gestured at the steaming hunks of dragon flesh.

"Yes."

"That's fantastic."

"You might not think so if you possessed the Gift."

"The Gift? What's that?"

Blast! I hadn't intended to reveal it so soon. "Never mind. Just trust me, please."

"Davian," Fosdric said, "We ought to think about moving away from the inn."

"Are you growing warm?" Brother Galthorn asked.

"Nah," said Fosdric. "But I'm thinking this blaze might bring some lookie-loos, see, and we don't know as how they'll be friendly."

"You're right," I said. For Orson's benefit, I added, "Fosdric said we should put some distance between us and the inn. The fire may attract—"

"Oh, no! Right, right! He's right! Let's go, go, go!"

Orson's sudden agitation surprised us. Fosdric, Brother Galthorn, and I looked at each other, unsure of what to think. "What is it?" I asked Orson.

"Look," Orson said, pointing to a misshapen lump of dragon. *"This dragon was under the control of one of these guys who can—one of the guys like you! He's using equipment from my— well, trust me. This guy was controlling the dragon's mind. The connection between them is broken, so I think he'll send another! Or two! We need to go, now!"*

"Controlling it? How?"

"No time! Explain later! Let's go!"

"Wait." Something occurred to me that might be important. "Orson, how far away can your communication device be heard?"

"Depends on weather, fluctuations in the (word) field, but pretty far. Many miles."

"And since this Master can communicate with dragons, as I can, then he can hear your device, too," I said.

"Yes, probably."

"And so can the dragons."

"Yes, yes. Oh…" Orson's eyes grew wide.

"So this Master found us by listening to your communication device."

Instead of answering, Commander Orson nodded and slapped the device. I heard a click in my mind as it was switched off.

"What is happening? What are you saying?" Brother Galthorn asked.

"We just realized," I answered, "That our friend from the sky is a lure for dragons."

CHAPTER SIXTEEN

The thought of doing battle with another dragon in short order was unappealing, to say the least. And yet that seemed likely, if our assumptions were correct.

Fosdric departed to collect Aeryx so we could load our gear for the journey to Stelnregon. Only then did I remember that everything we had carried with us was still inside the flaming wreck of the inn.

"What is it, Master Davian?" Brother Galthorn was ever sensitive to the moods of those around him, a valuable skill to one with his calling.

"Our gear is inside," I said. "Cooking gear, what little food we had—all gone."

"Perhaps not," Galthorn said. "Much of it was in the wing, and the fire seems worst here, over the great hall."

"But how—" I began, and then I understood what he was thinking. Without another word, Brother Galthorn and I hurried around the side of the inn, stepping carefully as the ground was slick with the inner fluids of the fallen dragon. After a moment's confusion, Commander Orson decided that following was better than being left alone, and he trailed behind.

A cry, a muffled thud, and a string of forceful exclamations in Orson's native tongue reached our ears almost immediately. The commander apparently misjudged his footing while rounding the corner of the inn. I briefly wondered about the kind of organization that would elevate such an awkward, unsure man to a position of authority.

Brother Galthorn and I arrived at the front of the burning building and found that the fire had not yet spread to the entire wing. Since the front door was already engulfed, however, we had to force an entry through heavy wooden shutters barred from the inside. My abilities are suited for such tasks, to a point.

The wooden shutters were mounted on sturdy iron hinges fastened to the stone walls of the inn. The hinges were fixed in a way as to prevent easy removal of the pins, and the hinges themselves seemed to have been set in the mortar to prevent an industrious thief from simply removing the shutters. I detected no metal on the bar inside that would allow me to manipulate it, so I concluded that our only hope of saving our gear was to attempt to burn through the shutters before our packs were incinerated by the rapidly spreading fire.

A shout from behind jolted me from my thoughts. I quickly turned to see Commander Orson yelling a word I did not understand, holding his weapon in his right hand and gesturing with his left. Focused on the problem before us, I failed to grasp what he was driving at.

Brother Galthorn understood. "I think he wants us to move out of the way," the priest said, gripping my arm and pulling me away from the inn.

We were no sooner removed from the line of fire than the commander raised his weapon, adjusted a small knob on its side, pointed it at the front wall of the inn, and fired. A pulse of light, no longer than the time it takes to blink, played across the wall just below the shutters I'd been studying. An instant later, a hole in the wall appeared with a roar and a cloud of dust and smoke.

Breathing through his loose-fitting sleeve, Brother Galthorn led us into the room where he'd retired for the night just a short time ago. It was our good fortune that we had put all of our gear in his room; the fire spread quickly along the hall outside the door, and it would not have been more than a few minutes until the whole of the inn was ablaze.

"Quickly!" Brother Galthorn shouted, but his encouragement was unnecessary. My eyes burned and watered from the smoke that flowed through the hole in the wall, and the heat of the fire sheeted across my face in ever-increasing intensity. I could have moderated the effect, of course, but I did not wish to take even a moment to stop and concentrate to redirect the energy of the fire. As it was, we were only in the room for a few seconds.

We made two trips into the room, carrying out our bedrolls and personal gear and dropping them on the opposite side of Naribor's main street, a distance we hoped was far enough from the tremendous bonfire that was formerly the inn. On our second trip, the young priest stumbled out of the smoke with my drag-onspear, nearly falling as he clumsily wrestled the long wooden pole through the ragged opening in the wall of the inn. Nearly collapsing to the ground, supporting himself only with the spear, the young man gasped, "Here you are, Master Davian. We can't lose this."

"Thank you, brother," I said, taking it from Galthorn. I hadn't the heart to tell him that the spear was the least of my worries. A few minutes with a stout piece of ash or oak and I could have replaced it. Setting it down in the street, I sat next to Brother Galthorn while we caught our wind. We desperately needed a moment of rest before continuing on into the night.

The sound of hooves approaching on the street heralded the arrival of Fosdric and Aeryx. The horse was surprisingly calm for all of the excitement that surrounded it. Normally, the presence of a dragon nearby, alive or dead, sends horses into a frenzy. Perhaps Aeryx had also sensed that this dragon was not behaving as it should and realized that he was safest if he kept quiet in his stall.

"Good men!" Fosdric said as he approached. "Maybe not too smart, running into a burning building, but good men, I say, for saving the gear."

"Come," Brother Galthorn said. "I'll help you load our things onto Aeryx."

"Much obliged, brother." Fosdric and Galthorn set to pack-ing our belongings for the final leg of our journey to Stelnregon. Commander Orson stood off to one side, alone, lost in his thoughts.

I sat on my haunches and stared into the flames dissolving the frame of The Happy Traveler across the street. The roar of the fire was deafening in my head, and its energy washed over me like water cascading over a cliff. Physically and emotionally, however, I was drained. How many more dragons would we face? Were we to battle dragons and a rogue Master as well? Even with Orson's dragon-killing weapon, our chances seemed dim.

Orson had hinted at some other piece of equipment now in the hands of the rogue. If it was as powerful as the commander's hand weapon, we had a serious problem. A dragon I could handle. I had no idea of where to begin against a device like that.

Rubbing my eyes, I realized how deeply fatigued I was. Worse, the dull, throbbing pain in my temples that had visited me so frequently of late threatened to return. Short of actually being in battle, I could not imagine a worse time for this weakness to present itself, and I cursed under my breath.

"Are you well, Master Davian?" Brother Galthorn hovered over me like a hen over an ailing chick.

"Yes," I lied. "I am just very tired."

"I was thinking about that," Fosdric said, as he finished tying off a bundle on Aeryx's back. "It seems to me as how we're not going to make much progress in the dark. I say we move just far enough away to be out of sight and then bed down the rest of the night."

"What's left of it," I grumbled.

"Better than nothing," Fosdric said.

"I think you're right," Galthorn said. "Davian looks as though he truly needs the rest."

Commander Orson slowly made his way back to our little group. In my mind, I heard the click that indicated he had switched on his communication device.

"I've been thinking," he said.

"And?" I did not feel up to a lengthy conversation.

"Your mind operates like my (word), right?"

"If you say so."

"Well, I think that's how it works," Orson said. *"Anyway, if this guy controlling the dragons can track my communicator signal, he might be able to track your thoughts when we're talking, too."*

That made sense. I should have thought of that.

"You are probably right," I said. "What do we do about that?"

"Let me think about that." And with another click, he was silent again.

"What did he say?" Fosdric asked.

"Orson thinks the rogue Master can hear my thoughts as well as his communicator."

"Oh, well, that's easy enough to fix," Fosdric said. "We just cut off your head."

On another day, that might have been amusing. Now, I just glowered at him.

"Or Galthorn can hit you with another rock," he continued.

"Let's be off," suggested Brother Galthorn.

* * *

We moved perhaps an hour down the road to Stelnregon, constantly on the alert for a rush of air propelled by giant bat-like wings. Fortunately, we were not observed—or at least, not approached.

At length we reached a wooded area atop a small rise. The combination of high ground and thick cover seemed advantageous, so we moved into the wood as best we could without light and settled down for a well-earned rest.

It was not nearly long enough. The pink glow on the horizon signaled the start of a new day just I was beginning to fully relax. We tried to sleep as long as we could, but the growing light of day mirrored the rising urgency of our mission. At last I rose, feeling as unsteady on my feet as I had the night I arrived in Marthwee. The morning dew was thick on the scrub that filled the gaps between the trees in our wooded shelter on the hill. A soft breeze brought with it the acrid scent of fire and death, reminding us all of our need to hurry.

The aching in my head had increased during the night. Retrieving a mug and some water from our supplies, I hurriedly heated a mug of tea, hoping that the brew would ease the pain in my temples. As I held the mug and focused on the water to heat it, I noticed Commander Orson watching me closely, studying me as one might examine an unusual insect under a glass. As I sipped my tea, too quickly made to be as strong as I liked, Orson approached and switched his communicator on.

"How do you feel?" Orson asked.

"My head is throbbing."

"Do you suffer from headaches often?"

"Not until recently," I said. "But lately, yes."

"I have an idea," he said. *"Do you have anything made of lead?"*

"Lead? Why?"

"I think I know what's causing your pain," he said. *"I might know how to stop it."*

I raised an eyebrow. "With lead?"

"Or something like it, yes."

Fosdric was slowly loading our belongings back onto Aeryx's broad back. Even the mighty horse looked as though he needed more sleep. "Fosdric," I said, "Do we have anything with us made of lead?"

He looked at me for a moment, eyes bleary and unfocused, before his face showed comprehension. "Ah, no," he said. "Cookware's iron. Haven't got anything else that's metal."

I turned back to Orson and shook my head. He frowned for a moment, and then brightened. *"Wait,"* he said. *"I've got it. Here."*

He fumbled with his skin-tight oversuit and somehow opened a pocket on his right hip where I would have sworn there was no seam a moment before. He withdrew a rectangular, gray pouch of some unknown material about the length of his forearm. He held the pouch with his fingers in an unusual alignment for a moment, and then it, too, opened. He pulled several small, thin, translucent discs from the pouch and dropped them back into his pocket.

"A (word) pouch, for shielding memory discs from the (word) force of your planet, he said. Doesn't matter if the discs survive if I don't make it home. Here." He handed the pouch to me. *"Put this over your head."*

The thin gray fabric of the pouch was much heavier than it appeared. "What is this?" I asked.

"Shielding," Orson said. *"Like lead, but lighter and more flexible."*

"And this will—"

"Hopefully shield you from them. Him. The other one like you."

It looked silly. I felt silly. I had no idea what he was talking about. But the throbbing in my head was getting worse, and anything seemed better than another episode that might leave me seeing demons where friends stood.

I slipped the pouch over my head and pulled it down until it covered everything above my ears and eyebrows. Instantly, as though a weight were lifted from me, the pain in my head was gone. Completely gone. But even more amazing, for the first time I can remember, the only sounds I heard came from outside my head.

It was unsettling. I felt blind. I hadn't realized until that moment how I'd taken the noise, my inner sense, for granted. Silence inside my head was not something I had ever experienced, or indeed, could have imagined.

My surprise showed, because when I looked up Orson was smiling, and Brother Galthorn and Fosdric were staring at me, open-mouthed—concerned or amused, I could not tell which.

"What?" Despite the relief from the pain, I was not in the mood to be the object of humor.

"I—well, I do not know what to say," Brother Galthorn stammered.

"Nice," Fosdric said. "You look like an abbot."

He was right. The corners of the pouch, sticking up above my ears, resembled the ceremonial cap worn by the learned clerics responsible for the abbeys in Aerwald. Turning to Orson, I asked, "Can we modify this to fit a bit better?"

Of course, I heard nothing. Orson only shrugged to indicate that he didn't understand. I took the pouch off my head, and again I heard the background noise to which I am accustomed. The buzz from the minds of the men around me; a quieter hum from Aeryx; and the unceasing static from smaller creatures moving about in the surrounding countryside. This sound has been a constant companion for all of my days. I repeated myself, and this time, without the "shield" around my head, Orson understood.

"Oh, yes," he said. *"That shouldn't change anything."*

"Brother Galthorn," I said, "Do you have any skill with needle and thread?"

"Why, no, not—"

"Here," Fosdric said. "Let me." He took the pouch, turning it over in his hands and rubbing the unusual fabric between his fingers. "You'll be wanting a skull cap, then?"

"Yes, I think so."

"What for?" he asked. "No disrespcct, Davian, but it seems a right unusual time to be worrying about headgear."

The pain was returning, strong enough this time to set my healing nose to throbbing once again. "It blocks the pain," I said, squinting. "Keeps out the noise."

"Ah," Fosdric said. "And maybe keep you on even keel."

I nodded.

"Well, the quickest thing to do is just lay these tabs over and—"

"Do it, quickly."

"Right." He hurried off to rummage through the bundles on Aeryx's back. Commander Orson, who'd been watching silently, intruded into my thoughts again with a click.

"Pain returning?" I nodded. *"Then we need to close communications, get you shielded, and move away from here. The other Master is looking for us, and he's probably getting close to finding us again."* He touched the patch, and with another click, he was silent again.

Sitting down, I put my head in my hands and waited for Fosdric while the pain blossomed. A swirl of sounds, roaring white noise, steadily increased inside my head. I wondered if this wasn't what had driven Eritan, Myath, Redakios, and Halteor out of their minds.

Suddenly, it was gone. Fosdric had slipped up behind me and fixed the improvised cap onto my head.

Gradually, the pain subsided, like water receding from the shore during low tide. I looked up, amazed and thankful for the swift relief from the crushing pressure inside my skull, and yet unnerved by the severance of the links to the world around me. Never before had I realized how much I depend on the Gift.

And yet it was more than that. With the cap in place, for the first time in my life I had no sense of where I was. It was most unusual and very disorienting. But with blinding headaches and possible madness as the alternative, I had no choice but to cope.

"Better, then?" Fosdric asked.

"Very much so. Thank you, Fosdric. And you, Orson," I added. He seemed to understand; a smile creased his chubby face and he nodded happily.

* * *

Breakfast was hard biscuits and water. I saw Brother Galthorn in prayer, giving thanks over his simple meal, and I saw that Orson watched him very closely. Orson watched all of us very closely. As far as I could tell, it was not from distrust, for if anything, Commander Orson was far more trusting of us than we were of him. No, it seemed that Orson was naturally curious about everything. That seemed to be the only explanation for his nearly psychotic need to record and categorize everything.

After biting into one of Fosdric's several-day-old biscuits and nearly chipping a tooth in the process, I asked Brother Galthorn why he felt it necessary to thank the Creator for such a thin meal. "Why, it is only natural," he said. "It is sustenance. It may be simple, but it will serve and I am grateful for it."

"Hmph," Fosdric said. "I'd be thankful for a bit of jam and a pint."

"His providence is sufficient for the day," Brother Galthorn said. "I have no doubt that we will find what we need along the way."

"Not likely," Fosdric grumbled. Indeed, the powerful sting of smoke in the air had probably frightened off nearly everything on hoof or wing worth eating. Because of the trees all around, it was hard to determine the source of the smoke. Most probably it was from the fires of Stelnregon that we had seen as a glow on the horizon. But it was also possible that the blaze that destroyed the

Happy Traveler had spread to the rest of the village, leaving nothing but smoldering heaps where Naribor had stood the day before. A depressing thought, but there was nothing the four of us could have done to prevent it.

Perhaps with more rest and nothing of importance ahead, I might have drained the fire of its energy even before the Happy Traveler was destroyed. It would have taken at least a day to recover my strength afterward, however, and with the likelihood that another dragon was soon to follow the one halved by Commander Orson, getting away and letting the fire burn itself out was the wisest course of action.

Our meal was quickly dispatched. Even with my thoughts shielded from a prowling dragon and this rogue Master, the countryside was so empty that one of the beasts would have had little trouble finding the four of us. We needed to move. While I still had no firm idea as to how we would combat whatever we would find in Stelnregon, at least now, thanks to Orson, my thoughts were not clouded by the noise and pain that had fogged me in recent days.

As we readied ourselves to leave our wooded bower, I happened upon Brother Galthorn, kneeling again in prayer. "Add a good word for me, brother," I said as I walked past.

"I have, Master Davian," he said, smiling. "Since before we met."

CHAPTER SEVENTEEN

We moved quickly, which added to our tension as we traveled. Our need to reach Stelnregon as soon as possible required staying on the main road, which we joined just outside Naribor the night before. However, this also meant exposing ourselves to the sky and the prying eyes of any dragon that might be overhead, searching for us.

There was little choice. Hacking our way through the forested country north of Stelnregon would have added several days to our journey. This Master, if he was waiting for us, knew that we must travel this route if we were coming to Stelnregon. Sooner or later, he would send a scout to search the road. We resolved to get as close to the burning city as we could before that encounter.

Something else had to be considered: We could not know how much control this Master exercised over the dragon that Orson killed, or how much communication there had been between them. If a dragon had been sent to search for its fallen comrade, which was a reasonable assumption, was it looking for one man—Orson—or four? If four, did it know I was in the group? I did not use my abilities against the dragon, but if the Master had fixed our location by tracking Orson's communicator, he would surely have reasoned that Orson was speaking to someone, and there are very few on Saramond who are able to answer.

As we drew nearer to Stelnregon, the occasional wisps of smoke carried on the southerly breeze grew thicker. Aeryx grew nervous, unwilling to walk into the danger he sensed ahead, and every few minutes another low growl emerged from Wolf, still riding in his pouch on Aeryx's back.

It was Fosdric who first spied Stelnregon. By late afternoon we had made the line of inland hills near the city, still without being seen as far as we knew. Acrid smoke drifted to us on the wind, burning our throats and stinging our eyes. Despite the warning carried by such a sign, we were utterly unprepared for what lay ahead.

"By the Creator's beard, it can't be!"

"What is it, Fosdric?" Brother Galthorn hurried to catch up to the smaller man, who had reached the crest of a small hill before us. But for once, Fosdric was speechless.

Walking behind them, holding Aeryx's lead, I saw the priest's thin frame reach the top of the hill and then sag, as if suddenly weighed down by some impossibly heavy burden. The young man fell to his knees, and as he did, Fosdric flew into a rage.

"The bloody bastards! The bloody, bloody bastards!" He kicked at the dust of the road and stormed about, lashing at the air with his fists and pulling at his hair while he raged like a man who has lost the command of his senses.

Commander Orson rushed forward to see what had prompted Galthorn and Fosdric to react as they had. At the crest of the hill, he stopped suddenly, as if he'd run into an invisible wall. He stood very still.

When at last I reached the top of the hill, I understood why Fosdric raved and Brother Galthorn prayed.

Stelnregon was no more.

From our vantage point atop the hill, fires burned as far as we could see from east to west. Over the length and breadth of the city, smoke hung low over what had once been homes, shops, and buildings of government. Difficult though it was to see through the thick, gray smoke, it was clear that very little of Stelnregon was still intact. Even formidable Tyngstaal Castle, rising above the city on a rocky point that commanded the entrance to Stelnregon harbor, appeared to have suffered heavy damage. Glimpses through the smoke revealed gaps in the outer wall, and a bright glow of fire was visible through the castle's breached defenses. One of the castle's towers was no longer visible, possibly cast down into the water, perhaps even blocking the harbor's passage to the great Southern Sea beyond.

It was as though the Creator himself had determined to burn this city of a quarter million souls down to the very ground.

As we stood there, frozen by the shock of the horror that lay before us, nearly overwhelmed by the stench of smoke and decay that rose from the ruins, a voice called to us from behind several large rocks that stood to the side of the road.

"Hey, there! Get off the road, you fools!"

A man emerged from behind a boulder nearly as tall as he was. His hair and countenance were dark and he was dressed in soldier's garb. Soot further darkened his lean face, and fatigue showed in the lines around his eyes. If he was part of Stelnregon's defense force, I did not envy what those eyes had seen in recent hours.

"I will not warn you again," he said. His voice was controlled, but there was no mistaking the underlying urgency. "It is not safe to be exposed here. Follow me if you want to live!" He turned and disappeared behind the rock.

The four of us looked at one another for a moment, and then followed. Commander Orson appeared to understand the stranger's words; in certain situations, the context makes any language easy to understand.

A path hidden from the road led into the trees and back down the hillside away from the city. The hill was the smallest in a line of low peaks that flanked the city, roughly parallel to the shoreline. Stelnregon's growth, fueled by abundant fishing and an excellent natural harbor, had been shaped by the hills inland; the generations that followed its original settlers found it easier to spread out along the shore of the Southern Sea rather than build on the sides of the gently sloping hills. The fact that Stelnregon was well inside the Kingdom of Aerwald made it unnecessary to fortify the ridge overlooking the coastal plain. Defensive fortifications here had always been designed to repel invaders from the sea.

Those defenses had offered little resistance to whatever caused the carnage we saw from the top of that hill.

The stranger, moving quickly, led us into a thickening stand of hardwoods on the inland side of the hill. The path was badly over-grown, and I had to work to maneuver my dragonspear through the low-hanging branches.

Fosdric, who had reclaimed Aeryx's lead, found it even more difficult to negotiate the trail, and he soon fell behind us.

"Hey, now!" Fosdric called called. "Slow down!"

Our guide turned to Brother Galthorn, who was two steps be-hind him, and gave him instructions I could not hear. Then he made his way back along the path. He cast a suspicious glance at Orson's weapon as he passed.

"Look," our guide said as he approached. "We need to get out of sight, now. Your horse is going to draw the beasts right to us. Best thing is to turn him loose, send him off in another direction as a decoy—Fosdric, is that you?"

"Talliver! Praise the Creator, you're alive!" Fosdric and the man embraced as old friends who had been reunited against all expectations.

Talliver pulled away first. "We do not have time to linger."

"Davian," Fosdric said, grinning, "This is Talliver, captain of the King's Guard hereabouts. He's the one I told you about. Now we'll see what we can do about this!"

"I am honored," I said, extending my hand. "I am Davian, a third-level Master of The Order. I hope we can be of service."

The captain shook my hand firmly, but looked at me warily. "Odd head gear."

"I am aware. It is, uh, medicinal."

Talliver nodded, not really accepting my explanation but un-willing to pursue it at the moment. Nodding toward our strange-ly-dressed traveling companion, he asked Fosdric, "Who's that, then?"

"Ran into him in Naribor," the little man answered. "Name's Orson. Not from these parts."

"I guessed that much."

"He talks funny, but Davian here can understand him," Fosdric said. "May not look like much, but he was surprisingly handy when we was jumped by a dragon."

Talliver's left eyebrow lifted, but he said nothing.

The captain of the Guard was tall and well-muscled. His piercing gray eyes were set in a face that was all planes and angles and framed by long dark hair. A beard, normally neatly trimmed, framed his mouth and chin. His unkempt appearance belied the strain of recent days, and I wondered how long it had been since he'd slept. Turning his attention back to me, he said, "I am glad you have come, although you may not be. I do not believe that even you have the power to withstand what has destroyed our city."

"Perhaps not," I agreed. "I have never seen a dragon cause such destruction."

"Not one dragon," Talliver said. "A dozen, at least. Working in concert. We were overwhelmed before we knew what we faced."

Fosdric let out a low whistle. "Dragons working together. Davian, have you ever heard of such a thing?"

"No," I said. "They are territorial. They fight one another as often as they fight men."

"Thank the Creator that they do, or it might be the end of human life," Talliver said. "But that day may be upon us. The dragons are cooperating now. They slaughtered thousands in the city. Tens of thousands. And I fear this is just the beginning." He glanced skyward, his eyes searching for the telltale shape of a dragon in the late afternoon sky. "They will count us among their victims if we do not get to cover. Fosdric, I will hold you personally responsible if this horse leads the monsters to us. Now move!" He turned and started again down the trail in the direction that Brother Galthorn and Orson had disappeared.

Fosdric and I followed as quickly as we could. Aeryx was still skittish, but he came along obediently. Wolf sniffed the wind, looking at the sky, but he kept silent.

We soon came to a place where the path led into a cleft in a steeply sloped rock face that led to the ridge overlooking the city. Sheltered by trees and the bulk of the hill, we could no longer smell the smoke from the fires still burning in Stelnregon. The cleft, on our approach, led into the hillside, a cave apparently being used as a place of refuge.

"Quickly!" A voice from inside the cave called out to us. "Our scout on the hill reports dragons in the air!"

"Have you room for my horse?" Fosdric asked.

"Yes, yes, but quickly!"

The entrance to the cave was narrow, barely enough to admit Aeryx. It was clear the horse did not want to enter the confined space. To Aeryx, the cave entrance must have looked like the mouth of a dragon, but at Fosdric's gentle urging, he followed his master into the darkness.

Following behind the horse into the cave, I felt a chill dampness in the air that hinted at an extensive network of caves or tunnels beneath the hill. After a moment, the light of a torch illuminated the space we occupied.

The cave was larger than it appeared from outside. It was twice as tall as a man, and the room we entered was at least six man-heights wide by four deep. A dozen men had gathered to greet us. Talliver was there, with Commander Orson and Brother Galthorn standing at his side. A younger man, thin, no taller than Fosdric, and obviously frightened, stood just inside the entrance with the torch.

"You see how we have been reduced to hiding under the earth, like moles," said Talliver. "We cannot abide this for long." He turned to the others, all dressed, like him, in the garb of fighting men. Even by the dim torchlight it was plain that they were in shock. The best of them looked fatigued; several wore bandages or slings.

"This is Master Davian. He is one of The Order," Talliver continued. "He and his comrades have come to help us." That drew no reaction from the small gathering of soldiers. Their eyes were dead; lifeless orbs set in the hollow faces of men who had lost all hope.

I was not surprised. The horrors they must have witnessed in recent days were fresh in their minds, and in contrast to the dragons, we seemed a poor lot—an undersized stable hand, an underfed priest, and an enigma. Even I, a third-level Master, surely seemed less than imposing with the ridiculous improvised cap on my head.

If I had been in their place, I would have been no more cheered by our arrival than they were.

"Talliver," I said, "Are these men all that are left?"

"Nearly," he said. "We have a few scouts hidden up above, and more deeper in the caves. There are some injured there, as well. All told, we have no more than three score."

"Sixty men," Brother Galthorn breathed. He appeared to be physically shaken. He had realized more quickly than I what that meant.

"Yes, brother," Talliver said. "All that remains of my command."

"Of how many?" I asked.

"Two thousand."

Brother Galthorn's shock now made sense. More than nineteen hundred men, professional soldiers of the elite King's Guard, eliminated in the span of a few days. I was numb. The priest bowed his head and murmured a prayer for those pitiful few who remained.

The goal of the madman who controlled the dragons was still a mystery, but this much was clear: Our situation was even more grave than it had appeared from the crest of the hill overlooking the ruins of Stelnregon.

CHAPTER EIGHTEEN

"Are you secure here?" I asked Talliver.

"Yes," Talliver said. "But let us move deeper into the caves. Although the dragons cannot enter the cave, they can cook us if we stay too close to the mouth." Turning to Fosdric, he said, "I am sorry, but your horse can go no further. He will not be able to negotiate the passages that lead inside."

"Then I stay here," Fosdric said. In his sling on Aeryx's back, Wolf barked once, as if in agreement with his master's decision.

Talliver's eyes narrowed, but he decided not to argue. "Fine," he said. "Just be alert. If one of the dragons alights outside the cave, leave the horse. Make no sound, and make your way down the passageway there. There are torches mounted further in. We take a great risk by bringing the horse here. I would not do it for anyone else, Fosdric."

"Much obliged, Talliver," Fosdric said. "I'm in your debt." Wolf barked again.

Talliver cast a disapproving eye over the small white dog. "And keep him quiet." Turning to his men, he said, "To the keep." Without a word, the weary group began filing through a passage at the back of the cave.

Following Captain Talliver, Galthorn, Orson, and I passed through a confined passageway, dimly lit by a torch carried by the young man at the head of the line. It was difficult to see, and I misjudged the height of the passage once, which left me with a painful reminder to be more alert.

Bumping against the stone ceiling of the tunnel also knocked the makeshift cap from my head. I caught the cap as it fell, but as soon as the cap was removed, I stopped in my tracks, surprised by the relative quiet in my mind despite the removal of the shield.

I heard the noise I expected from the men around me, but the painful background noise that I had endured almost since leaving Darnaatha was much reduced, muffled into a nearly inaudible rumble. Tucking the cap inside the leather belt around my waist, I hurried to rejoin the group ahead.

After several minutes of maneuvering through the cool, damp, twisting passageways, we emerged into a cavern large enough for several hundred. Torches mounted along the walls cast a dim light that illuminated the space with an flickering orange glow.

The space was enormous, a great hollow in the rock beneath the hill where we had first encountered Talliver. The dome of the cave soared above us, no less than a dozen man-heights or more, before meeting in the darkness overhead. Talliver and his men had clearly retreated here as a last, desperate refuge from the dragons outside. Wounded men were arranged on a flat shelf along the far wall and were attended by those who had escaped injury. Brother Galthorn immediately led Commander Orson to the injured to ask the attendants how they might be of assistance.

Sadly, it appeared that at least a dozen of the threescore who remained of Talliver's command were too badly hurt to be of any use in battle. Then I realized that if we truly faced an organized assault by a force of dragons, there was no battle we could fight that any of these men would survive in any case.

Looking around the makeshift command center, I saw how truly desperate our situation was. There was no store of provisions in sight, but they might have been secreted in another cave. I hoped so, for while clean water might be had in the complex of caves, it would be extremely difficult to secure additional food from outside with the threat of dragons ever present.

Perhaps that was why Talliver allowed Aeryx to be brought into the cave. If all else failed, the white horse might hold off starvation for a while. I shuddered and put the thought from my mind.

Talliver was occupied, giving orders to a junior officer. He seemed competent and confident, though surely he saw the gravity of his situation. I waited until he dismissed his subordinate before I approached.

"Talliver," I said quietly, "I am not a military man. How do you see the situation?"

He glanced around to be sure we were not overheard. "I will not lie," he said quietly. "It is grave. I have set the men to work, given them tasks to keep them occupied. We have scouts hidden on the hills above, and there is a team working to re-open a long-abandoned tunnel that connects these caves to Tyngstaal Castle in the city. Perhaps we can find some provisions or weapons there that will sustain us for a time. But I have no illusions of driving the dragons from the land, not if they are working together. And we may not reach the castle before our limited stores here are gone."

"You say there are at least a dozen?"

"Yes," he said. "They came upon us four days ago. I was awakened that morning by a runner from a sentry in one of the guard towers at Tyngstaal. Dragons had been sighted. After I satisfied myself that the sentry truly meant more than one, I mobilized my men. And then one of your Order arrived at the gates, demanding an audience with the governor."

"Herdryk? Where is he now?"

"Dead," Talliver said. "Governor Herdryk met with him, of course. It is not every day a Master makes demands of the king or his appointed governors."

"No," I said. "People have enough fear of us as it is. Who was this Master—his name?"

"Arandor."

His name was unknown to me, which was a bit of a surprise. While the Order is a loose confederation of men scattered about the lands of Saramond, it is not a large fraternity. We tend to know to know the names of our brothers who live nearest us. There are a few who leave the care of The Order each year, and it has been more than ten years since I struck out on my own. The mountains that are home to The Order are several months' journey to the west, in a remote corner of the Kingdom of Loanda. We do not often return to the place we were raised, except for those called to train the next generations of boys with The Gift. It would not do to have all of us gathered together, leaving the dragons to ravage those places left unguarded.

So, this Arandor was a new problem. It has happened rarely, but Masters have gone rogue, rejected the tenets and teachings of The Order. When it has happened, they have caused a great deal of damage before The Order was able to dispatch teams to restrain them. Never before, however, had a Master sought to ally himself with our mortal enemies, the dragons. Indeed, as Talliver had observed, it is well for us that the dragons had not, until now, learned to cooperate with one another.

"This Arandor," I said, "What were his demands?"

"Immediate and unconditional surrender," Talliver said.

"And Herdryk's reply?"

"He refused."

"Even with dragons circling overhead?"

"There were none at the time, Talliver said. "No one believed that he truly controlled them."

"Understandable," I said. "I would not have believed it myself. What then?"

"Arandor left the city. And then the dragons attacked," Talliver said. "It was slaughter. They were not interested in engaging my troops. They delighted in destroying and killing wherever we were not. Just as we arrived at a place to confront a dragon, it would fly off, leaving us nothing to fight but fire. When we finally tired from running to and fro, they began to pick us off. A squad here, a patrol there. They toyed with us as cats do with mice." His eyes grew distant and his jaw clenched as the sights, sounds, and smells returned to him. "I finally realized that trying to fight them on their terms meant certain death for the few men still left to me, and so we made for these caves. The few you see here, except for our scouts, are all that remain."

"I have seen what individual dragons can do to those unfortunate enough to be captured," I said. "What a dozen could do, I do not wish to contemplate." I looked around at the weary, broken men, moving slowly in the damp chill of the cave, or lying on the floor moaning in agony with burns and broken bones. They would not be there at all if not for their loyalty to Talliver. It was a credit to his ability as a commander of men that he'd been able to save even these few.

His eyes belied the weight of his misery. A lesser man would have collapsed under such a burden.

"We may have some hope," I said. "The unusual device you see in the hands of our strange companion is a weapon—a weapon more powerful than any I have seen, and I have no doubt you will say the same."

Talliver's eyes were suddenly fixed on mine. "How powerful?"

"In truth, I do not know it's full potential," I said. "But I can tell you this: With my own eyes, I saw Commander Orson slice a dragon in half as though it were a heated knife passing through butter."

The eyes of the King's Guard opened wide. "Davian," he said, "This is not a time for jest."

"It is hard to believe," I agreed. "But it is the truth. The device emits a beam of light, so bright it is painful to the eye. But it is more than light, because the beam passes through whatever it touches."

"Is such a thing possible?"

"I have seen it."

"Where did he obtain such a weapon?"

"That is difficult to explain," I said. "He claims to have come from another world, beyond the stars."

Talliver's brows furrowed. "You do not mean he is a Messenger from the Creator?"

"No," I said, watching Commander Orson stumbling after Galthorn as they carried water to the wounded. "Although Brother Galthorn has his hopes."

In response to Talliver's puzzled expression, I said, "Forgive me. You are right, this is not a time for humor. Orson says he has traveled from a far distant land. It seems to have advanced far beyond anything we know in the sciences and mechanical abilities."

"These people would be a formidable ally," Talliver said. "How do you know him?"

"We encountered him in Naribor," I said, "but the particulars would take too long. What is Arandor's next move?"

"I do not know. My guess is that he is making an example of Stelnregon, to intimidate anyone else who might consider challenging him. He is still in the area, clearly, or we would not still see dragons in the air."

"They are looking for us, I think."

"Why?"

"Orson believes Arandor has the ability to perceive his whereabouts," I said. I opted not to disclose that Arandor might also hear my thoughts, which was in part the reason for my odd skullcap. "And Arandor must know that we killed one of his dragons." Remembering the carcass we discovered before we reached Naribor, I corrected myself. "No—two of his dragons."

Talliver nodded. "Maybe there is still hope after all."

A click in my mind was followed by the metallic voice of Orson. *"Davian? I think it is safe to talk down here."*

I turned and found the pudgy commander standing behind me. "Are you sure?"

"I don't think the (word) waves can penetrate the rock," he said. *"I noticed you took off your cap. How is your head?"*

"Fine. The pressure and pain are gone."

"It will probably return when we go outside again," Orson said. *"Don't lose that cap. I don't have any more of those pouches."*

Talliver placed his hand on my shoulder. "You understand his speech?" He masked his feelings well, but he was decidedly uneasy.

"Yes," I said. "It has something to do with that device on his uniform."

"I see," he said, although his frown made it clear he did not. "Ask the commander if he can help us defeat the dragons."

Turning back to Orson, I said, "Talliver wants to know if you can help us defeat the dragons."

It may have been the dim light in the cave, but I thought Orson's fair skin became even more pale. *"Defeat them?"*

"Yes," I said. "In case you hadn't noticed, dragons seem to have declared war on us."

Orson blinked. *"War?"*

"Yes, yes," I said, growing irritated. "You are familiar with the concept?"

He nodded weakly.

"You saw what they did to the city outside?"

He nodded again.

"We cannot allow this to happen again! Will you help us?"

"I—What can I… I mean, I don't…"

There is no way to say it charitably. Commander Orson was terrified.

His reticence at such a critical moment was shocking. It seemed hardly conceivable that his people could have crossed the vast emptiness between the stars with men such as Orson in command. My anger boiled over. "Orson, now is the time for action! What sort of commander are you?"

Orson looked at me blankly, plainly confused. I glanced at Talliver; his was the face of a man whose last hope had just been crushed.

"Do you not understand? How did your people see fit to name you commander?"

"I—oh, no," Orson said. *"There has been a misunderstanding."* And then he began to giggle.

It is not unheard of for men in times of terrible stress to laugh when they should weep. Often it is a sign of mental instability. I began to wonder how difficult it would be to learn to use Orson's weapon without his assistance. Surely an experienced soldier like Talliver could master it in time—if the dragons would allow us any.

"Orson," I said, "I fail to see humor in our situation." And yet he continued to laugh, his giggles growing into full belly laughter that nearly brought the commander to his knees.

"You don't…hoo hah…I'm not…ha ha ha…oh, this is too much…hee hee hee…"

"Tell him to stop laughing." The color in Talliver's face had deepened to a dark crimson.

"Orson," I said, "Let me be clear: This is inappropriate. Besides the tens of thousands who are probably dead in the city, Captain Talliver has lost more than nine-tenths of the men under his command. It would be wise to stop laughing. Now."

"Ha, ha, ha...I'm sorry, This is too much," he said, wiping at his eye with the back of his hand. Orson appeared to be losing his grip on sanity. *"We crash, get ambushed by a dragon, and who back home would believe it? I mean, those things are huge! It's a nightmare come to life! And they breathe fire and everything! And by sheer luck I survive not one, but two of those blasted things. They will haunt my dreams forever! I'm no soldier! They told me this would be an easy mission. Nothing to worry about, they said. But those things are all over, and I finally find you guys and think, hey, maybe I can live through this. And all the while you thought my name was a title! Like* I'm *the guy who will beat the dragons! Ah, ha ha ha..."*

Talliver's mood was growing worse. "What is he babbling about?"

It was another moment before Orson composed himself. *"I'm not a commander,"* he said. *"In one of the ancient languages on my world, my name is a word that translates as 'army commander.' But that's my* name, *not my* rank.*"*

I was confused. "What?"

"My name is..." He switched off his device so that I would hear only his voice and not the communicator. The word he spoke sounded like, "Hahr'ohld."

"Hahr'ohld?"

He nodded and switched the communicator on again.

"So you are not a commander among your people?"

"Heavens, no," Orson said. *"I was the plant (word) on the mission."* When he saw I didn't understand, he tried again to explain. *"My job was to study the plants that grow on your world, take samples, and write a report to take home to our people."*

I stared. "You are a gardener?"

He thought for a moment. *"Well, yes, in a way."*

It was inappropriate, I know, but I couldn't help myself. Orson was right—it was simply too much. I began to laugh.

For reasons beyond my understanding, the Creator had seen fit to place the fate of Saramond in the hands of a captain with no troops, a dragonslayer who was losing his mind, and a gardener from beyond the stars.

CHAPTER NINETEEN

Talliver fumed. "Have you taken leave of your senses?" His dark eyes flashed with barely controlled fury. "With all due respect, Master Davian, unless we can form a plan, and quickly, we are doomed. And perhaps all of Aerwald with us."

"I know," I said, regaining control of myself. "I apologize, Talliver. You and your men have suffered much, and I do not make light of our situation. It is just—this situation has grown more bizarre with each passing hour. Talliver—no, I will spare the details until we have time. Hahr'ohld," I said, turning back to Orson, "We desperately need your help. You knew we were coming here, and you knew why the city was in flames. Why did you come along if you did not intend to fight?"

His voice was quiet and he stared at the ground. *"I want to find my ship,"* he said. *"I want to go home."*

I closed my eyes for a moment and took several deep breaths. "Hahr'ohld," I said, "The situation is this: Our kingdom, and perhaps all of Saramond, faces potential annihilation. You have a weapon which may be of some help. You are the only one who knows how to use it."

"But dragons…"

"Can be killed like any other enemy," I interrupted. "It's just a bit more difficult. We need to form an intelligent plan that utilizes our strengths and exploits our enemy's weaknesses." Orson did not appear to be convinced.

"And faith that the Creator will not abandon us in our hour of need." Brother Galthorn joined our conversation, still carrying a pitcher of water.

"Yes, of course," said Talliver, a bit irritably. "What are their weaknesses?

"Their weaknesses," I repeated. "Well—I don't know yet. In truth, Talliver, I have never battled more than one dragon at a time. For a single dragon, I can strategize. I do not believe The Order has trained anyone fighting more than one, because it is something we have never encountered."

"Wonderful," said Talliver. "See me if you have an idea. I must attend to my men."

"Talliver." I reached out and put my hand on his shoulder. He glared at me from beneath arched eyebrows. "Please," I said, "Give us a few hours. We slept little last night because of our fight with the dragon. We have traveled for seventeen days to reach you. Our journey has been difficult. Let us rest awhile, and then we shall sit and determine how to save the world."

* * *

In the darkness outside, something searched for me. Its footsteps were audible, but muffled. Huddled in on myself, I wrapped the darkness around me like a cocoon. I wished for the dawn to drive the thing away, back to its den, where it would hide from the purifying light of day.

And yet, somehow I knew the thing that sought me would not rest or take refuge during the day. Its desire to find me was great, and I felt its frustration grow with each muffled step. My blanket of darkness kept me safe for now, but it would not hide me forever. The thing would not, could not leave until I was found.

Why was it so intent on finding me out? Was I a threat? What did it know of me? I began to sense that I would soon learn the answers to these questions.

Suddenly, all grew quiet. I listened carefully, not daring to breathe, but the silence was unbroken. Gratefully, I relaxed and slipped deeper into darkness, and remembered nothing more.

* * *

Hours passed while I tried to recover the rest that we were cheated the previous night. To his credit, Talliver waited patiently while his wounded troops lay on the floor of the damp cave, suffering and dying. When I opened my eyes at last, I was soon aware that there were fewer men among the wounded than when I had dozed off.

As I sat up and stretched to work the stiffness from my limbs, I discovered, to my surprise, that the makeshift cap had been placed on my head. I removed it and tucked it back into my belt.

"Did you rest well, Davian?" Talliver asked as I approached. He was seated on a low, round rock, with several maps and charts spread before him on another, larger rock.

"As well as one can in these conditions, thank you," I said. "I see that several men are missing from the wounded. Are they—"

"Dead," Talliver finished. "Yes. We have no medicines and few supplies with which to treat them." He looked up at the re- maining wounded, most of whom were now sleeping. "Fosdric and Galthorn have been a help, though. Fosdric somehow pro- vided some rum, which eased the suffering of some of the men. Enough to let them sleep, in any case."

That Fosdric had managed to rescue a bottle of rum from the burning inn was not terribly surprising.

Sure enough, Brother Galthorn still tended to the injured, ex- amining each man with concern to see whether any might need his assistance. "Has he been there all the while I slept?" I asked Talliver.

"Yes," he said. "He refused my suggestion that he rest himself. That has allowed several others to get their first sleep in days."

"And where is Hahr'ohld Orson?" I asked.

"He is still asleep, over there." Talliver pointed to a shallow recess in the cave wall about seven man-heights away. Orson was curled into the fetal position with his back against the contour of the cave's wall.

"And what of you, Talliver? How are you?"

"I will rest when this is over," he said. "Or when we are dead."

"I hope it will not come to that."

"You must admit that the prospect is very real."

"As it always is for those of us who must fight," I said.

Talliver nodded. "I have considered our situation, and I have an idea."

"I am glad. I have none that give me much hope."

He motioned for me to look over his shoulder at the maps spread before him. "See," he tapped the nearest chart, "We are here, under this hill. A network of caves runs through this line of hills, which has been expanded through the centuries by miners digging for iron ore. At least one tunnel was dug all the way under the city to Tyngstaal Castle, but it has been decades since it was used. It may take days or weeks to dig through sections that have collapsed and to shore them up. But truthfully, Davian, we may not have the time to do it. What food we have here will be gone in four or five days."

"I do not think there will be much help for you at Tyngstaal Castle," I said. "From the top of the hill, the castle appeared to be in ruins."

"Perhaps," Talliver said, "But there were stores in cellars below the castle in the event of a siege. I doubt that even the dragons could dig through that much rock."

"Well," I said, "it is worth the effort. It may mean keep the men alive long enough to—to do what? That is the question."

"Indeed," Talliver said. "I have given this much thought over the last few hours. What is the unique nature of the danger we face?"

That was obvious. "The fact that the dragons are cooperating."

"Exactly. And what else?"

"That they appear to be directed by a man who knows the weaknesses of men better than a dragon would."

"Just so," Talliver said. "It would seem, then, that our energies need to be directed first and fully toward eliminating Arandor."

"Logical," I said. "But killing a Master of The Order is difficult. Not impossible, but difficult," I added, remembering my own folly at being taken unawares and kidnapped. However, that ordeal would not have lasted long if I had been willing to sacrifice Fosdric and Brother Galthorn to Elgyrn's henchmen.

Based on the carnage outside, I had little doubt that Arandor would go to much greater lengths to protect himself than I had.

"How do we get to him, Davian?" Talliver asked. "Can you help us?"

"I—don't know."

"What do you mean?"

"Arandor seems to be doing something to control the dragons that interferes with my ability to think. It causes debilitating pain."

"Hmm," Talliver said. "Is it simply that he is extraordinarily powerful?"

"It's unlikely," I said. "I am certain I would have heard of him before now."

"Perhaps he has some device that magnifies his abilities."

"I hope not. Too much power is not healthy for Masters of The Order." I debated whether to continue, and decided that keeping secrets from Talliver at this point served no good purpose. "For example, we are very careful to avoid lightning storms. The energy within those storms seems to overload our senses. It can cause hallucinations that are difficult to discern from reality. We were caught in the open by storm during our journey and I very nearly killed Fosdric and Brother Galthorn, thinking they were monsters of some sort."

"But you came to your senses in time," Talliver said.

"No. Brother Galthorn caught me from behind and knocked me unconscious with a large rock."

Talliver's raised his eyebrows as he considered the weary priest, still attending the injured on the far side of the gloomy cave. "Bested a Master, eh? Truly, this is a young man who has won the favor of the Creator."

"Remind me to tell you sometime how he killed the dragon at Marthwee." Talliver simply stared at Galthorn, unable to respond.

"I must confess," I continued, "That I opposed the idea of bringing him with us at first. But I am glad that we did."

"So," Talliver said, shaking his head in disbelief, "Back to business. Our men on the surface have indicated that the dragons seem to be concentrated west of the city. We must assume that Arandor is there also."

"Reasonable," I said. "What is there that would attract Arandor?"

Talliver's eyes narrowed. "I suspect it has something to do with the coastal road. That's the main highway to Beirgryn," he said, "It is the path most refugees would take when the dragons fell upon us—the few who escaped the city."

I didn't follow his thoughts. "And?"

"There is a box canyon skirted by the road," Talliver continued. "One that essentially has only one entry, there at the road. It would be an easily guarded place in which to hold hundreds—thousands—as prisoners. Perhaps as many as four or five thousand."

I saw then where he was leading, and my insides turned cold. "Or—"

"Or as food." His tone and his face were grim.

Dragons are extremely territorial. It does not require a great deal of thought to realize that the land could not support many of the great beasts; even one dragon can quickly depopulate the countryside for miles around. But a dozen or more in one place—the need to keep that many of the monsters fed must be the reason Arandor brought them to Stelnregon. It was the largest city in Aerwald after Beirgryn, the capital.

And why, I realized with a jolt, we had seen no refugees on the road from Darnaatha. There were none. No one had escaped—at least not that way.

"By the heavens," I said, "Arandor is mad."

"Perhaps," Talliver said, "But he is out there, and we are in here."

"We must get to him as soon as possible," I said. "He must be stopped."

"Yes. I believe I said that."

I stood and went to the place where Hahr'ohld Orson slept. He was curled around his weapon, apparently fearing the thought of it in our curious hands while he slept. Remembering the power of his device, I was grateful that he did not toss in his sleep.

"Hahr'ohld." I knelt down and nudged him, taking care to stay away from the front of his weapon.

He jolted awake, gripping the device. From his wide and unfocused eyes, it appeared that he did not know where he was for a moment. After a few seconds, he focused on me and relaxed. He tapped the symbol on his shirt. *"It's you,"* he said.

"Yes," I said. "We need to plan."

Hahr'ohld sighed. *"I guess so."* He slowly stood, stretching and yawning. He followed, carrying his weapon, as I led back across the cave to Talliver. The King's Guard was rubbing his eyes.

"Are you well, Talliver?" I asked.

"Tired," he said. "This is a very trying time."

"I do not doubt it," I said. "Here is the situation, Hahr'ohld: We must eliminate this Master, Arandor. Without his control, the dragons will likely disperse. At the very least, they will no longer work in concert, and they will be much less difficult to dispatch."

"But—he'll probably use the dragons to defend himself," Hahr'ohld said.

"Almost certainly."

"How can we get past them?"

"I had hoped that you would help us with that problem."

"I'm not a soldier," he protested. *"I'm just an expert on plants. I don't know anything about tactics or strategy or anything like that."* He was clearly shaken by the prospect of having to face the monsters again, but I did not care. Without Hahr'ohld—or at least his powerful weapon—we might as well join those whose only remaining purpose in life was to sate a dragon's hunger.

"Hahr'ohld, your assistance is crucial," I said. "We need your weapon, and we do not know how to use it." A thought occurred to me. "You said you were on a ship. How many others were in your crew?"

He looked up sharply at that. *"There were six of us in all."*

"And where are they?"

Hahr'ohld looked down. *"I don't know. Two are dead for sure. Dragon got them just as we finished repairs on the ship after we crashed. I panicked and ran. Got separated from the other three. I went back to where we landed, but the ship was gone."*

I pondered a moment, and considered the agony that Orson's distress beacon had inflicted on me and, apparently, the dragon at Naribor as well. "Could Arandor operate equipment from your ship without the help of at least one of your crew mates?"

"Ship?" asked Talliver. "What sort of ship?"

"A ship of metal," I said. "Hahr'ohld says they flew to Saramond from another world beyond the stars."

Talliver rolled his eyes. He had yet to see proof of Hahr'ohld's weapon in action. Was he now beginning to doubt my sanity? So be it. I was not inclined to ask Hahr'ohld to demonstrate in the cave; there was no way to know what an explosion might shake loose above us.

"I doubt it," Hahr'ohld said, a glimmer of hope in his eye. *"I hope so. It's possible to fly the ship alone, but it's really designed to be controlled by two, at least."* His face fell. *"But I'm not a very good pilot."*

"You see? You have a vested interest in helping us find and destroy Arandor. And, perhaps, finding your crew."

"And we have an interest in survival," Talliver said. "Can we dispense with persuasion? It is very simple: We kill Arandor and drive off the dragons, or we die. Davian, ask him what his weapon can do."

"Hahr'ohld," I said, "Talliver wants—"

"I think I understood," Hahr'ohld said. *"I've been tweaking my communicator so I can almost make out what you hear when others speak. Tell him, basically, this is a (word) (word), a…"*

I held up my hand to stop him. "Assume for a moment that I am an ignorant savage. Explain in simple terms, please."

"This device emits a beam of highly concentrated light," Hahr'ohld said.

"That's better."

"The beam is so intensely hot that it will cut through any-thing."

"Anything?"

"Wood, metal, rock—pretty much anything."

I relayed Hahr'ohld's words to Talliver, who gaped. "Is this true?"

"I have seen it," I replied. "If we had two days to spare, I would show you the pieces of the dragon Hahr'ohld brought to ground in Naribor. The beam of light from his device lasted no more than two heartbeats. The beast was cleaved nearly in two."

"If this is true," Talliver said, "Then we need not—"

With a sudden shock, like a slap across my face, I felt a powerful shift of energy nearby. "Wait," I said. "Something is wrong."

Talliver lifted his eyebrows but said nothing. I sensed a disturbance in the energy again, a surge pushing through the space around me like waves in a thick, syrupy fluid.

"That way," I said, pointing to the opening in the cave's wall that led back to the entrance.

"What is it?" Hahr'ohld asked. *"What's happening?"*

"I…"

"Hey! Hey!" Thin and distant, the frantic voice of Fosdric echoed down the passageway.

"Come!" Talliver's single word was command enough for a half-dozen men to quickly arm themselves with swords and make for the passage at a dead run.

Grabbing a torch from the wall without breaking stride, Talliver plunged into the passageway. I followed with Talliver's men close behind.

"Hey, I say!" Fosdric's frantic voice was closer now, and I wondered if we would collide with him in the narrow tunnel. We nearly did, but Fosdric saw Talliver's torch and flattened himself against the wall of the passage.

As we reached him, the source of the energy disturbance became evident. The smell of scorched leather and fabric made it plain that Fosdric had been in close company of an open flame. A moment later, our suspicion was confirmed; a deafening roar thundered through tunnel, setting the rock walls to resonating as though the very hills above us were about to collapse.

The dragons had found us.

CHAPTER TWENTY

Wisps of smoke curled from Fosdric's clothing in spots, and it was plain, even in the thin light of Talliver's torch, that Fosdric's hair was singed. He stood stiffly against the wall, eyes wide and breathing hard.

"Fosdric," Talliver said, "Are you hurt?"

"Nah," the little man gasped, "But it were a near thing."

"What happened?" I asked.

"I was resting," Fosdric said, "And all of a sudden, Aeryx gets real skittish, like. I try to quiet him down, see, and suddenly, the whole cave is on fire! Aeryx starts to jumping and bucking, and I try to pull him down the passage here, and—" His voice broke as he realized what had probably become of his horse—his friend. Fosdric bowed his head into his hands and could speak no more.

Brother Galthorn appeared from behind us. The priest put an arm around Fosdric and gently led him back down the passage to the refuge Talliver and his men had found deep in the cave.

Another roar echoed through the tunnel as the dragon tried to claw its way in. Briefly, the tunnel was lit from afar as the monster again seared the entryway with its infernal breath, trying to scorch what it could not grasp.

An anger that had been slowly building in me, kindled by the death and destruction just outside the rocky walls of our underground prison, now burst into flame. Pushing past Talliver, I stormed upward through the tunnel toward the entrance of the cave, determined to blast the foul beast's head clear of its body.

"Wait!" Hahr'ohld's voice echoed off the walls and through my mind, but I paid no heed. Breathing deeply, I focused my

mind, drawing from the energy around me, feeding my anger and directing it at the vile creature that I could hear even now stamping and pawing at the mouth of the cave.

"Davian, wait!" Hahr'ohld cried again. I heard him, but that part of my mind was no longer in control of my actions.

I opened my mind and sought the dragon—and heard nothing. At least, not what I expected to hear.

There was a roar, an overpowering hiss of white noise, and then—

"Ah, there you are." A voice in my mind, not a dragon's, but a man's. Deafening, irresistible. I tried, but I could not block it out.

"I have expended a great deal of time and energy searching for you. You seem to be the only one of my so-called brothers still in the area. The only one who isn't a drooling idiot, that is."

Forward, slowly, I was drawn toward the dragon. Against my will, I placed one foot in front of the other, moving ever closer to the dragon who waited patiently now outside the mouth of the cave.

"I am Arandor, as you have no doubt already guessed. Time is short. Dragons are difficult to control when they are hungry, and there are only so many people left to feed them. So I will not waste time with you, Master Davian. The dragon waiting outside the cave, whose name, I gather, is Sallagthiss, will dispatch you quickly. That will leave me free to concentrate on other matters."

Step by step, my unwilling feet moved closer to the light, the glowing portal that would lead me into the jaws of the dragon.

Suddenly, my head was violated by a mind-rending shriek, a banshee wail that rose and fell in rhythmic pulses, a cacophony that would surely rouse the dead from slumber if such a thing were possible.

My forward progress ceased and I fell to my knees, clutching my head and hoping against hope that the noise would stop before my very mind was lost to me forever.

The dragon outside the cave roared with a weird and unnatural cry. It was pain, not anger or hunger or challenge, the sounds normally heard from the beasts. Clearly, the dragon also heard the head-shattering wail that threatened to leave me senseless.

Just as suddenly as it began, it ended. I felt other hands about my head and looked up to see the concerned face of Hahr'ohld Orson, pulling the makeshift cap over my head. He pointed to the emblem on his chest, and I understood—the sound was coming from his communicating device.

Then Hahr'ohld picked up his weapon from where he had dropped it and moved cautiously to the mouth of cave. I tried to protest, but I found myself too weak to move.

I looked up in time to see Hahr'ohld peer out of the cave as the dragon continued to roar in agony. He stepped into the entry, leveled his weapon, and a thin beam of red light emerged from the device.

The roaring outside instantly ceased.

Talliver ran to the cave mouth to see for himself what had transpired. He looked out of the cave, then at Hahr'ohld, and then at the device. His expression was one of awe.

"Praise the Creator," Talliver said. "Perhaps you are a Messenger, after all."

Hahr'ohld, who did not understand, merely smiled and nodded happily.

From a narrow crevice along the wall directly opposite where I lay sprawled, a small, bedraggled thing extricated itself and ran to the mouth of the cave. It was Wolf, fur singed and blackened in spots, but still defiant. He broadcast a challenge to the world with his sharp, high-pitched bark, telling all who heard that despite the dragon's best effort, he, Wolf, still survived.

Two young men wearing the colors of the King's Guard helped me to my feet. As I brushed the dirt from my clothing, Fosdric burst from the passage that led to the keep. "Wolf!" he cried. "Creator be praised, I nearly forgot! Come here, boy!"

Wolf yipped at the outdoors one last time before turning and running into the arms of his master. In truth, Fosdric looked as dreadful as Wolf. Clearly, it had been a very near thing when the dragon surprised them outside the cave mouth.

Talliver approached with Hahr'ohld at his heels. "What happened, Davian? What was that all about?"

My head still rang with the memory of the inhuman wail. I rubbed my temples and tried to compose myself. "I thought to confront the dragon," I said, slowly. "But I was brought under the same power, I think, as the dragons that have set upon you. My feet moved me forward against my will. It was only Hahr'ohld's presence of mind to distract the dragon with that head-splitting noise from his communicator—which caused my weakness, as you saw—that saved me from the teeth of the monster."

Talliver frowned. "We heard nothing."

"Be grateful," I said. "My head feels as though it will crack like an egg if I move too quickly."

Signaling with his hands, Hahr'ohld indicated that he wanted to move back into the cave so that we could speak again. I understood. Deep in the cave, I would be shielded from the thoughts of Arandor.

"Talliver," I said, "Let us return to the keep. Hahr'ohld may have some insight on what Arandor is doing, but I cannot talk with him here."

Talliver motioned to his men and once again we prepared to descend into the bowels of the hill. From outside, however, came a crashing and commotion that caused us all to stop, prepared to run at the first hint of the presence of another dragon.

"Ho, there! Men of Stelnregon, I say, ho!"

Definitely not a dragon. Indeed, Talliver seemed to know the voice. Moving quickly to the mouth of the cave, his stern face broke into a smile for the first time since I had see him.

"Can it be?" Talliver stepped outside the cave, and it was impossible to see who it was he greeted against the bright summer sun. Nor did I care to look, as the light hurt my eyes, which made my aching head hurt all the more.

"Talliver! Praise the Creator, it's you! When we saw the city, I feared the worst. Man, it is good to see you!" The voice was familiar. A moment later, the shadows resolved into men.

"And you, my friend," Talliver said, entering the cave. "In truth, the sight of you and your men is a greater blessing than I could have hoped for." A moment later, I saw why I recognized the voice of Talliver's companion: Leading a small group of armed men was the captain of the Darnaathan contingent of the King's Guard, Caedwulf.

"Greetings, captain," I said. "Welcome to the festivities."

Caedwulf blinked, staring in my direction, waiting for his eyes to adjust to the dim light inside the mouth of the cave. Finally he said, "Master Davian?"

Wolf, from the safety of Fosdric's arms, barked at the half-dozen newcomers that crowded into the cave mouth. Caedwulf looked around, his eyes coming to rest for a long moment on Hahr'ohld, before finding the source of the noice.

"Ah," said Caedwulf. "Fosdric. I should have guessed."

"Hello again, there, captain," Fosdric said. "Pardon the appearance. Had a little scrum with the beastie outside."

"So I see," Caedwulf said. "The priest is here too, then?"

"I see you know these men," Talliver interrupted. "No doubt the story is a good one, Caedwulf, but it will have to wait. How many are with you?"

"A full company," Caedwulf said. "A hundred men on horse."

"And we shall need every one, Talliver said. "Dragons, at least a dozen, are working together. And they are being controlled by a brother of The Order."

"Not of The Order," I interjected. "The Order is not a part of this. Arandor is rogue, acting alone."

"Your pardon," Talliver said. "However it may be, our immediate problem is this: Arandor is no doubt aware that his pet outside is dead. Others will come, and probably soon."

Caedwulf frowned. "Is not Davian a Master? Can we not offer our arrows and spears in assistance to his Gift?"

"Not at present," I said. "This Arandor has somehow amplified his power so that he overwhelms all with the Gift. Outside this cave, without this strange cap, my thoughts are not my own. Just now, Arandor very nearly walked me into right the dragon's mouth. No, until we find and eliminate Arandor, the dragons are his to command, and I can do very little to help."

Turning to the man at his side, Caedwulf immediately detailed orders for the men still outside the cave. "Get the men to the cave I described to you on the way here," he said. "About two miles further down the line of hills. Get the horses well inside and wait for word from me."

"Sir," the aide said, "How will you get to us, moving in the open with dragons above?"

Talliver said, "There is an entrance to this network of caves fewer than a hundred yards from the cave that Caedwulf speaks of. Our messenger will come to you that way."

Caedwulf nodded. "Worry about the men outside now, Janver. Go quickly." The young man snapped his right arm to his chest in salute and departed to carry out Caedwulf's command.

"And now," he said, turning back to Talliver, "I am at your disposal, Talliver. How can we help?"

* * *

After returning to the depths of the cave, Talliver summarized the situation for Caedwulf, whose face grew more drawn and determined as Talliver spoke. It was a fair guess that Caedwulf was no stranger to Stelnregon, and may well have friends or family among the dead or missing.

We sat in a circle on the floor of the cave, listening to Talliver's summary of our position. At length, he turned and asked me to describe for Caedwulf the means by which Hahr'ohld Orson came to be our traveling companion, and the power of the strange metallic device that never left his side.

"So, this Hahr'ohld," Caedwulf said, nodding in his direction, "was part of a voyage of discovery that traveled to Saramond from a world somewhere among the stars?"

"That is what he says," I replied. Hahr'ohld, sitting to my left, smiled and nodded politely. It was not clear whether he understood or was just being polite. "Certainly, his clothing, his speech, and his devices are like nothing on this world."

"He looks like us—although strange."

"True," I said. "But you saw what his weapon is capable of."

"Yes, I did," Caedwulf said. "We heard the dragon roaring and tearing at the ground as it tried to enter the cave. We approached with caution, hoping to move into range for a shot at its eyes while it was occupied with digging out whoever was inside. Without warning, the dragon went into a fit, clawing at its head as though desperate to free something trapped inside its skull. And then a shaft of light, brighter than any I have ever seen, burst from the cave and pierced the dragon through the head, like a spear. Just like that, it was dead." Caedwulf shook his head, as though disbelieving his own memory. "Is he truly willing to help us?"

"Not exactly," I said. At Caedwulf's questioning look, I added, "Hahr'ohld is no soldier. But he wants to return home, and his best chance of doing so is to find his ship. We assume that Arandor somehow came into possession of this ship and is using it, or one of its machines, to somehow amplify his abilities."

"How is that possible?"

"I have no idea. Hahr'ohld," I said, turning to include him in the conversation, "Are we correct in assuming that your ship is being used by Arandor to increase his power?"

"It has to be," Hahr'ohld said. *"The (word) energy on your world is unbelievable. You can use it, Davian, and the others like you, and the dragons use it, too. In fact, they must use it to fly, because nothing that big could fly with those flimsy wings."* Hahr'ohld's eyes took on a faraway look as he continued to speak, although I was not entirely sure that he was still talking to me. The others in the circle, hearing only the nonsense jabbering of the outsider's speech, gawked openly at the two of us, taken aback by Hahr'ohld's strange tongue and the fact that I seemed to understand him.

"I mean, yeah, they move a lot of air, but there's no way their wings generate enough lift to get off the ground. I wonder if the dragons even realize they're doing it. And if they can manipulate enough energy to lift that much mass, I wonder what they could do if—," He stopped suddenly. His face had the same traumatized expression it had when he described his first encounter with a dragon.

"Is something wrong?" I asked.

Hahr'ohld turned his attention back to me. *"Davian, can you fly?"*

"What?"

"You can't fly, can you?"

"Of course not! Do I have wings? No man can fly!"

"Dragons shouldn't be able to fly, either," Hahr'ohld said. *"They are way too big for those wings."*

I frowned. He made no sense. "And yet you see that they do."

"And you tell me you can do things with your mind I can only do with the help of mechanical devices," he said.

"What is your point?"

"Don't you see? The dragons do what you do, but in a different way! That's probably how they make fire, too, with their minds, and they probably don't even know it. Davian," he said excitedly, grabbing my arm, *"The dragons fly with their* minds, *not their wings! Do you understand? Their minds! Can you imagine what they could do if they knew they had the same powers as you?"*

"Do you mean—"

"Maybe it requires so much concentration to fly that the dragons can't use the power for anything else," Hahr'ohld interrupted. *"Maybe their brains are just wired differently, or—I don't know. But maybe—maybe they don't do what you can do simply because they don't realize they can do it."*

I considered Hahr'ohld's words for a moment. Dragons with the power of Masters? Creator forbid! The beasts are deadly enough with just their claws, teeth, and flame.

"Perhaps," I said slowly, "it would be best not to tell them."

Hahr'ohld stared, unsure of whether I was jesting. Talliver, Caedwulf, and Fosdric stared at both of us, trying to determine what had just passed between us.

"Orson is sharing his theory of what gives the dragons their power," I explained, "And speculated about some abilities have not yet seen. Interesting, but not entirely relevant. What we know is that dragons have never shown the ability to do anything but fly, bite, claw, and burn. Thankfully so. Let us assume that these are the dangers we must overcome—complicated by their newfound ability to cooperate under the influence of an external power. So, how do we counter them?"

"Well," Hahr-ohld said, *"You saw how the distress signal on my communicator affected the dragon outside the cave?"*

"I know how it affected me."

"Trust me, it did the same to the dragon," he said. *"I think there's a way to amplify the noise to disrupt Arandor's control of all the dragons at once. Maybe even incapacitate them."*

I relayed Hahr'ohld's words to Caedwulf, Talliver, and Fosdric. Caedwulf nodded. Talliver asked, "What then?"

"Then," I said, standing and leaning on my dragonspear, "While the dragons thrash about, senseless, we take our weapons and kill them."

CHAPTER TWENTY-ONE

The plan proposed by Hahr'ohld was accepted, his lack of military experience notwithstanding. As long as Arandor controlled the dragons, nothing was free to move above ground. Just wresting the dragons from Arandor's control, even if we were not able to kill them, would be an improvement. If they were free, the dragons would be as likely to fight one another as us.

The problem we faced was generating the distress beacon that Hahr'ohld said would accomplish the task. As he explained it, the energy of the device on his clothing was not sufficient to interfere with the signal being used by Arandor unless the dragon was almost literally on top of us. Clearly, that was a dangerous proposition.

"Can we boost the strength of his device?" Talliver asked. Hahr'ohld responded before I could translate.

"I need to find a device that we sent ahead of us," Hahr'ohld said. *"It was a probe, an unmanned ship, that we sent to scout the land and take soil and animal samples."*

The shock on our faces must have been plain. The pudgy stranger beamed and said, *"I figured out how to adjust my communicator to hear the sounds passing through your mind. So you don't need to think at me."*

I wasn't sure if I like that, but I relayed that to Talliver, Caedwulf, and Fosdric, who laughed.

"What's funny?" I asked.

"Well, it's simple, isn't it?" Fosdric said. "This adventure gets more unreal by the hour. You're the Master of the Order, the big, bad dragonslayer, but at every turn it's the priest and the gardener here who's getting the drop on you!"

"Yes, very amusing."

Caedwulf looked suspiciously at Orson. "So, you mean to say he can hear your thoughts?"

"No, not exactly," Hahr'ohld interjected. *"His mind—I mean, your mind, Davian—must process the words of others, and apparently that throws off enough energy for my device to hear and translate. Like a (word)."*

I relayed his explanation to Caedwulf. And going forward in this tale, for the sake of time (and my aching fingers, as I commit this account to parchment), you may assume that I repeated Orson's words to my companions whenever it was necessary.

"Why?" Caedwulf asked.

"To see if we could survive down here," Hahr'ohld explained. *"We needed to know if the plants and animals were poisonous to us. So this device would move from place to place, cloaked so it wouldn't be seen, and it sent reports back to our ship in the sky with a communicating device like mine, but a lot more powerful."*

"What do you mean, 'cloaked'?" I asked.

"It's hard to explain," Hahr'ohld said. *"I don't really understand it myself. It's a way for something to be invisible."*

"Invisible?"

"A device inside the probe bends the light around it so that when you look at it, you see what's behind it. So it's invisible."

A puzzle piece fell into place. To confirm my hunch, I asked, "And what do you mean, 'animal samples'?"

Orson looked puzzled by my line of questioning. *"Smaller ones, like insects, were captured and studied inside the probe,"* he replied. *"Larger ones were killed with a device similar to my weapon and dissected. Some of the internal organs were removed to analyze by a small (word) inside the probe. You know, it's surprising how similar the life-forms are here..."*

"And when this probe travels, how does it move?"

"Well, standard (word) (word) drive, of course."

"Simpler terms, please."

"It flies by ejecting hot gas through a tube, and it controls its flight by the use of smaller tubes through which gases can be ejected to push it in different directions."

A mystery was beginning to resolve itself in my mind. "How hot is the gas? Would it leave scorch marks on the ground?"

"Most likely."

I rubbed my eyes. As if our situation was not already unbelievable enough, the cause of the crisis that had prompted my journey from Marthwee to Stelnregon had just dropped from the sky in the form of Hahr'ohld Orson. There was never an invisible dragon—it was a device sent from Hahr'ohld's flying ship to study our livestock.

And searching for the non-existent invisible dragon had landed us in the middle of a desperate war with a man who controlled real ones.

Talliver was less than pleased to learn that the mutilated livestock that had terrified farmers in his district was the product of scientific experiments by Hahr'ohld's people. Hahr'ohld smiled apologetically.

"Hahr'ohld," I said, "How do you know this probe is not being used by Arandor to control the dragons?"

"Would you know how to use it if you found it?"

"No."

"Then I bet Arandor doesn't, either," he said. *"He probably found our ship after... after I ran away. At least one of the crew must still be alive, and Arandor is forcing him to operate the (word)."* As he spoke, his pudgy face fell, and he looked again as though he were about to cry. *"Davian, I'm truly sorry about all the trouble our people caused by coming here, and I'm ashamed I ran away and left my crewmates to that dragon and whatever Arandor is doing to them. I want to make things right. I'll do anything I can."*

"All right," I said. "Tell us how to find this invisible probe."

"Actually," Hahr'ohld said, *"We don't have to find it. I can send a signal to it that will bring it to us."*

"Will not Arandor's signal interfere with yours?"

"Don't think so. It should be on a different (word)."

I raised my eyebrows and waited for a simpler explanation. Hahr'ohld sighed and tried again. *"The signal takes a different—path through the air."*

Caedwulf and Talliver glanced at one another, understanding no better than I did. But they, like I, cared not how it worked so long as it did.

"Master Davian!" It was Fosdric, calling from the far side of the cave. "Come quickly!"

The little man was bent over someone on the floor of the cave. Talliver, Caedwulf, and Hahr'ohld followed as I hurried to him. It became evident that the form on the ground, covered with a fraying, dirt-brown robe, was Brother Galthorn.

"He wouldn't eat, and he wouldn't rest, and he wouldn't listen, neither," Fosdric said. He was examining the priest for injuries he might have sustained when he fell. Thankfully, there were none we could see.

"What happened?" Talliver asked.

"He was looking after your wounded, sir, and he just give this man here some water when he stands up, drops the water gourd there, and falls over," Fosdric said. "He's been looking none too good, but he wouldn't stop for food or rest."

"Find him a place to sleep, over there." Talliver pointed to a spot near a small fire. "Keep him warm, and when he wakes, make him eat. Tie him down, if you must."

"Straight away, sir," Fosdric said. He went in search of a healthy man to help him move Brother Galthorn to the place indicated by Talliver.

"Remarkable young man," Talliver said.

"Would that all priests were like him," I said.

"Would that all men were like him," corrected Caedwulf.

"Is he all right?" Hahr'ohld asked.

"I think so," I said. "He needs food and rest. He has been assisting the wounded since we arrived, even while we slept."

Hahr'ohld looked surprised, but he said nothing.

Talliver turned to me and asked, "When can we begin? When can your friend summon his machine?"

"Right now," he said. *"We just need to go outside for a minute so my communicator can, uh, speak to it."*

Talliver, after I relayed Hahr'ohld's reply, said, "I will send a dozen men, archers, to guard against interruption. And we will go by a different route. I suspect the mouth of the cave may have another sentry soon, if not already. We'll use the exit closest to the cave where Caewulf's men are hidden. Caedwulf, you can let them know that there will be action soon. Hahr'ohld, you have my thanks—if we are not killed."

* * *

The trek through the warren of tunnels honeycombing the underside of the hills north of Stelnregon was tiring. The air underground was damp and cool, but the footing was uneven and slick, so that each step had to be carefully placed to avoid a turned ankle, or worse. Being carried out by others under such conditions would have made the journey much more hazardous than it was for one man alone. And needless to say, emergency medical care is hard to come by in a dank, dimly lit cave.

Eventually, after an hour and a half of careful stepping, crouching, and groping our way through the tunnels behind the lone man with a torch, we spied daylight seeping around a bend in the tunnel ahead.

"Hold," said Talliver, second in line behind the young man with the torch. "Pelgar, scout ahead. Carefully! We don't know whether the Guards in the cave outside have drawn attention with their horses. A dragon would not be able to get into this cave, but its flame would. Go now, and be quick."

The young man said, "Yes sir." Handing the torch to Talliver, he crept down the passage toward the cave mouth, keeping to the shadows.

Someone nudged me in the ribs, and I turned to find Hahr'ohld pantomiming the act of putting something on my head. I had nearly forgotten. I pulled the shield cap from my belt and slipped it onto my head, and the whispers of sound I had begun to hear in my mind, almost without noticing, were stilled.

Then I realized that I should be the one to scout ahead. "Talliver," I said, "Call your man back. Let me go."

"Why? We need you."

"If a dragon sits outside, it won't need to see or hear him," I said. "It will sense his mind. This cap shields me from them."

Talliver thought for a moment, and then hissed, "Pelgar! Stop!"

The young man stopped and looked over his shoulder. Talliver called him back with a wave of his hand. As I started forward, Talliver put his hand on my shoulder and said, "Be careful, Davian."

I smiled. "Dragons are easy. Women are difficult." He managed a half-smile in return.

The passageway leveled out in the last few man-heights before the exit to the outdoors. A soft breeze blew into the cave, carrying with it the warm scent of growing things, smells sadly absent from the depths of the caves into which Talliver and his last few soldiers had taken refuge. I resolved to be more appreciative of simple things such as leaves and blades of grass henceforth, if we ever escaped the cold, damp security of the caves.

Slowly I advanced, allowing my eyes time to adjust to sunlight. My ears heard only the slow rustling of dry leaves in the breeze. So accustomed am I to sensing my surroundings with my mind that I briefly considered removing the cap, but remembering what had happened the last time I ventured near the mouth of a cave without it, I decided against it.

Step by step I moved closer to the irregular oval that framed our portal to the world outside. As I crept nearer, I sensed an odd tingling around my scalp as though some force was trying to bypass the shield cap to access my mind. No doubt that was the case, as Arandor was by now aware that his dragon had failed to eliminate me or Hahr'ohld Orson as threats to whatever he had planned.

Or perhaps it was simply nervous sweat as I crept toward I knew not what, deprived of the Gift.

At last, I reached the opening that filled this last segment of the passageway with light. Peering outdoors, I steeled myself to jump back into the tunnel if I saw anything out of the ordinary.

Behind me a sharp noise suddenly burst from the tunnel, causing me to start and bump my head smartly against the overhanging rock.

It was Wolf, barking and wagging his tail happily.

"Blasted dog," I grumbled. From the tunnel, I heard the sounds of smothered laughter. My companions had advanced far enough to witness my near-braining because of a dog the size of a shoe.

"All clear," I called down the tunnel, rubbing the lump on the top of my head. In truth, it was a beautiful day outside. The soft light streaming through the trees surrounding the path in front of the cave created a dappled effect on the carpet of fallen leaves. Small yellow flowers growing nearby seemed to reflect the radiance of the sun. On any other day, this place would have been a peaceful refuge to rest and reflect. I would not enjoy returning to the cave, if need arose.

Hahr'ohld came forward, blinking in the sunlight and filling his lungs with the warm, pleasantly scented air. Though I could not hear his communicator, it was easy enough to see that his thoughts were very close to mine. Returning to the caves would be something we would do only grudgingly.

The strange gardener from the stars set his weapon at his feet and reached into a pocket hidden on his silver garment. As Hahr'ohld fiddled with the small device he had retrieved, Caedwulf and his aide, Janver, crossed quickly to a cave hidden from the path by an outcropping of rock. A few moments later, several others dressed in the garb of the King's Guard followed Caedwulf back to where we stood.

I was uneasy. We were exposed, and if, as Talliver's sentries had reported, dragons patrolled the skies, we would surely be detected quickly. But with the shield cap on my head, I had no sense of where the monsters were and could give no more warning than any other man with a good pair of eyes.

"Hahr'ohld," I said—and then I realized that we would not understand each other until I removed the cap, which I dared not do until we returned underground.

He raised a hand to stay my tongue as he monitored the tiny device in his other hand. I had no choice but to trust that he knew what he was doing.

Looking anxiously to the sky, I saw nothing but blue through the leaves. I was thankful for the cover offered by the canopy of green, though a dragon would probably scent the presence of so many men and horses together. There was no way to know how the dragons were affected by artificially amplified mind of Arandor. Perhaps they were reduced to automatons, going only where he directed, unable to react to any stimulus other than his thoughts.

So I hoped, at any rate.

Suddenly, Hahr'ohld pointed to the east, the direction of the cave where Caedwulf's men had hidden their mounts. We turned to follow the direction of his hand and saw nothing, at first. Slowly we recognized a shimmer in the air just above the trees, and a wind that seemed to blow through the upper branches, causing the leaves to dance vigorously, like a man celebrating a successful hunt with too much wine and song.

Hahr'ohld moved to the front of the knot of onlookers that watched in fascination as the unseen thing floating over the trees drew closer. Waving his arms excitedly, he communicated his earnest desire that we move closer to the mouth of the cave, leaving an open space directly beneath a clearing in the covering of leaves above us.

Once we were away from the open area, Hahr'ohld manipulated the device in his hand again, and at once, the shimmer in the air parted and disappeared. In its place was a silver-gray cylinder, perhaps two man-heights from top to bottom, riding on a cone of yellow-orange flame.

The thing seemed to hover weightlessly until Hahr'ohld again tapped at his device. Then slowly, the cylinder began to lower itself to the ground.

I turned at the sound of footsteps behind me. Fosdric had emerged from the cave, blinking at the sunlight as he walked. Wolf barked happily and ran to greet his master, who bent and gave him a welcoming scratch behind the ears.

"Just wanted you to know, Davian, that Brother Galthorn's going to be—what in creation is that?" Fosdric stared at Hahr'ohld's probe, now just a man-height above the ground. The grass and leaves below crisped and ignited as the flame from the probe played across the turf.

"That is Hahr'ohld's probe machine," I said.

"By the Creator's beard," Fosdric said slowly, his eyes wide. "It's the iron dragon."

The gray machine settled to the ground, touching down on three spider-like legs that extended from the body of the thing with a soft thump. After it settled, the flame playing across the turf ceased as whatever powered the probe switched itself off. Hahr'ohld manipulated the small device in his hand, and then crossing to the probe, he retrieved a tool from a pocket hidden against his right leg and began to remove a panel on the side of the probe.

"How many pockets you got in there?" Fosdric asked.

Hahr'ohld, not understanding a word, merely smiled and nodded as he removed the panel and set it on the ground. He began to work at something inside the probe.

I glanced again at the sky. It seemed wrong that we had been outdoors now for nearly half an hour with no sight of a dragon. Either Arandor had lost interest in us or he was not as thorough as I had feared. Or he had something planned.

That was it.

Without warning, three of the monstrous beasts exploded over the far side of the hill, no more than three or four man-heights above us, spraying flame in all directions and setting the forest around us ablaze.

"To the cave!" Talliver shouted, and his men leapt to obey. His twenty archers might have succeeded in slowing or even killing one dragon, if an arrow managed to pierce an eye or the sensitive underbelly, but against three there was no time for a second shot.

I ground my teeth in frustration, dearly yearning for a chance to hold our ground for even a few minutes until Hahr'ohld could complete whatever it was he was doing. I looked at the man from space, and he was sweating profusely as he worked furiously at something inside the probe.

"Hurry!" I shouted. I am sure he understood, even without translation. A burning branch dropped within arms' reach, and the leaves above us leapt and danced in crimson waves as the fire spread from tree to tree. The dragons had circled about and were bearing down on us again. Talliver's men had gained the mouth of the cave, but I doubted that many would get far enough inside to escape a dragon's breath.

Desperate, I reached for the cap on my head. If Arandor was occupied with the three monsters converging on us, perhaps I would be able to save at least a few of the men before falling under his control myself.

"Ha!" Hahr'ohld beamed, exultant, and he slapped the emblem on his chest. My scalp tingled, and I was thankful I had not yet removed the cap. The dragons, however, were not so protected.

All three of the beasts appeared to have suddenly forgotten how to fly. Twisting and rolling in mid-air, clawing at their heads in agony, the beasts were propelled through the air now only by momentum.

And once again, I found myself standing at the projected point of impact of a dragon hurtling from the sky.

Hahr'ohld was entranced, frozen in place, staring at the twisting, rolling behemoth that threatened to crush him where he stood.

"Run!" I yelled, and I grabbed his arm as I turned and dashed for the cave.

The first dragon crashed through the trees and smashed against the very place we'd stood only moments before, impacting the ground with a meaty, ground-shaking thud. As it rolled, the beast's clawed hind legs came near to decapitating us. I heard a _whuff_, and Hahr'ohld fell to the ground behind me. I turned to look, and a tangled mass of scales and claws suddenly filled my vision and I threw myself down, arms over my head. The rush of air as the creature tumbled past was so great that for a moment I felt as though I had been caught in a whirlwind.

The second and third dragons collided with the ground mere moments after the first. One pounded the hillside, rolling down the slope and nearly blocking the cave in which Talliver and his men had retreated, while the other hit at such an angle that it was impaled on a particularly stout oak. The denuded tree, slicked red with the dragon's blood, protruded nearly a man-height from the beast's armored back.

Rising slowly, I searched each of the dragons carefully for signs of movement. It would not do for one to unexpectedly spring to life after calling Talliver, Caedwulf, and their men out of the caves.

Hahr'ohld lay unmoving on the turf, curled into a ball like an infant. I feared the worst, knowing how close the dragon had been. As I approached, however, he slowly uncurled, looking dazed. With a start, he jumped to his feet, eyes wide as they took in the three quivering hulks littering the ground nearby.

I motioned to Hahr'ohld for quiet as I watched the dragons carefully. Unfortunately, I had little time to examine the beasts as the fires around us were growing hotter. Finally determining that the beasts were well and truly dead, I signaled Hahr'ohld that all was well, and I turned to call Talliver.

"Aagh!" A cry of anguish from Hahr'ohld spun me around again. He stood where the first dragon had nearly flattened us. It missed us—but it had landed squarely on top of Hahr'ohld's probe, which lay scattered in pieces across the turf at Hahr'ohld's feet.

He bent down and gently retrieved an item from the ground, which he held up for my inspection. It was a twisted piece of metal, bent like a man's arm at the elbow, almost artistic in its smooth lines. Its color was that of the probe. A moment passed before I recognized the item and the reason for the crestfallen expression on Hahr'ohld's face.

It was his weapon. He had forgotten to pick it up when we ran from the falling dragon. And from its mangled appearance, I was certain that it would never work again.

CHAPTER TWENTY-TWO

Hahr'ohld stared helplessly at the useless collection of metal in front of him. When he turned back to me, his face was a mask of disbelief.

While I shared his disappointment, we had little time to consider the situation. The dragons had clearly been sent by Arandor, and so he must know about the deaths of his beasts. He would probably also know about the signal Hahr'ohld had used to defeat them.

It occurred to me then that Arandor was likely nursing a headache even more painful than the ones I endured after being subjected to the weaker version of Hahr'ohld's distress beacon. He might even be incapacitated. If there was ever a time to seek out this villain, it was now.

We no longer had the advantage of Hahr'ohld's weapon. We did, however, have his communicator. If we encountered dragons on the way, we would have to deal with them at close range, and with conventional means.

Another burning branch cracked and fell to ground, nearly braining Hahr'ohld, who seemed unable to move. I rushed to him, grabbed his arm, and pulled him to the cave. Talliver and Caedwulf had emerged, drawn by the relative quiet. The roar of one dragon can be nearly deafening; three at once is an experience I hope never to repeat.

"Are they—" Talliver began.

"Dead, yes," I said. "All of them. Once again, Master Davian is present while another slays the dragons. Hahr'ohld has now claimed five in the short time I have known him."

The King's Guard eyed the pudgy gardener with confusion, unable to give credence to my words. "How—"

"The noise from his machine," I said. "The pain was so intense that it nearly drove them mad. Unfortunately for them, they were in mid-flight."

Caedwulf surveyed the landscape and noticed that a number of his men had emerged from the other cave. The sound of horses whinnying with fear came from the cave.

"We must get our men out of the cave before the fire makes it impossible," Caedwulf said.

"Yes, but where?" Talliver said. His brow furrowed as he lost himself in thought.

"Captain," I said.

"Yes?"

"Now may be the time to find Arandor."

"Explain."

"He was most likely affected by Hahr'ohld's device as the dragons were," I said. "Judging by my reaction to the weaker signal, the effect is probably temporary, but he may never be this vulnerable again."

"Why not?"

"One of the falling dragons smashed Hahr'ohld's machine."

A moment passed while Talliver considered his options. He was apparently not afraid to cast the die when it was handed to him. He wasted no time.

"Caedwulf, get your men," he said. "I need mounts for myself, Davian, Hahr'ohld, and twenty of my men. Can you spare that many?"

"I will. Janver, come here." Caedwulf turned and gave a series of orders to his aide, who thumped his chest in salute and left at a run for the cave where the horses grew ever more skittish.

"There is one thing more, Talliver."

Talliver turned back to me with an expression that plainly read, *What now?*

"Hahr'ohld's weapon was also damaged by the dragon," I said. "I do not believe we can repair it."

Talliver sighed and looked skyward for a moment. "Davian," he said, "Is it your opinion that we can move about outside for the time being?"

"Yes, I think so."

"Good," he said. "Men, let's move. This fire grows too warm for my liking." With that, he started up the path that led toward the entrance of the cave we had used at first, where a dead dragon still lay outside the mouth.

The fire above was indeed growing warm. It would not be long before the dragons lying dead outside the caves would be roasted by the blaze they had started. A fitting end.

As we walked the narrow path at the base of the hills, I decided to risk removing the shield cap for a moment. Hahr'ohld was right behind me; if my guess about Arandor was wrong, Orson was the only one among us who would know to replace the cap before I caused anyone harm.

I slid the cap off of my head slowly, prepared to pull it back on quickly if I sensed anything unexpected. There was no need. While the level of energy in the air felt stronger than normal, I sensed only the men around me, and farther away, the men and horses following us away from the fire.

Turning to Hahr'ohld, I replaced the cap on my head and pantomimed the message that he should under no circumstances activate his communicator. If and when Arandor came to his senses, I preferred that he wonder whether we had survived the encounter with his three dragons. Hahr'ohld appeared confused for a moment, but then he nodded agreement, apparently understanding my reasoning.

We smelled our destination before we saw it. Dragons carry a lot of flesh, and when a dragon dies, it gives off a powerful stink. Dragons smell none too pleasant when alive, and like humans, they void their bowels at the moment of death.

Killing dragons is no easy task, but I say truthfully that I prefer it to butchering them. My stomach is not that strong.

Caedwulf and his men arrived at the entrance to the cave just behind us. As we had traveled the distance on foot, it was only the width of the path that kept them behind us during the three quarters of an hour it took to reach the dead dragon.

"Caedwulf," Talliver said, "We depart from here. I thank you for allowing my men to make use of your horses."

"We will be glad to have the skilled archers of Stelnregon with us," Caedwulf said. Turning to his men, he said, "The men who are staying, dismount. Follow Fosdric here to the keep. Post a sentry here—upwind if you can." There were chuckles from his men. "You have your orders, now go."

Fosdric, carrying Wolf, led a small procession of soldiers to the mouth of the cave. "Come along, gents," he called over his shoulder. "Mind the dragon."

Talliver turned to me and asked, "Is there a mount you prefer?"

"They are all the same to me," I said. "I am not as comfortable on horseback as on foot, but I will manage."

A powerful walnut brown horse with a splash of white on his muzzle named Champion was assigned to me, or I to him, and I was soon riding with the King's Guards toward the ruins of Stelnregon. Behind me on Champion was Hahr'ohld, who had refused to mount a horse of his own.

To be truthful, Talliver had difficulty understanding why a man who claimed to sail the vast empty spaces between the stars was afraid to ride a horse. To defuse Talliver's frustration, I volunteered to carry Hahr'ohld with me.

The choice of Champion was a good one. The stallion responded quickly and surely to my commands, and he was sturdily built, thankfully. While I am of average size and build, Hahr'ohld was padded more thickly than most. The added burden seemed not to affect Champion at all.

As we rode, Hahr'ohld's arms around my chest constricted until it felt as though I were in the coils of a giant snake. I tugged at his interlocked fingers until he understood and relaxed somewhat. It seemed bizarre, but it occurred to me that Hahr'ohld may not have ridden a horse before. It was even possible that there were no horses wherever he was from.

The warmth of the sunlight would have been pleasant had not the gentle inland breeze carried a hint of smoke, a reminder of the reason we rode. The hills screened Stelnregon from our view, so we saw only the trees of the wooded hillside and the softly filtered light of the mid-afternoon sun.

It was difficult, I confess, to escape the nagging thought that it might be the last afternoon of our lives. I was also bothered by the fact that our journey through the caves earlier had forced me to leave my dragonspear behind. Carrying that length of timber through the tight quarters of the tunnels would have been difficult at best. I felt defenseless—no spear, and unless I was able to remove my cap safely, the Gift was useless.

I began to sweat, something a Master of The Order does not normally do unless he chooses. For the first time, I could soon face a dragon as an ordinary man. And I was suddenly afraid.

Forcing the thought from my mind, I tried to tally our strengths. Numbers, certainly: We had roughly one hundred well-trained soldiers of the King's Guard who were tested and brave, trained in swordplay and steady hands with a bow; men who would not flee at the sight of a dragon. Experience, too: Caedwulf and Talliver commanded the respect of their men, and they both seemed capable. And Hahr'ohld: Though the Guards regarded him with suspicion, fearing that his courage would fail when tested, Hahr'ohld carried with him the means by which we might defeat the dragons without my abilities: the distress signal generated by his communicator.

We saw the first dragon as we began to descend the last hill on the road leading into Darnaatha. It was a middle-sized beast perhaps two miles ahead of us, flying slowly from our right to our left over the smoking, blackened remains of Stelnregon. The dragon's motion through the air was smooth, fluid, as though it were an aquatic snake swimming lazily through the water of a slow-moving river.

The horses of Caedwulf's command were well-trained. Not a single one flinched or shied, even though they must have been aware of the dragon's presence.

Hahr'ohld saw it a moment after I did. I heard a sharp intake of breath, and his arms tightened again around my chest.

Talliver, leading the column on a chestnut mount with a regal bearing, held up his hand as a signal to stop. He turned in his saddle and motioned for me to come forward. Pulling Champion from the line, I rode to the head of the column and stopped next to the captain. Caedwulf sat astride a horse of pure white on the other side of Talliver.

"Why has it not noticed us?" Talliver asked.

"That is a good question," I said. "At this distance, it should have sensed us. It should have changed direction and come to scout us, if nothing else."

"And yet it does not."

"So it seems."

Caedwulf frowned and said, "I do not like this. First the dragons cooperate for the first time in memory, and now we see one ignore a force of one hundred men nearly within spitting distance."

Behind me, Hahr'ohld was clearly fixed on the dragon. His bear hug made it difficult to breathe. I rapped his knuckles to advise him that I needed to inhale. He finally understood and relaxed.

"Perhaps the dragon is dazed, confused by the blast from Hahr'ohld's probe device," I said.

"It is flying over the road," Talliver pointed out. "We will have to deal with it."

"There is no way around?"

"Are you afraid, Master Davian?" Talliver eyes hinted at amusement.

I shook my head. "It seems wiser to avoid a fight. We don't know how long this effect may last. If we fail to reach Arandor before he recovers, it matters little whether we kill this dragon."

Talliver frowned.

"And," I said, "If we are forced to activate Hahr'ohld's beacon, we may summon other dragons. We may kill the first one only to be killed in turn by the second, third, or fourth beast to arrive."

Talliver nodded. "There is another route over the hills. But it would take another full day of riding along the far side of the ridge." He pointed to the west. "It would bring us across on the far side of the valley we seek." Looking back at me, he asked, "How long until Arandor recovers his senses and we are set upon by a squadron of dragons?"

"I have no way to know."

Talliver looked down into the valley, considering with his dark eyes the scaly obstacle lazily flying above the ruins of his city.

"All right," he said at last. "Caedwulf, we will risk riding beneath the dragon."

Caedwulf's mouth tightened and his eyes narrowed, but he nodded agreement. There was little choice. We had to find Arandor as quickly as possible.

Turning to his men, Talliver issued the order. Their unease was plain, but no one questioned their captain, a testament to their faith in his judgment and ability.

Hahr'ohld suddenly realized what was happening, and he began to speak excitedly in his tongue. I turned to look, and his round face was contorted with fear.

Risking detection by Arandor seemed a worthwhile risk. If Hahr'ohld panicked, his communicating device might become useless to us. That distress beacon might be the difference between success and falling prey to Arandor's army of dragons.

As we began to move again, I removed the cap from my head. Silence.

No, not quite silence, but a roaring, hissing noise. No sound, and yet all sound. My mind submerged beneath the weight of sound, and I was unable to think, to see, to speak.

Through the torrent of sound-that-was-no-sound, I heard Hahr'ohld's voice: *"What are you trying to do?"*

"I wanted to talk to you."

"Fine. Let me try something."

At once the deluge of noise was sharply reduced. My senses returned, and I became aware that I was losing my balance in the saddle. I quickly righted myself.

Hahr'ohld had partially replaced my cap, and his fingers circled my scalp under the edges of the cap.

"I think we can talk this way without exposing you to the (word) from the ship."

"I hear you," I said. "Thank you."

"Davian," he said shakily, *"Please tell me why in the name of the Creator we're riding straight toward that dragon."*

"We are taking a chance that the dragon ahead is not aware of our presence," I said. "Based on what I just experienced, I would say that the dragon probably does not know where it is, much less where we are."

"Isn't there another way?" he asked. *"Do we have to go right under it?"*

"We have already considered that," I said. "It would take us at least a day out of our way. We do not have the time for such a detour."

Hahr'ohld sighed in resignation. *"Right,"* he said. *"Arandor might wake up."* After a moment's pause, he asked, *"What exactly happened to you?"*

"My mind was drowning in a flood of noise."

"Oh. Good." He withdrew his fingers and replaced my cap, and my mind was again cut off from the world outside.

The smoke from the fires still burning in Stelnregon grew thicker as we descended to the coastal plain. My eyes began to water, and the odor that reached us was burnt wood mixed with the stench of death and decay.

Scenes of horror beyond my imagining passed before us as we rode through the outskirts of Stelnregon. Houses burned to cinders; men and women crushed beneath collapsing beams; carcasses of horses, pigs, and cattle ripped and torn with a mindless, savage fury. The only sounds were the crackling of fires still burning themselves out and the buzzing of insects hovering over their gory feast. As we passed one particularly gruesome sight, I felt Hahr'ohld struggling to hold down his last meal. We held sleeves, kerchiefs, or any scrap of cloth we could find over our noses and mouths, and rode on in silence.

All the while, nervous eyes tracked the dragon as it marked its curious path across the sky. Eerie it was; the beast floated slowly through the air, back and forth over the breadth of the city. But so far, it showed no sign of being aware of our presence.

The archers, distributed through the column of riders, kept their bows at the ready. They were equipped with stone-tipped arrows, which were more effective against a dragon's scales. Their goal, however, would be to lodge an arrow in one of the small vulnerable spots on the beast, in the throat, the lower abdomen, inside its mouth, or its eyes. A well-placed shot could bring down a dragon, since the arrowheads were dipped in a powerful poison that induced paralysis within a few minutes.

However, it was a only very skilled or a very lucky archer that could hit a moving dragon in one of these areas. Even with twenty of the best in the district taking aim, success was no sure thing. And a dragon was sometimes most dangerous while it thrashed about as the poison took effect, flailing about and convulsing in violent, unpredictable ways.

"Davian." It was Talliver at the head of the column. I guided Champion alongside. "Do you have any sense of whether it knows we are here?"

"No," I said. "I do not believe it does."

"You believe, or you know?"

"That is my guess. I took off this cap to find out and I was rendered senseless. Hahr'old Orson kept me from falling off the horse. I think the dragon is experiencing the same thing."

Talliver nodded. "Let us hope it remains so."

* * *

After a time, even the most sensitive of men can become hardened to the carnage of battle. It was more difficult to remain unaffected by the horrors that confronted us, however, because the dead and mutilated had not been soldiers, but unwilling innocents slaughtered to satisfy the whim of a madman. There was so much death in Stelnregon that we were forced to withdraw into ourselves, ignoring the obscenities that stared lifelessly at the five score soldiers who rode silently by.

After a seemingly endless ride through the funeral pyre that was once a city, eyes constantly on the sky for any hint of change in the behavior of the dragon that glided through the smoke overhead, we reached the western edge of Stelnregon. We began a gentle climb as we joined the road to Beirgryn, the royal city of Aerwald.

Hahr'ohld, who had been swiveling his head to and fro since the dragon had first been spotted, suddenly jerked. He loosed his grip on me and began to frantically fumble with my cap. He placed his fingers again on both sides of my head, and his voice intruded into my mind: *"I think the dragon is coming."* He removed his hands, turned, and pointed behind us and to our right.

Just as I turned to look in the direction Hahr'ohld was pointing, some of the men at the tail of the column raised a shout. "Dragon! Dragon!"

True enough. The beast had somehow broken free of whatever held it in thrall, and it was now approaching rapidly. From directly over the heart of the city, the hill upon which stood the broken walls of Tyngstaal Castle, the dragon burst through a column of smoke at murderous speed. Though I could not sense its thoughts, they were plain enough. It meant to add us to the tens of thousands of corpses lying unburied among the ruins of Stelnregon.

CHAPTER TWENTY-THREE

"Defensive positions!" Talliver reacted immediately and his men leapt to respond. Unfortunately, the western edge of Stelnregon was hemmed by hills that ran down to the sea, and the road followed the only pass through that line of hills. It was not broad, and it was flanked by steep slopes on either side.

In short, we had been funneled into a space that allowed us to deploy no more than ten men side by side. The dragon might be able to roast half of us in a single pass.

The archers at the front of the column quickly dismounted, grabbed their bows, and began to run toward the dragon. Caedwulf's horsemen did their best to clear lanes for the archers, understanding that they would need to join together and fire coordinated volleys to have any hope of striking a sensitive target.

I cursed the device in Arandor's possession that gave him the power to render me useless. This fight should be mine. Alone, I could bring this dragon to ground as I have done with a score of others.

It was possible, I realized, that Arandor had recovered enough to direct the beast bearing down on us. That did not bode well. If this dragon occupied us long, there would soon be others, and we might be forced to run a gauntlet of the beasts before we reached their master. If we survived.

Our immediate concern, however, was now a half-mile off and closing fast. I dismounted and held out my hand to help Hahr'ohld dismount. However, he simply stared at the monster in the sky, frozen with fear. There was no time to waste; I grabbed his arm and pulled him from Champion's back.

The archers formed a ragged battle formation at the rear of our column and drew their bows, measuring the distance to the onrushing creature. Our horses, sensing the approach of the monstrous thing, began to panic, and a few bolted up the road. One unfortunate soldier was caught dismounting when his horse reared, and he was dragged away by the terrified beast, oblivious to the cries of his rider.

Standing Hahr'ohld upright, I pointed at his communicating device, and then at the beast. He gazed at me stupidly, trying to force thoughts through channels in his mind that had been barricaded by fear of the creature that was just moments from unleashing fiery doom.

Suddenly, he understood. Hahr'ohld twisted at the insignia on his chest and then slapped it. The dragon, now only a long bow shot from the archers, immediately soared straight upward, as though yanked heavenward by a chain pulled by the Creator himself.

A few of the archers, who had been timing their shots, released their arrows into the space the dragon would have occupied had it not suddenly changed course. Instead, their missiles sailed through empty air, one or two glancing harmlessly off the beast's armored underbelly.

The dragon continued upward, rising high into the air before leveling its flight and arcing back toward Stelnregon. It roared a challenge and began to circle well above us, perhaps a hundred or more man-heights over our heads.

"What happened?" Talliver yelled, running to us from the head of the column.

"Apparently," I said, "The noise from Hahr'ohld's communicator is enough to keep the dragon at bay."

"Why didn't the dragon outside the cave fly away when he used it?" Talliver asked.

"I don't know. Too close, perhaps. I will ask Hahr'ohld when I can, but I think the power of his device weakens with distance, and it can be blocked by certain substances, such as the rock in the caves and whatever this cap is made of."

Glancing skyward for a moment, Talliver asked, "Can he keep that thing going while we ride?"

"I think so."

"Good. Mount up."

Caedwulf had assisted several of his men in catching the horse that had run off dragging its rider. Thankfully, the horse had been caught only a short distance up the road. The young soldier, a fair-haired young man named Balmagoun, suffered a broken wrist in the fall, but considering the powerful horse from which he'd fallen, he was fortunate. His injuries could have been much worse.

We mounted our horses and resumed our trek westward along the Beirgryn road. As it was late in the afternoon, the sun would soon be directly in our eyes.

"Talliver," I said, riding up to join him and Caedwulf, "How long until we reach this valley?"

"Not much farther," he said. "Another hour."

The road wound through the hills, following the path of least resistance. The slope was not a steep one, but it slowed the horses who were weary from the distance already covered, as well as the stress of being much too close to the creature feared most by horse and man alike.

All the while, the dragon circled above us. Occasionally, it bellowed its frustration at the little device in Hahr'ohld's garment that kept it from approaching the feast spread out along the road below.

A shout from behind jolted the company to alertness again, but I could not see what prompted the call. Then, suddenly, a fleeting shadow was followed instantly by a crushing impact behind us. I whirled to see horses and men leaping in all directions, and a boulder as tall as a man bouncing and rolling through the column.

Screams; a spray of blood, impossibly red; more shouts; horses rearing in panic. Another cry: "Look out!"

There was a brief glimpse of another shadow low overhead, so close I felt a rush of wind as it passed. This boulder was not so well aimed, and it smashed into the wood alongside the road, snapping several middling trees as it fell.

I looked up. Where there had been one dragon, now there were five. "Dragons!" I shouted, without need. The beasts, unable to get close to us because of the device on Hahr'ohld's chest, were determined to crush us with boulders dropped from above—or, perhaps, smash the cursed noisemaker, and then feast at will.

Another rock the size of a cottage slammed into the rear of the column. More screams, from men and horses. I screamed in anger and frustration. There was no way to reach the dragons. They would be free to crush us at their leisure until Hahr'ohld was hit, and then they would descend on the survivors like ravens on the dead.

Talliver and Caedwulf came at full gallop. "We cannot stay here!" Caedwulf shouted. He continued on toward the injured.

"We cannot leave the wounded," I said to Talliver. "Without Hahr'ohld's device, they'll be slaughtered!"

"I know that!" Talliver shouted. "Give me an option!"

Another rock buried itself in the ground, missing the side of the road by less than a man-height. Only one dragon was in sight. The others must have gone in search of more boulders.

The ugly truth was that the injured men were probably dead already. We had no time to treat them, and we could not slow our pace to bring them along. Leaving them at the mercy of the pitiless monsters was unthinkable, but there was little choice. We had to reach Arandor to sever his link with the dragons or all was lost.

Another shadow passed over us, a dragon flying between us and the setting sun, preparing to loose another chunk of granite. Hahr'ohld tracked the beast with his eyes, tensing to leap if it appeared a boulder was aimed too close.

"Well?" Talliver loomed large in my sight, demanding, pleading for an alternative. I had none to offer. I shook my head. Nothing would have compelled me to trade places with Talliver, to make the decision he faced at that moment.

Without warning, one of the archers wearing the red and white garb of the King's Guard rode up at full gallop. "I will draw them away!" he shouted, and then he was past.

"No!" I cried, but I was too late. The uniform of the rider fit badly. It was much too broad across the shoulders and chest, and not nearly as long as it should have been. The unruly dark hair blowing wildly in the wind was a sight I had seen often in recent weeks. And there was no mistaking the powerful white horse on which he rode.

Disappearing over the hill was Brother Galthorn, and he rode the horse that we thought had been lost, Aeryx.

Talliver turned to me in disbelief. "Was that—"

"The priest, yes," I said.

"We must follow!" Turning to his men, he shouted, "Back on your mounts! We ride!" I turned away to find Champion.

"Aiee!" It was Hahr'ohld, behind me. I whirled and a silver-gray blur flew past, tumbling and rolling along the road. With a shudder, a boulder as long as a horse embedded itself into the tracked dirt surface of the road exactly where Hahr'ohld had been standing a moment before.

Talliver leapt to his horse, his decision made. "Come! There is no time to lose!"

The faces looking back at Talliver registered shock and dismay as they realized what his command meant for those who had not been able to avoid the falling rock. Caedwulf's powerful voice echoed Talliver's command from the back of the column, urging his men to obey his fellow captain.

More shadows in front of the sun. The dragons were eight now. It was impossible to see whether any had followed Galthorn. I began to despair of even reaching the top of this hill and crossing the ridge, much less finding the man who'd sent the monsters to destroy us.

Another rock that might have served as the base of a monumental statue struck nearby, thankfully off target, crashing through the trees along the roadside.

Screams still filled the air, punctuating the metallic scent of blood that was impossible to escape. From the corner of my eye, I saw Caedwulf draw his sword and mercifully dispatch a horse that had been critically injured.

Hahr'ohld was lying on the road, curled in on himself. I reached down and pulled him to his feet. His face was ashen, nearly the color of his garment. Half pulling, half dragging, I maneuvered

Orson to our horse, threw him across Champion's back and vaulted up after him. I looked about until I found Talliver, standing in the stirrups and calling for us to follow.

I gave Champion the command to move, and then quickly pulled the reins hard to the right as yet another boulder crashed into the road directly in front of us, bouncing away into the trees. Looking up, I saw three of the beasts, but I could not see whether they carried anything. Giving Champion my heels again, we quickly drew alongside Talliver. Perhaps four score followed; twenty lay shattered and bleeding on the road, crying for us to stay or for release from their suffering.

Above, a dragon bellowed in triumph, perceiving that we were confused and divided. A shadow rose before us, yet another dragon backlit by the disk of the sun.

And then something changed. Another bellow echoed from above, but it was one of rage or challenge. It was answered by one in kind. At least eighty pairs of eyes turned to the sky.

Two of the beasts above us now circled a third, larger dragon, which hovered in place, bellowing and swinging its great head to face first one and then the other. A fourth dragon flew off at speed, heading out to sea. The others had seemingly vanished, nowhere to be seen. I fervently hoped they had not given chase to the foolish priest.

As we watched the scene in the sky above, it became clear that the dragons had again lost interest in us, but this time for a different reason. They now engaged one another in a struggle to the death, for there is only one thing a dragon will tolerate less than the presence of a Master, and that is another dragon.

I knew not how or why, but Arandor was no longer master of the dragons.

The two smaller beasts began to harry the third, always keeping it between them to prevent it from defending itself against both snapping, slashing antagonists at once. The middle dragon, the oldest and largest of the three, realized its untenable position and decided to flee. Without warning, it swiftly folded its wings and dove to gain speed to escape. The path of its flight carried it directly over our heads, barely above the tops of the trees lining the road. We huddled against our horses, who shivered and whinnied with fright, but the dragon had other concerns.

Its attackers screamed with rage and followed close behind, determined not to allow their victim to slip away. In an instant, all three disappeared to the north, blocked from view by the wooded hillside that flanked the road. The crash of snapping trees reached our ears, and the muffled cries of the monsters echoed in the distance as the dragons continued their struggle out of our sight.

Talliver, his eyes fixed in the direction of the battling dragons, shouted, "Davian, what is this?" His meaning was clear: *Are we safe?*

I thought for a moment. The dragons had returned to normal behavior, so Arandor's device no longer functioned. Perhaps, I might finally be of some use on this quest. I reached up and removed my cap.

Stupid. I had forgotten Hahr'ohld's distress signal.

For a moment, my head felt as though it had exploded. The scream in my mind threatened to shatter every bone in my skull. Mercifully, Hahr'ohld was quick to silence the shriek.

It throbbed, but I felt nothing else inside my head. My thoughts were my own. Whatever power Arandor had was broken, at least for the moment.

"Hahr'ohld," I said, "Can you hear me?"

"Yes."

"Get down and stay here with the wounded. Get them off the road and into the trees if you can. Use your device if the dragons return to keep them away from the men. But please wait until we are out of sight."

"Understood." Hahr'ohld clumsily maneuvered himself down from Champion. *"Actually, we should be able to stay in contact for awhile. I can give you warning before I activate the signal."*

I nodded. A roar echoed along the road from the battle taking place on the far side of the hills. Out of sight, yes, but still too close. "Perhaps the battling dragons will deter others."

"What now?" Talliver asked.

"Something has happened," I said. "Chance, fate, luck, or divine intervention, whatever you choose to call it. Arandor's power over the dragons is broken. We need to ride now. I can protect us from the beasts, and Hahr'ohld can keep them away from the wounded."

Talliver and Caedwulf needed only a glance and a nod to reach agreement. Caedwulf quickly detailed twenty men, including five of Talliver's archers, to stay with the wounded. Too few, but hopefully to keep the monsters at bay with the help of Hahr'ohld's strange device. Janver, Caedwulf's lieutenant, saluted and began to direct the removal of the injured and dead from the road. Hahr'ohld accompanied Janver, eyes on the sky in case a dragon should return.

We took off at a gallop toward the top of the hill. The road leveled and curled gently to the left past the summit. Talliver and I led the three score of King's Guards who followed. I was relieved to be free of the shielding provided by the cap, but apprehensive as well. I kept it close at hand, ready to slap it back into place at the first hint of Arandor's return.

The presence of so many dragons in the area was another reason for my unease. My sense was that all of the beasts nearby were occupied with one another, but that could change if one were to emerge victorious.

Sounds of trees crashing and deafening, deep-throated roars from the road ahead caused Talliver to instantly signal a halt. He looked to me. I sensed two more of the beasts ahead, and signaled as such. Talliver ordered the Guards off the road and into the cover of the trees, and then motioned for me to join him in scouting ahead.

The thunderous battle before us shook the ground as if the dragons meant to split open Saramond itself. Talliver and I approached on foot, not wishing to risk the horses—or injury, if the horses panicked.

We jogged toward a gentle rise, when the sky before us erupted in flame. The blast was answered by a roar of challenge that set my ears to ringing. Trees crashed and fell, and two fully-grown dragons, locked tooth and claw, rolled out of the trees to our right and directly into our path. Their minds were nearly deafening inside my head, unintelligible, and white-hot with rage.

Talliver jumped for the trees on the opposite side of the road. Knowing the dragons would sense my presence no matter where I ran, I stood my ground and watched, gathering my strength from the powerful waves of energy surging around me. It felt good to be free of the shackles of that cap, and I breathed deeply to calm myself for the confrontation to come.

One of the dragons was seriously wounded. Blood flowed freely from a gaping wound at its throat, and I knew enough about the beasts to recognize the wound as fatal. It had minutes to live before the loss of blood claimed its life, but while it breathed, it used every last ounce of energy in an attempt to dispatch its enemy.

All the better for us.

The dominant dragon emerged atop the other squarely in the middle of the road, not five man-heights from where I stood. Crazed with blood lust and furious that its dying opponent refused to surrender, the stronger beast swiped at its foe's eyes with a foreclaw, and then reared back and loosed a blast of fire at the dying dragon's head.

The wounded beast managed to squirm away, eyes tightly closed against the flame, and using its tail for leverage it succeeded in throwing its enemy aside—and right at me.

Marshaling my strength, I directed a bolt of energy at the approaching dragon's midsection. My goal was not to harm it, but to keep from being crushed by its bulk. With a resounding explosion, the beast's skidding roll came to a sudden stop, as though it had hit a wall.

A wise man once said, "There is no time like the present." That proverb was never truer for me than at that particular moment.

Stunned, the dragon jerked its head to see what had inflicted the blow. Its eyes widened when they found me, the very last thing it expected to see; the very last thing it would ever see.

I did not waste time by introducing myself. Before it could react, I hit the beast with every ounce of strength I could muster right between its eyes.

The effect of an intense, tightly focused burst of heat energy on a pair of eyes is not pleasant, and I will not disturb you with a description of it here. Given a dragon's heavy armor, however, its eyes are its most vulnerable point—a direct and lethal pathway into its brain.

A clear shot at a dragon's eyes are not easily gained. They sense changes in the energy around them just as I do, and they will shield their vulnerable eyes by closing their thick, armored lids. Fortunately, this dragon was too surprised to react quickly enough to save itself.

The dragon shuddered and was dead in a moment. Wisps of sickly gray smoke curled from the empty sockets where its eyes had been.

A bellow of rage erupted from the wounded dragon. A cold, dry voice entered my mind: *You have cheated me, and so you shall die!*

The dragon's words were defiant, but it was already near death. Great arcs of steaming red marked the ground of its final battle as its lifeblood streamed from its neck. The injured beast struggled to its feet, but before it was able to tense the muscles of its hind legs, it collapsed. The dragon curled to one side, and the hideous gray-green lizard fell forward, across the corpse of its slain foe.

The world was silent. Even the distant sounds of the battle between the three dragons had ceased. I waited patiently until I was sure that both of the great beasts were dead, and to be sure that another had not been attracted by the sounds of the struggle.

Nothing.

Satisfied, I called to Talliver, "They are dead."

He emerged from the trees, picking his way through the undergrowth that clutched at his boots. "So quickly?"

"One was mortally wounded. I did nothing to help it along," I said. "The other was exhausted and distracted. It didn't know I was here until too late. My battles are rarely so quick."

Talliver nodded. "Thank the Creator. We need to press on."

In my mind, a familiar click was followed by the voice of Hahr'ohld: *"Davian? Are you all right?"*

"I am fine, Hahr'ohld," I said. "The dragons are dead." Talliver raised his eyebrows in surprise. He had not realized that

Hahr'ohld's communicating device worked even when he was out of sight.

"I heard it, Davian, I heard it just like you do! On my communicator! How can you stand it? That thing was so…"

"Hahr'ohld, quiet!" There was a noise, outside my head. Talliver heard it, too.

"Hey! Hey, I say! Over here!"

"Someone is here, hurt," I said to Hahr'ohld. "Be quiet until I call you."

The voice was weak, but steady. It came from the roadside, just beyond the point where the dragons had crashed out of the trees and into the road.

Without a word, Talliver and I ran toward the voice. Leading the way, I vaulted the tail of the dragon I had killed. Talliver followed close by.

"Hey! Please, help!"

Not fifty paces beyond the hulking corpses lie a man on the side of the road, wounded, blood soiling a broad crimson swath across the white jerkin of the King's Guard. A bow lay broken nearby. It was one of Talliver's Guardsmen—or so I thought at first.

And then I remembered that only one man wearing the uniform of the Guard had advanced this far along the Beirgryn road.

"Brother Galthorn," I cried, rushing to his side. He lay at an awkward angle just off the side of the road. The priest's thin face was pale and he was clearly in great pain. I knelt and took his hand.

"Brother Galthorn," I said again, my voice catching in my throat. "You—you brave-hearted fool."

CHAPTER TWENTY-FOUR

"What's going on? What's happening?"

"Quiet, Hahr'ohld," I said. "It's Brother Galthorn. He's hurt." The priest was pale, sweating, and his breathing was labored. His shirt was torn across his right side, where it was stained deep red with his blood.

"Is he all right?"

"Be quiet, Hahr'ohld!"

"We must remove his shirt," Talliver said, producing a knife with a blade as long as my hand. "Here, step back. How did you come by this, brother?" I moved out of the way, and the captain began to cut open Brother Galthorn's shirt where it was ripped.

"Please do not be angry with the man who lent it to me," the priest said. "He was hurt and in no condition to travel."

Talliver tore open the fabric, revealing an ugly gash that bled from Brother Galthorn's sternum to his armpit. If the wound healed, Galthorn would have a spectacular memento of his foolhardy adventure.

"And you made a bargain with him for his uniform?" Talliver said, continuing to remove the ruined shirt.

"Not exactly," Galthorn said, weakly. "He was unconscious. But I intend to return it—ow!"

Talliver used the wadded fabric of the Guard's uniform to slow the bleeding along Brother Galthorn's ribs. "Does that hurt, brother?"

"Yes," Galthorn said through clenched teeth. "Did I draw—are the dragons gone?"

I am ashamed to confess that I began to answer Brother Galthorn truthfully. *No, brother,* I nearly said, *the dragons were released from their thrall and fell in to fighting one another. It was a good thought, but your wounds were for nothing.* It would have been unkind, and perhaps worse. At that moment, we did not know whether the young priest would survive his wounds or no.

It is well that Captain Talliver spoke first.

"Yes, brother, you drew the dragons away from the wounded men," he said gently. "You gave us time to move them to cover. That was the most valiant and courageous act I have ever seen."

The captain spoke truly. I was grateful that he saved me from a thoughtless act toward a young man who had been selfless to a fault since the day he arrived at my home to request my help. The gift of words that inspire and encourage others is rare, and I envy those who possess it.

Closing his eyes, Galthorn said, "I had ridden only this far when a dragon came from nowhere and knocked me off—where is Aeryx? Ow!" Brother Galthorn tried to sit, but was forced to abandon the attempt. No doctor am I, but clearly something in the young man's lean frame was broken.

"We have not seen him," Talliver said. "But the dragons were so soon occupied with one another that there is a good chance he escaped."

I knelt again and asked, "Why did you do it?"

"What do you mean?"

"Why did you borrow the uniform and ride with us?"

Through his pain, a smile creased the young man's thin face. "I thought you needed help."

I shook my head. "You, brother, are a very unusual priest."

"Not at all," he said. "Whatever happened, I was in the Creator's hands."

Hooves pounding up the road drew our attention from the wounded young man. Emerging from behind the fallen dragons was Caedwulf and his lieutenant, Janver.

"We heard an explosion," he said. "Are you—who is hurt?"

"The priest," Talliver said. "It was he who rode off alone."

"The priest?" Dismounting, his eyes full of disbelief, Caedwulf approached and knelt next to Galthorn, considering the wound which Talliver still tended. "Does it hurt?"

Smiling ruefully, Galthorn nodded. "The dragon knocked me from the saddle with its tail." He grimaced as Talliver dabbed again at the wound. "I think my ribs are broken."

Caedwulf glanced at Talliver, who nodded. Turning to his lieutenant, he said, "Janver, get back to the men. Rig a field litter and carry Galthorn back to the others. Bring a half-dozen of the archers when you return." Janver saluted and rode off.

"Brother Galthorn," Caedwulf said, "That was the bravest thing I have ever seen. Also the stupidest. If you truly wore that uniform, I would have you scrubbing stables for months. After presenting you with the Silver Sword."

"The stable at the monastery where I trained is the cleanest in Aerwald," Galthorn said. "The abbot blessed me with a great deal of experience."

* * *

Janver returned soon with help, though I am sure it felt like an eternity to Brother Galthorn. He was truly fortunate if broken ribs were his only injury. A dragon can crush a man with its tail with very little effort.

As Talliver and Caedwulf conferred, one of the Guards bandaged Galthorn's wound with a clean dressing. I stood, stretched my legs, and looked to the west. There was nothing nearby that troubled me, but I wondered how much time we had before Arandor regained control over the dragons.

"Davian," Talliver said. "We must be away."

"I agree," I said. "This may only be a reprieve. Arandor may be dead, but we cannot know until we find him."

After a brief farewell to Brother Galthorn, we mounted our horses, and, with half a dozen of his archers, Talliver and I started westward down the Beirgryn road. Caedwulf would ride back to the rest of the column and follow as quickly as he was able.

The sun was low now in the western sky, making it difficult at times to see a great distance ahead. "How much farther, Talliver?"

"The valley is just ahead, past the bend," he said.

I squinted, seeing nothing but the glare of the setting sun. But I sensed something, a low crackle rising above the background noise in my mind. It was people—a great many. They were agitated, and coming closer.

"Talliver," I said. "I hear them."

"Who?"

"Your people, I think. They are coming."

He did not hesitate, but immediately gave his horse the word and he was off at a gallop. I followed with the archers close behind.

It was only a few moments until we made the bend Talliver had spoken of. The sun cast long shadows along the road, and the woods to either side grew dark a short distance into the trees. To our right, a break in the trees marked what must have been the trail that led down into the valley we sought.

A moment later, that was confirmed as someone burst from the shadows, stopping at the road to turn and exhort someone following to hurry. Backlit by the sun, it was impossible to see anything but a silhouette, but clearly Talliver was taken aback.

"Quickly! Move!" It was a woman's voice.

Others came scrambling out onto the road—men, women, children, some carried by adults. Their fear rolled before them like a great wave, washing across me like an ice-cold breaker crashing onto the shore at Stelnregon.

All of them were bedraggled and dirty, their clothing torn. And they were deathly afraid of whoever, or whatever, they fled.

"Hold!" Talliver's voice was commanding, and it stopped those who had reached the road in their tracks. Standing in the stirrups, he said, "We seek one called Arandor. Where is he?"

The leader, the female, turned and addressed Talliver with a strong, full voice. "Who are you?" There was no fear in her. Strangely, I sensed in her a growing anger.

Frowning, Talliver said, "I am Talliver, captain of the King's Guard in Stelnregon."

Against the setting sun, I saw only the silhouette of a person with hands on hips, defiant. She fairly shouted, "A fine job you've done protecting these people! Where were you when they were being fed to the dragons a score at a time?"

Talliver was livid. "Watch your tongue, woman! We have lost many good men in recent days, men who died valiantly in battles they could not win. Now, quickly: Where is Arandor?"

"I left him in the valley below," the woman said. "He may be dead. I did not wait to find out. These people need to get away, now. There may still be dragons about."

"Not at the moment," I said.

"And how would you know?" the woman demanded, whirling to face me.

"I am Davian, a third-level Master of The Order."

She said nothing, but simply stared at me for a long moment. Finally she said, "How is your nose?"

Squinting, I looked closer. And then my jaw dropped.

It was Lareina, the daughter of the headman in Marthwee. Her long, dark hair was tied at the back of her neck and she wore the clothes of a woodsman, but her flashing eyes and full lips were unmistakable.

"What are you doing here?" I asked.

"Saving these people from one of your brothers."

I clenched my teeth. There was no time to argue.

"Mykhos, lead the lady and these people to Caedwulf," Talliver said to one of the archers. "Ask Caedwulf to escort them to Tyngstaal Castle. Get a team to work opening the tunnels and recovering the stores below. See about opening the tunnels to the caves. There should be food enough and some shelter, at least, if the dragons return. We will return to you there. The rest of you, let's go."

"I am coming with you," Lareina said, as she walked toward where I sat on Champion.

"No," I said.

"Do not argue," she said, vaulting up onto Champion's back behind me. "I know where Arandor is. Go."

Such disrespect to a Master is uncommon. Even Talliver, with far superior knowledge of military tactics, had been courteous enough to ask my opinion as we hastily planned this operation. But this woman brooked no disagreement once she had made a decision, even from a Master of The Order.

It was maddening.

Nevertheless, time was of the essence, and we had lost too much of it to the dragons we encountered on the road. To Talliver's questioning glance, I simply nodded.

Talliver stood in the saddle again and addressed the growing crowd of frightened refugees. "People! Please, move to one side. Follow this man. He will guide you to safety. Go, now, quickly!"

As the throng moved to obey, Talliver led the way down the path, urging his mount to as much speed as he dared. There were dozens, scores, hundreds of frightened, hungry, hollow-eyed people scrambling along the trail, moving as quickly as they were able to escape whatever horror was in the valley. I followed, with five of Talliver's archers, and Lareina on Champion behind me.

"I ask again, what are you doing here?" I said over my shoulder.

"There was nothing left for me in Marthwee," Lareina said. "So, I followed you. I thought perhaps I would see you die."

"I am sorry to disappoint you."

"The day is not over."

We rode in silence for several minutes as the trail that descended into a narrow ravine. We moved more quickly now that we were past the flood of survivors escaping Arandor's outdoor prison, the larder for his stable of monstrous servants. The only entrance to the valley, according to Talliver, was this path, and the sides of the ravine flanking the valley were so steep that blocking this exit made escape from the valley nearly impossible.

"How did you follow us?" I asked Lareina.

"You arrogant swine," she said. "All I had to do was follow the trail of burned and ruined buildings. It will be some time before you are welcome again in Darnaatha. And Naribor no longer exists, but no doubt that was not your doing. Is it because I am a woman that you assume tracking you would be difficult?"

"That is not what I meant," I said.

"Oh, of course."

"Cursed woman, I—"

"You see? It *is* because I am a woman."

Fuming, I followed Talliver in the growing darkness in silence. When I spoke, I resolved to turn the conversation to something that might prove useful. "How did you find Arandor?"

"I followed the survivors from Stelnregon as his dragons herded them here."

"And the dragons took no notice of you?"

"I am here, am I not?"

"How does Arandor control the dragons?"

"He carried a device like a small black box with a stick on the top," Lareina said. "Arandor put his hand on it and the dragons would do what he asked."

"He spoke to the dragons?"

"Not aloud. He told his captives that he controlled the dragons. I believe him."

"Hahr'ohld? Can you hear me?"

"Who is Hahr'ohld?" Lareina asked.

"Hush," I said. Lareina snorted. In the recesses of my mind, I heard Hahr'ohld's voice very faintly, as if calling from a great distance.

"Davian? Are you there?" His voice was barely audible.

"Hahr'ohld, do you know of a device that looks like a black box with a stick on the top? Something Arandor might use to amplify his abilities?"

"...trouble hearing...but I think...asking." His voice grew more faint as we descended further into the valley. *"Probably... communicating device...power...distances."*

The words "communicating device" confirmed my suspicion. Arandor had come into possession of a larger, more powerful version of the thing attached to Hahr'ohld's uniform.

To Lareina, I asked, "Where was Arandor when you saw him last?"

Before she could answer, a shock wave of sound exploded inside my head. I reeled with the impact, and I barely felt Lareina pull me upright again. My mind was being ripped from my body, removed from control and forced into a quarantined space from which there was no exit.

Struggle was to no avail. My senses were overwhelmed by the noise, which, as before, was a blend of no sound and all sound at once. My self-awareness was a leaf spinning and bobbing on a raging torrent, struggling to stay afloat, swept away by a flood that roared through my consciousness.

And then suddenly it stopped.

I found myself lying on my back. With effort, I opened my eyes and looked up into the dark, searching face of Talliver. Our horses snorted and fidgeted nearby, disquieted.

Talliver took hold of my arms and pulled me to my feet. "I am sorry, but I assume this means Arandor is still alive and we have very little time," he said. "I replaced the cap on your head. Are you well enough to move?"

My head throbbed, but at least my thoughts were again my own. I nodded.

Standing behind Talliver, Lareina said, "This way." She turned and started down the path on foot.

The archers looked to Talliver for direction. He shook his head in frustration and said, "Dismount and follow."

"Talliver," I said, trying to clear my head as we walked.

"What is it?" Talliver asked.

"Your archers have stone-tipped arrows?"

"Of course."

"When we find Arandor, position them in an arc around him," I said. "He will not be able to strike at all of them at once. Perhaps one of them will draw a killing shot."

"You have found me," a loud voice said from a small clearing ahead. "Shall we have some light?" Suddenly, a ball of flame leapt into being about three man-heights above us with a loud report. A ball of white flame illuminated the clearing and the path with a light that was somehow devoid of cheer.

Startled by the noise, our horses behind us whinnied in fright. Talliver turned to his men and hissed, "Spread out! Half circle around the clearing, now!"

As the archers hurried to obey, a tall, thin man appeared in the center of the field of light. "Greetings," he said. "I am Arandor. I trust you are ready to die."

CHAPTER TWENTY-FIVE

Blinking while my eyes adjusted to the sudden blaze of light, I gazed into the clearing. My eyes found a thin, sharp-nosed man with eyes that glittered with barely concealed madness. Like me, his head was shaved, but he had chosen to adorn himself with a garment that was self-aggrandizing, to say the least.

A long robe of purple wore Arandor, trimmed in red and white. Jeweled rings on several fingers reflected the light from above. As Talliver and I approached, he regarded us coolly, with a trace of a smile upon his lips. In his left hand was the small, black box that Lareina had described. He was more than confident; he was arrogant. He appeared to believe that he would be the only one to survive this encounter.

Surprisingly, although she had led us to this place, Lareina was nowhere to be seen. Talliver and I looked at one another briefly, each of us deciding that her whereabouts were better unknown for the moment. If the dragons had taken no notice of her, then perhaps Arandor did not know she was here.

"You must be Davian," Arandor said to me. "Clever of you to have found a way to shield yourself. You look ridiculous."

"My compliments to your tailor," I said.

"Thank you." He turned to Talliver. "And you must be the captain of the local garrison. How pathetic. Perhaps, I will allow you to live so that you may explain to King Ednorwain the futility of resistance when we arrive in Beirgryn."

"Never," growled Talliver.

Arandor looked past us into the darkness. In a raised voice, he said, "I know your men are out there. Tell them to lower their weapons or I will cook their captain from the inside out!" I noted that he did not mention Lareina. Was she truly hidden from his senses?

"Do not listen—augh!" Suddenly, Talliver doubled over in pain, collapsing to his knees. I knelt and took hold of Talliver's shoulders to steady him. Heat radiated from his body as though he were a walking furnace. I cursed under my breath. With the cap on my head, I could do nothing.

"You see I have the power," Arandor said. "Lower your weapons!"

Sounds of movement from the darkness indicated that Talliver's men obeyed to save their captain.

To my left, there was the unmistakable twang of a bowstring being released. A soft whistle in the air was cut short by a flash of light as the arrow burst into flame in mid-flight. Its path was changed just enough to miss Arandor's torso. The fiend stared along the direction of the arrow's flight, and the night was instantly rent by a scream of such intense agony that I was chilled to the marrow.

A moment later, there was a muffled *pop* in the darkness, and the scream was silenced.

Seeing Arandor's handiwork in the ruins of Stelnregon was to walk through a living nightmare. Standing by helplessly as he murdered a man in that way was even worse.

"The rest of you, step into the light where I can see you," Arandor called. "Come, now, don't be shy." Slowly, the four remaining archers, bows empty, stepped into the pool of light.

"Do be so kind as to set your bows on the ground in front of you," Arandor said. The archers slowly obeyed.

"You are sick," I said to Arandor. "How can you…"

"Oh, do shut up." Arandor turned to face me. "Let me ask you something, brother," he said, emphasizing the word as a taunt. "How can you willingly place yourself in servitude to inferior beings when you have it within you to be a king? A god?"

"Like you?" My face twisted in distaste.

"Yes! And why not? What have these creatures done for you? Tear you from your home, send you away, isolate you, fear you, avoid you—yes, until they're threatened by a dragon. And then they cry for you, demand that you save them and their meaningless lives, and curse you that you didn't arrive sooner!" Arandor's face was animated with a loathing more repugnant than any dragon I have encountered.

"What do gain, Arandor, by declaring yourself a god?" The madman took two steps toward where I knelt with Talliver, whose overheated body was now slick with sweat. His eyes were closed and he shook. I could not tell whether he was still conscious.

"I gain the world," Arandor hissed, leaning toward us. "No one dares oppose me—no man and no Master. I will destroy The Order if it tries, and with the device from the outsiders to command the dragons, there is no army on Saramond that can muster the force to stop me."

"You are mad," I said.

"The learned elders of The Order said so," he replied. "They tried to imprison me when I would not conform to their rules. Why do we have this power if not to *use* it? But they were wrong. You are wrong! I could not be more sane. It is you who are deluded!" His eyes gleamed with. If I had believed in such things, I would have said they glowed with the light of an inner demon. "You will never be accepted by these lessers. You are different, better—but in their eyes, a freak, a monster. You will never be one of them. Never!"

Arandor suddenly covered the distance between us and knelt to look directly into my eyes. "Join me," he said, his eyes gleaming. "Join me, and we will rule the world."

Talliver groaned and sagged. "Stop what you are doing to him," I said. "He's dying, you filth."

The madman stood and sighed. "Ah, well. I tried. You shall die as well," Arandor said. "You killed more of my pets than I expected, but not all of them. And there are others on Saramond. I will recruit them as I need them, and we shall sweep across Saramond like a flood." He turned and looked at me. "And one of them will join us momentarily."

I leapt at him. "You bastard!"

A hammer blow knocked me aside, as though I were a fly brushed aside by the hand of a giant. Stunned, I lay helpless on the ground, trying to catch my breath. I heard movement, and Arandor shouted, "Stay back!" Talliver's men stayed, frozen with fear. The thought of a dragon arriving to do Arandor's bidding was terrifying, but so was whatever Arandor had done to the brave man who had dared to let fly an arrow.

The rogue Master bent over me, looking into my eyes for a long moment. "You sad, misguided fool. You won't need this any more. " He reached down and pulled the cap from my head.

Once again, my mind was overwhelmed by a torrent of sound that drowned my thoughts and my will beneath an ocean of agony.

And just as suddenly, all was silent again.

I opened my eyes and found that it was suddenly dark. Sensing someone at my side, I quickly rolled to find Arandor on the ground close by, dazed and senseless, his eyes unfocused. Standing over him was Lareina, holding a branch the length and thickness of my arm.

"Well?" she said. "Get up!"

I did, and a blast of heat washed over me from behind. Turning, I found that Arandor's pet had arrived. A great, gray-black dragon had landed in the clearing and was now advancing on us with hunger in its eyes. My head was still spinning, but there was no time to collect my strength. I mustered what power I could and sent a pulse of energy at the beast's snout. It drew back, absorbed the blow, shook its head, and continued lumbering toward us with a murderous roar.

Behind me the archers scrambled to nock arrows. Lareina moved quickly to assist Talliver, who was in harm's way. As she pulled Talliver from the dragon's path, the beast brought forth another burst of flame, aimed directly at my head. I gathered the energy, collected it, and drew strength from it. Clearing my mind, I redirected the monster's flame against it in an intense, tightly focused beam. It struck the beast squarely in the center of its forehead with a resounding crack.

The dragon closed it eyes against the blast, recoiling and rolling backward. The archers struggled to find a target as the winged serpent regained its feet with a defiant roar. I focused my mind and formed a ball of intense light, which I launched at the dragon's eyes, hoping to dazzle and perhaps blind it temporarily. As I did, I realized that I might also blind the archers.

Too late. It was done. I am accustomed to fighting alone.

The dragon was caught unawares by the burst of white-hot flame that exploded close in front of its eyes just as it recovered its feet. It shook its head, blinking rapidly as it tried to clear its vision.

Tricks! You fight with tricksss! I heard in my mind. The creature swiped at its eyes with a foreclaw, struggling to regain its sight before it was too late.

"I fight with the weapons I am given," I said, moving quickly to my right in case the dragon attempted a blind charge.

Instead, the dragon decided that flying blind was better than fighting a Master it could not see, and its wings unfurled as it attempted to take to the air. A bowstring strummed. One of the archers found a target and let fly. The dragon jerked, and the arrow bounced harmlessly off its knobby, armored head.

Gathering my strength once again, I directed a burst of intense heat at the dragon's left wing, hoping to shred its leathery skin and force the dragon to fight on the ground. The burst impacted just as the dragon began its first downstroke.

The dragon screamed with rage and pain as its wing exploded in flame. It fell to one side, the damaged wing beneath it. There was a sickening crack as the dragon's bulk crushed its wing as it fell and rolled. The beast roared again, and I sensed it was no longer thinking rationally, but was consumed with pain, hatred, and mind-numbing rage.

"Light! Give them light!" It was Lareina, calling from behind me. Having pulled Talliver to relative safety behind several large trees, she apparently felt free to offer advice on how to fight a dragon.

It was not a convenient time to discuss tactics with Lareina. Besides, she was right; the archers could not hit what they could not see. I projected a ball of light into the air high above the clearing, illuminating an area at least a score of man-heights in all directions. That was enough for the archers to draw a fix on the dragons head, and the four bowmen set to work peppering the beast with their arrows.

Thus distracted, the dragon was unable to mount a direct charge. Instead, it was forced to dodge the annoying missiles that, to the archers credit, came near enough to hitting its eyes to hold the beast's attention. In response, the great lizard tried to burn the brave soldiers where they stood, but I again redirected the dragon's blast back into its own face.

With a wing shattered, the dragon was as good as dead. The beasts are powerful, but they are slow and cumbersome on the ground. It is difficult for a dragon to feed when it cannot swoop from the sky onto unsuspecting prey. They are still difficult to kill, but over time, a team of archers with stone-tipped, poisoned arrows can bring down and kill even the largest dragon.

That assumes, of course, that Hahr'ohld Orson's theory about dragon flight is incorrect. If dragons truly fly because they control a power similar to the Gift, well, then, The Order has much research to do—but there was no time to ponder such things just then. I was focused on surviving beyond the next few moments.

With Talliver down and one of his men dead, we had only four archers and a limited number of arrows. I could not allow the battle to drag on. I waited until the dragon was nearly mad with the frustration of dodging the arrows fired by the archers, who surely proved their valor against the malevolent beast.

The dragon had all but forgotten me. I directed my thoughts at it and screamed a high-pitched battle cry, one that has been used by the warriors of Aerwald for centuries when riding into battle. It swung its great head around and stumbled toward me, bellowing a response to my challenge.

Again I marshaled my strength and focused a pulse of intense heat on the dragon's face. As I had hoped, frustration and pain made the beast careless, and this time its eyes were open and exposed. With a powerful crack, the dragon's head was enveloped in a brilliant light, and then, its brain burned to cinders, the monster fell forward, collapsing dead at my feet.

All was silent for a moment while the dragon twitched once, twice, thrice, and then lay still.

The archers erupted in cheers, celebrating a great victory, and no doubt relieved that they had just survived a close encounter with the most dangerous beast on Saramond. I closed my eyes and leaned forward with my hands on my knees, breathing heavily. The energy I expend during a battle is great, and I often do not realize how great until afterward. I felt as though I had just finished running a great distance, and I needed to sleep.

As I stood, I felt a disturbance in the energy around me. Reacting rather than thinking, I threw up a shield in the direction from which the disturbance came, and just in time. A powerful bolt of yellow-blue light split the darkness, intensely hot. I was driven from my feet. The spot of ground where I had been standing was in flames, the turf and organic litter ignited by the bolt intended for me.

Arandor had regained his senses and was swiftly walking towards me. The archers, stunned, began to reach again for their bows. Arandor waved his hand and the four soldiers were thrown backward by a violent explosion, a superheating of the air in front of them.

I struggled to regain my senses. Arandor bent and picked something off the ground—the communicator box. He touched it, and again my head was filled with sound from outside. And then, just like that, my thoughts were Arandor's.

Enough, I heard in my mind, crushingly loud. It was as if the Creator Himself had manifested within the confines of my skull. *You have delayed my conquest long enough. You are done. I will not make the mistake this woman has made twice now by allowing me to live when I was within her power.* As he approached, carrying the communicating box in one hand, Arandor withdrew a knife with a long, curved blade from his robe. *Do you know what I always say, Davian? Kill a Master when you have the chance, because you will surely never have another. Too bad that female dog of yours doesn't live by that rule or you might have seen another sunrise.* Holding the wicked instrument high in the air, Arandor looked down into my face with spiteful grin. "Farewell, Davian."

I tried to move but I was paralyzed, as helpless as an insect in a spider's web. Arandor drew back the knife, the blade gleaming as it reflected the light of—of what? The sun had set, the moons had not risen, and the light I generated for the archers had been snuffed when Arandor attacked.

Suddenly, Arandor screamed as a ball of yellow light exploded around him, setting his purple robe ablaze. Able to move again, I quickly rolled to my right, away from Arandor. He recovered from his surprise, absorbed the energy of the fire, and directed it in a stream of flame toward me.

I dodged his attack and launched one of my own, a pulse of heat aimed at the ground beneath his feet. The turf exploded under him and he tumbled forward, the knife falling from his hand. As he stood, another ball of yellow light caught him unawares, lifting from his feet and dropping him heavily to the ground.

What had saved me? Who directed these bolts of energy? Had another Master arrived from The Order?

No. The only other person in the clearing was Lareina. She appeared as stunned as me. What we had just witnessed could not possibly be, and yet it was.

Lareina had the Gift.

A shift in the energy field around me. Too late I reacted, spinning and shielding myself as a scorching blast of heat exploded along my right side, blistering the skin on my shoulder and driving me to the turf. I rolled as I hit, and the pain in my shoulder blossomed and spread along my back and side. It came to me slowly that my shirt was afire. I rolled again until it was out.

Pulling myself to my feet, my shoulder screaming in agony, I cursed the bad luck that forced me into successive battles with a dragon and a fellow Master. Arandor was not as fatigued as I, and for all my experience, the strain of the day's events might be my undoing. The villain approached with his arm raised, pieces of his charred robe flaking off and drifting away into the night air as he came. I sensed another shift in the energy around me. A pulse of heat washed over me, but I was able to deflect the worst of it. There was another, which I deflected, and yet another, which I blocked, but not as well as before. Arandor was wearing me down, and soon I would have naught to defend against his assault.

Suddenly Arandor stopped and picked up the box he had dropped. "You lose, Davian," he said.

He extended a finger, preparing to touch the box as he had done before. My heart sank. With even a moment's respite after the dragon, I might have thought to recover the infernal device and keep it from Arandor. Now, I despaired that anyone would again have such an opportunity to put an end to this madman's dream of ruling the world.

Strangely, he did not touch the box, and my thoughts were not swept away by the power of the communicating device brought to our world by Hahr'ohld and his people. Instead, there was a whisper of movement through the air and the solid *thunk* of something colliding with flesh and bone. Arandor stiffened and his eyes grew wide. Sinking to his knees, he let out a long, high-pitched wail, and then he fell forward onto his face.

Protruding from his back was the short wooden handle of a stone-headed axe, the type used by the woodsmen who travel the wilds of Aerwald.

I stood motionless for a long moment, hardly daring to believe what I saw. But my senses confirmed it; without touching him, I knew with a certainty that Arandor, would-be ruler of all Saramond, was dead.

Behind Arandor was Lareina, swaying where she stood. She stared, eyes unseeing, as though in shock. I ran to her and reached her just in time to catch her as she collapsed.

CHAPTER TWENTY-SIX

Fosdric was among those waiting to greet us at Tyngstaal Castle as we returned to Stelnregon the following night. It was a slow journey, as those of us who returned from the valley were bruised and sore. We also had a score of wounded and dead from the attack on the road, and some the injured could not be moved easily.

It was a quiet journey. Although we had succeeded in eliminating a madman who had killed tens of thousands, and might have killed millions more, the deaths of all those people so recently and so near made it difficult to be of good cheer.

Another reason for the somber mood, for me, was the presence of the beautiful Lareina. She and I knew that something of great import had occurred. Never in memory, as far as anyone knew, had a woman possessed the Gift. It was impossible to know how The Order would react, much less the good people of Marthwee. Life with the Gift is difficult enough as a man. We are tolerated because we are needed. How people would respond to a woman with such powers, I could not say.

There were other things I dearly wished to discuss with Lareina, but I despaired of her willingness to listen. After I caught her as she fell, I could not bring myself to let her go. Upon awakening and finding herself in my arms, she immediately fought free, obviously displeased to find herself in that position. I do not know whether she was ashamed to have displayed weakness or angry that I had assumed she needed help. Perhaps she simply detested me.

As we rode back to Stelnregon, I found, to my surprise, that it was the last question I wanted answered most of all.

* * *

Wolf was the first to herald our arrival at Tyngstaal Castle. The small white dog barked and spun excitedly as we appeared before the castle's gate at the last light of day. The little dog proudly led our bedraggled party through the gate and into the courtyard as though he were the bailiff himself. Caedwulf, commanding in Talliver's absence, quickly organized a party to bring the wounded into a sheltered area of the castle for treatment.

A feast in our honor was hurriedly assembled from the stores that had been cached in the depths of the castle. Tables were set up in the courtyard, as many parts of the castle itself were not considered safe after the furious assault of the dragons.

I was forced to recount the tale of Arandor's defeat. There was no pleasure in the telling. I had no wish to accept credit that was not mine, but I was still unsure that revealing Lareina's Gift was wise. With some twisting and editing of the facts, I presented a passable account that satisfied the assembly.

During the tale, and afterward, I noticed Lareina watching me with a strange and unreadable expression upon her face.

Hahr'ohld Orson was decidedly cheerful, especially upon the return of the communicator box I retrieved from the clearing in the valley. I had been tempted to leave it there, fearing that the power I might wield with such a device would turn me into a monster like Arandor. Rather than tempt myself, I asked one of Talliver's archers to carry it when we prepared to leave the valley.

In any case, Hahr'ohld said it might allow him to signal the ship in which his crew traveled from his own world, which might dispatch what he called an "escape pod."

"When will you do this?" I asked Hahr'ohld during the feast.

"Oh, I don't know, he said. *"Now that I know I can get away if I want to, it doesn't seem as important to do it right away. There is still a lot to learn about your world. And maybe I can help you with some useful advice."*

"I thought going home was your goal."

"Well, it was," he said. *"But we still haven't found the rest of my crew. Unless we do, I'll have to make the trip alone. By the*

time I get back home, everyone I know will be old or dead." A shadow fell across Hahr'ohld's face.

"What do you mean?"

"Relativity—oh, forget it." Hahr'ohld sighed. *"It's complicated. I'll try to explain it sometime."* He took a long pull of the ale that an enterprising soldier had managed to provide.

A pair of guardsmen had formed an impromptu musical group and energetically performed an up-tempo drinking song with fiddle and flute. A brave few had broken the ice and begun to dance. The flickering torchlight gave the shattered castle's courtyard a festival atmosphere. A pretty young lady walked past our table—for the third time, I noticed. Her shy smile was for the pudgy gardener from the stars. Hahr'ohld noticed, too. His face had turned several shades of crimson.

"You know," he said, *"I could just use the ship (word) to relay my research by back home. I'm sure there's a lot to learn about Saramond. What with the dragons and all, I really haven't had a chance to do any research at all. And I really should learn your language,"* he added, grinning.

I noted, happily, that Brother Galthorn was honored with a hero's welcome by the soldiers of the King's Guard upon our return. The story of his mad dash on Aeryx, offering himself as a willing sacrifice to draw the dragons away from the wounded on the Beirgryn road, reached Stelnregon ahead of us. Though he was confined to bed, there was no end to the line of men who wanted to meet the courageous dragon-slaying priest who was so well protected by the Creator.

Fosdric, of course, had added to the priest's reputation by recounting Brother Galthorn's victories, in his colorful way, over the dragon in Marthwee and the half-mad wizard who mistook him for a demon. I overheard one of the Guards say that Brother Galthorn must surely be one of the Creator's Chosen Ones.

"And who's to say he's not?" asked Fosdric. I had excused myself from the feast after taking the liberty of introducing Hahr'ohld Orson to the young lady who had seemed so interested in the visitor from the stars. She had promised to teach him the local dances without keeping him out too late. Fosdric found me looking out over the crenelations on one of the castle walls that was still intact. Moonlight rippled across the water in the harbor with hypnotic effect. Wolf, well fed on table scraps, curled up sleepily at Fosdric's feet.

"I suppose you could make that case," I said, "But it does not change the fact that the dragons left us when Lareina clubbed Arandor. The Creator had nothing to do with that."

"Right," Fosdric said. "Tell me again: How'd she sneak up on Arandor? I thought you Masters had a special way of hearing people inside your heads."

"We do," I said. "How she surprised him, I cannot say."

"She's got the Gift, ain't she?" Fosdric looked at me with one eyebrow arched.

I took a long look at the stable hand and part-time street actor. "How could you possibly think that?"

"It's simple, isn't it? Your story about how you took out Arandor had holes you could drive a wagon through. Not that most people noticed," Fosdric added. "Credit the ale for that. But she'd have never got close to Arandor if she couldn't hide herself from him. Not to mention the dragons. And besides, she followed us so easy, I bet she was hearing you in her head and maybe didn't even know it herself. And you didn't know she was there, neither."

After a long moment, I said, "Tell me again why you are a stable hand and not a counselor to King Ednorwain."

Fosdric laughed. "Horses are easier to get along with than some people," he said. "Specially kings. No, if I got to deal with a horse's hind end, it's better I don't have to take orders from it."

"All right," I said, laughing. "But please tell no one until Lareina herself decides to make her Gift public knowledge."

"Done and done."

The sounds of the celebration in the courtyard below did little to lift my spirits. Below us, outside the walls lay the skeletal remains of a city that once housed a quarter-million souls. It probably would again, but it would be many long and painful years until that day.

"Look out over the city there, Fosdric," I said. "What is the point? If the Creator is good and all-powerful, why did this happen?"

"Don't rightly know," Fosdric said.

"How can anyone expect a rational, thinking man to believe in a good and righteous Creator of all, when there is so much senseless cruelty and death in the world?"

"Well," Fosdric said, "If I was a priest, I might say, 'Look at it this way: How do you explain Brother Galthorn being in the right place to drop that dragon for you at Marthwee; and me stopping that door with my head that night in Elocin; and us getting away from Darnaatha with naught but a few bumps and bruises; and Hahr'ohld turning up just in time to blast a couple more dragons, and give you that cap that saved your brain, and that probey thing that give you the time to find Arandor? And most of all, what about Lareina turning up with the Gift, which neither she nor nobody else has ever heard of a lass having until now, and without which you and Talliver and a devil of a lot more people would be dead tonight? What are the odds of *any* of those things happening, forget about all of 'em?' How would you answer me that?"

"Chance," I said.

"Ha! Then you got more faith than I do," Fosdric said, "Except yours is blind."

"All right, then," I said, "If the Creator has a hand in our affairs, then why are there dragons at all? Why create something so dangerous that without a freakish few like me, the dragons would overwhelm us?"

Fosdric leaned on the rough stone of the battlement and looked over the ruined city, where a few fires still smoldered. "I been thinking about that," he said. "It seems to me that the dragons is more of a nuisance than anything."

"What?"

"Okay, a right awful nuisance, I'll give you that," Fosdric said. "But look, they can't live too close together or they fight to the death, right?"

"True."

"So, that puts a lid on how much trouble they can cause. You know as well as I do that armies of men can leave a lot more death behind 'em than a dragon."

"Also true."

"And it wasn't until one of you blokes got it in his head to rule the world that the balance was knocked off kilter and the dragons caused real trouble."

"Yes, but..." Fosdric had a point, but I was too tired to unravel it for myself. "I am weary, Fosdric. What are you saying?"

"Well, it seems to me you Masters think you're here to save us from the dragons. And don't think I'm not grateful, because I am," Fosdric said. "But after all this mess, I wonder what you fellows would do if you didn't have dragons to fight. Or—or if one of your brothers got too strong for his own good." He turned to me, his face highlighted by the glow of the torches illuminating the feast in the courtyard.

"What if the Creator made dragons to give The Order something to keep busy so you lot wouldn't get it in your heads to turn the rest of us into slaves?"

That was a jolt. It had never occurred to me: How many of us in The Order, without our single-minded focus on training up the next generation of dragonslayers, would find the temptation to profit from our abilities too great to resist?

It was not a pleasant thought. There are few enough in The Order that if the people of Saramond wanted to rid the world of us, they could—but it would be a long and bloody fight.

Perhaps the Creator established the world with balance in mind—dragons and Masters of The Order locked in an eternal battle simply to prevent one side or the other from imposing its will on everything else. Why would the Creator do such a thing? Would the world be better off without dragons *and* the likes of me?

It was far too late and I was much too tired to think things through. I bid Fosdric and Wolf a good night and went off in search of a place to sleep.

* * *

And that is the way of it. Six months have passed since the events related here, and life has at least begun to find a routine in Stelnregon and the surrounding district. One cannot say that things have returned to normal as that word no longer has meaning for the few who survived Arandor's ungodly scheme. There was no celebration for the survivors; of the quarter-million in the city the night that the dragons attacked, only ten thousand returned to a city that was utterly destroyed. It will be some time before the city is restored to anything like its former state.

King Ednorwain has placed all of the kingdom's resources into rebuilding Stelnregon. It was a crucial port, and neighboring kingdoms are only too willing to take advantage of a rival's misfortune. Thankfully, Captain Talliver has proven to be an able interim governor. He may be appointed to the post on a permanent basis once the crisis is past, and I, for one, think he would do well.

As for me, I plan a long journey; a quest, if you will. Questions were raised during these trials that require answers. Am I here to fight the dragons, or do the dragons give me purpose to keep me from becoming another Arandor? What would I do if there were no dragons? Come to that, what would I do without the Gift?

Without the Gift, what could I offer a woman like Lareina?

My soul is unsettled. Questions burn in my heart, and self-examination has not revealed the answers I seek. While there is quiet in the land, I am off to study with the learned brothers at Dunswallat Abbey. They are not entirely comfortable with my visit, but I have convinced them of my sincerity.

Of all in this world that is noble and true, I have seen those qualities shine brightest in a young priest from a small riverside village, one who risked his life for others without hesitation—not once, but over and again. I leave in the morning to learn his secret. Perhaps I will find it at the abbey.

More than anything, I must know this: Why is Brother Galthorn, who is more content and satisfied in this life than any man I have known, so willing to let loose the reins of his life when there is a chance it might save the life of another?

ABOUT THE AUTHOR

 DEREK P. GILBERT hosts *SkyWatchTV* and co-hosts the weekly video programs *SciFriday* and *Unraveling Revelation* with his wife, Sharon K. Gilbert, author of *The Redwing Saga* series of supernatural fiction.

Derek is a Christian, a husband and father, and the author of the groundbreaking books *Bad Moon Rising*, an analysis of the spiritual forces behind Islam, *The Great Inception*, which explores the importance of sacred mountains in the Bible, and *Last Clash of the Titans*, which shows that the Hebrew prophets understood that the gods of the pagans were real and have a prophesied role in the end times.

He and Sharon are the co-authors of *Veneration*, a deep dive into the cult of the dead in ancient Israel, the origin of demons, and the Bible's prophecies of the return of the evil dead at Armageddon; and *Giants, Gods and Dragons*, which unmasks the supernatural forces plotting the final war of the ages. Derek also teamed with Josh Peck to write *The Day the Earth Stands Still*, a book that documents the occult origins of "ancient aliens."

Derek is a lifelong fan of the Chicago Cubs, prefers glasses to contacts, and has been known to sing the high part in barbershop and gospel quartets.

On the web:
www.gilberthouse.org
www.derekpgilbert.com